EASY

MONEY

EASY

MONEY

John C. Boland

ST. MARTIN'S PRESS
NEW YORK

Design by Glen M. Edelstein

Library of Congress Cataloging-in-Publication Data

Boland, John C.
    Easy money / John Boland.
        p.   cm.
    "A Thomas Dunne book."
    ISBN 0-312-05859-4
    I. Title.
PS3552.O575E27   1991
813'.54—dc20   91-4486
                                                             CIP

10 9 8 7 6 5 4 3 2

for Mira

EASY

MONEY

1

FORGETFULNESS brought me back to the office. In the January dusk, the financial district had emptied out, as life and money flowed uptown. Even the sidewalk vendors had rolled up their blankets and gone home. I crossed William Street at a run, meeting a wind that roared like a flash flood down granite channels from the river.

My own fault I was doubling back. An old client, Professor Potter, had called in the afternoon worrying that he owned too many petroleum stocks and I had said I would check. Then I had walked out at five without his file. Barney Potter wouldn't take his money and stomp off because I had gotten forgetful, but I liked him and felt the one percent he paid us entitled him to an answer.

The deskbound evening guard nodded as I brought the icy wind into the lobby. Since a round-the-clock commodities trading house had taken over the twentieth floor in October, the building showed signs of life at all hours. As I reached the elevators, a multinational platoon of brokers, most of them Chinese in jogging suits and barely into their twenties, poured off and raced for the door.

We were on the fourteenth floor. I opened the hallway door with its pebbled glass and flipped on the lights. The outer office was a snug oblong, deliberately old-fashioned in its decor, where a four-day-a-week secretary and our collection of statistical reference

1

books competed for the space. Gail maintained an upper hand by stripping the rosewood shelves of things she hoped we wouldn't miss.

I closed the door thinking the cleaning woman had gotten sloppy. A wire basket lay on the floor with brokerage house reports spilled across the carpet.

Then the rest of the room registered. It had changed a lot in an hour. A gale had swept in from the frozen Lower Manhattan streets, ripping books from shelves, scattering stock charts, tipping over the coffee maker, smashing a computer screen.

There was a feel of debris barely settled.

The inner office held clients' records, our research files, the safe, more computers. I pushed open the door between rooms with a queasy feeling.

The chaos was a little nastier, as if the visitor had gotten impatient when turning the place upside down was failing to yield any cash. File drawers had been dumped, desks ransacked, computer disks strewn about along with files, paper clips, rubber bands, coffee cart change. Even a couple of steamship etchings had found their way onto the floor, the glass splintered. I picked the frames up by the edges and set them on my desk.

Frustration and anger were written all over the mess.

The safe bore a few new scratches, but it hadn't opened. There wasn't much in it.

Suddenly edgy, I went into the front office and locked the hall door—then remembered it had been locked when I arrived. I tilted a chair under the knob, suspecting it was too loose to help.

What were they after?

Money, stocks, bonds, perhaps unregistered Deutschemark bearer notes that could trade as anonymously as cash overseas. . . . We kept nothing of the sort. Canning & McCarthy Investment Counsel managed portfolios by telephone and telex, leaving the handling of cash, checks and securities to the brokers we used.

An addict starving for twenty dollars wouldn't know that.

I sat on a corner of my desk, pulled the phone up from the floor and punched my senior partner's number. The voice that answered was Barbara Canning's, high-pitched, nicely elegant.

"Hello? Oh, Benny . . ." She sounded disappointed and impatient.

"Can I talk to Jack?"

"Yes, of course." She set the phone down and I heard music in the background, classical and busy. If I knew my partner's wife, the composer was notable for his obscurity, which provided a subject for dinner-table erudition by Barbara.

Jack came on. His voice was nasal and upper-crusty, suited to being fussy about small things. It would have been hard to take if you didn't like the man. "What's up, Ben?" he said.

"We've been burglarized."

"You and Martha? That's dreadful." He was too polite to ask why I was calling him.

"I'm at the office. It's you and I who were hit."

His response was muted, too muted. "Is there anything missing?"

I swallowed, not feeling well. "It's impossible to tell."

"Did they steal the hard drive?"

We had years of trading records on the computer's hard memory. "No. Gail's terminal is caved in. Otherwise no serious damage."

"Well, there's nothing negotiable on hand. I suppose I'd better come down and see the damage."

"I'll call the police."

He hemmed. "Don't get carried away. Burglaries make clients nervous."

For good reason. Who would want a burglar knowing he had a million-dollar portfolio? Ninety percent of our clients had more than that with us. Quality, not quantity, was Jack's unspoken motto in just about everything. He seemed not to notice that he measured a client's quality by the weight of his checkbook.

"Burglaries make me nervous too," I said.

He ignored any submerged meaning he heard in that.

I hung up and spent the next forty minutes wondering about my partner—boss really, partner by generous technicality. He had hired me two years earlier as an assistant portfolio manager without experience, had taught me in the intervening time as much as he could of the art of buying and selling stocks without inviting ruin. He said I showed promise at managing money; at handling clients

3

I probably was hopeless. No matter. Three months ago he announced that Canning Investment Counsel was henceforth Canning & McCarthy and that the new name on the door entitled me to a fifteen-percent partnership with no further questions. The bonus was unnecessary, unexpected, not at all standard business practice, in which partnerships were more often sold than given away. Least of all had Jack needed to surrender part of the firm. Clients walked through the door to have Andrew Jackson Canning, not his thirty-two-year-old apprentice, manage their money. They brought him inheritances and pension plans because in the insular financial community, Canning had a reputation as a conservative investor whose clients' wealth grew a reliable twenty percent a year.

Besides quality, he believed in consistency. "Anyone who chases last year's fad will lose money," he told his weekly finance class at Columbia. "Investors need to develop a discipline and stick to it."

Besides quality and consistency, he believed in integrity. That made him a Boy Scout by Wall Street's standards, a reasonable gentleman by his own.

He treated me with paternal fondness, and I responded with distancing casualness. This was mostly a defensive measure. One father in a lifetime had been half too many. Besides, I told myself, Jack's wisdom outside the stock market was naive and hardly reliable. At fifty-three he assumed the underlying decency of human nature. His attitude was matter-of-fact, more a surgeon's confidence in finding an appendix than a preacher's faith in a soul.

Not the sort of man to be unsurprised by a burglary.

Not the sort to withdraw confidence without a reason.

I collected stock charts off the floor, cursing the service that sent out the hundreds of pages unbound. One pattern and name caught my eye. The chart showed two years of price swings, mostly downward, in Seattle Aviation, a small aerospace company that had been knocking down well-larded defense contracts for jet trainers. The market had been sloppy lately, and Seattle Avy shares had gotten dumped out of nervous portfolios like everything else. Now the stock could be bought for about six times its net income. If the government hadn't canceled a contract, I decided to buy a few hundred shares for my own account.

4

I found Professor Potter's file in the jumble and set it aside with the Seattle Avy chart.

The hall door crashed into Gail's chair as Jack arrived. He set the overturned chair upright, unamused by the fumbling precaution. He surveyed the wreckage from an ascetic's narrow face, remote blue eyes, a long nose, wavy white hair. He stood over six feet, and his shoulders were wide but frail-looking.

He sighed. "Let's call in Gail tomorrow."

She normally didn't work on Tuesdays. I said, "Okay," and stepped aside to let him into the inner office.

He shook his head. "The bastards didn't miss much."

"Except the safe."

He stooped and picked up a couple of file jackets. The records they had sheltered might show up in the next day or two. He tossed the folders onto his desk. The street was dark, and the window reflected his black-coated figure bending and rising like an elegant ragpicker. His face was creased and grim, and in a moment of charity I thought there might be no explanation deeper than the fact he had had a lousy day.

"The timing couldn't be much worse," he complained. "We've got to get the tax statements out."

I supposed a few of our clients solemnly shredded our summary of their transactions and whipped up a less expensive version for the IRS. It was something I didn't have to know about.

"Does this make any sense to you?" I asked.

"How could it? Some damned fool must assume we keep a mountain of bonds lying around."

I listened, nodded, didn't believe him.

Somehow, something was wrong. Occupying the same office, you know if your partner has started accepting accounts from Bogotá. Jack hadn't. You know if he has squandered a widow's nest egg in the commodity markets. He hadn't. But he was looking at trouble of some kind. I hoped it didn't concern me.

"We had better get the locks changed," I said. "Either the latch got jimmied or our friends had a key."

"You'll attend to it?"

I nodded.

5

He spotted something. "Is that the Wrather file?"

"Whose?"

"Wrather." He spelled it.

The folder that I had come back for lay on my desk. "It's Barney Potter's. I think we should sell some things for him, shift a little into utility bonds."

"That sounds reasonable," he said. He came over and unobtrusively made sure about the file. "We have dinner guests coming—already arrived, I imagine. Will you lock up, Ben? . . . assuming it matters."

"All right."

He tugged on a dark tweed cap that looked rakish atop the white hair. "Don't spend all night here, Ben. I'll see you in the morning."

"All right," I repeated.

I could have thrown an arm around his neck and choked the truth loose. Could have but didn't, because I was annoyed that after two years he didn't trust me enough to say what was bugging him.

In a way he was right.

2

I went back to Delmonico's, where the financial press hangs its hat. Two hours earlier a big-bottomed blonde had been swearing that Coca-Cola was a goner; whether bankrupt or merged she wasn't making clear. Her bray was missing from the subdued murmur that had taken over. The secrets had thinned, and the weary listeners were sorting through an evening of relentless talk—the absurd, the useless, the plausible.

If word was out on Canning & McCarthy, maybe I would pick up a whisper tonight. My in-laws could wait to throw a crepe-hanging party until they opened their morning papers.

From the door I saw Peter Bagley, who wrote the "Street Smarts" column for *Investor's Week*. He was sharing his wisdom on the intertwinings of politics and stock prices. "If you want prosperity, you've got to bet on a middle-of-the-roader, not an ideologue," Peter said. "Your basic pragmatic hack believes in promoting American industry. That keeps the voters tranquil. And no matter how often Wall Street genuflects to free trade, stock buyers like economic nationalism."

When the bartender brought me a beer, I hauled myself deeper into the place. It was three-quarters empty, populated mainly by serious drinkers and a handful of people who didn't like the other places they had to go to. Not an ideal spot to reflect about Jack's behavior. But a familiar place.

Peter was red-faced and beefy, dressed in an English suit, an alligator belt and three-hundred-dollar shoes. He wasn't noticeably more adamant than he had been when I left. But his audience had changed. On one side was a broker I half recognized. On the other was a pretty girl who looked like a recruit at *Investor's Week*. Peter liked to play mentor to the new ones. If he had his way, her education would be fast and unsentimental.

Peter Bagley and the girl stood close, while the broker wobbled on a stool. "You have to understand politics if you want to understand the stock market," Peter said. "The whole economic process is political. You can't buy a bolt today without paying a tariff."

The broker didn't turn his head. "So what?"

"So the price of bolts is not decided by the market anymore. The bureaucratic infrastructure decides. That's a fact, and there is no point crying for the old days."

The broker shook his head. "I wasn't crying for them. And I don't give a fuck about bolt prices."

Peter saw me and clapped my shoulder, his grin hazy. He had heavy dark features and gentle eyes, and he must have been handsome before all the years of expense-account dinners. His hairline and chin were sliding in opposite directions, elongating the face. He nodded between the girl and me. "Back again, huh Benj? Nancy Scott, meet our journal's twenty-third most famous alumnus. Benjamin McCarthy was a contender for my column when he left."

I said, "You'd have gotten the column anyway." It was probably true.

The girl had honey-colored hair and luminous gray eyes that widened in disbelief. "Why would anyone leave *Investor's Week*, Mr. McCarthy?" Her accent was vaguely border states. She wasn't used to drinking.

Peter answered for me. "Ben liked to play stocks and got angry having to ride the elevator six floors to find a quote machine. Would you believe it, Ben? We still don't have one in the office."

I made a sympathetic noise. *Investor's Week* hit the streets on

Saturday mornings, giving its two hundred thousand readers a slick mixture of news about corporations, interviews with stock analysts and ruminations by its columnists. I had been on the staff for six years and had kept in touch with Peter and a couple of other writers.

"Actually," Peter said, "it was the siren song of more money that lured Ben away."

"Also no deadlines," I said.

Nancy Scott wrinkled her nose in disapproval. Not only was I greedy by Peter's account but also lazy by my own.

"What's the gossip?" I said. Peter heard a lot of the idle talk that wound through the small interlocked streets.

"It's been a dull winter since Markey Wahl," Peter complained, putting his drink down. "Remember that?"

"Vaguely," I said.

He turned to the girl. "They were a small stock-trading house, pretty well regarded until they collapsed in November. A week later the senior partner suffered a fatal stroke. Scandals since then have lacked the poignant touches." Peter lowered his voice and said, "Now if you're asking about stocks, Benj, I know a couple that could make you money."

Peter's stocks seldom made anyone money, but I said, "Let's hear them."

"Can't do," he pounced, with a delighted smile. "You're an outsider now, McCarthy, and I'm honor-bound to secrecy about the crud that fills the magazine."

The girl scowled at me across her drink. "Do you always ask reporters for stock tips?"

"Only Peter," I said. "He's got the best contacts on Wall Street."

"It sounds unethical," the girl said.

"It's that only if he tells me."

"Ah'm surprised the Securities and Exchange Commission hasn't arrested you," she said, trying to swallow a hiccup.

The SEC didn't arrest people. They could yank my license, almost as damaging. I started to tell her the distinction, but it seemed like splitting hairs.

Peter's grin wavered, as it often did when talk turned to the SEC. There was always a risk someone would ask to see his own trading records. Buying a stock before touting it in the magazine was frowned on. "Ben and I kid each other," he said. "I was just about to tell Nancy my war story about Continental Minerals. Remember that one?"

"It was Peter's finest hour," I said.

She laughed. He was eager to impress her, and she was nervous but enjoyed it. "Tell me about Continental Minerals," she said.

"It was a dinky mining company out in Denver," Peter said. "I scribbled a column suggesting that the company had inflated the size of its ore reserves. Monday morning the stock fell apart. People couldn't sell it fast enough. A group of crafty young guys uptown, who had sold short about three-quarters of a million shares, made a bundle. The SEC wanted to know how I got wind of it—whether I was in cahoots with the short sellers. First I told them to piss off, reporter's confidentiality and all that. Then the editors decreed I was looking bad for the magazine. So I fessed up. I sat down with two SEC lawyers and told them the company's officers had been selling their stock for months and I looked around for a reason. The chairman himself had dumped a half-million shares. He was floating rumors of a big ore lode so he could get top dollar. And yeah, the short sellers might have tipped me, but that was their right and mine." He chuckled in satisfaction.

"What happened to the chairman?" the girl prodded.

Peter's smile vanished. "Continental's chairman was a contributor to the Colorado reform Democrats. After reflection it was decided that the ore estimates were the fault of an incompetent geologist. Life on Wall Street is consistent. Even the watchdogs know how to cut a deal."

I'd heard variations on that theme a dozen times from Peter. *Nothing in this world is fair and aboveboard, Benj.* It was his way of justifying his own shortcuts. Peter could tell himself, *Everyone does it, why not me?*

Nancy Scott tilted her head close to me, looking up questioningly. "Have those watchdogs come sniffin' after you?"

Peter chuckled. "Ben is too virtuous. Or too clever to be suspected."

"Too clever, I'd guess," she said.

The broker sitting beside Peter, who had been staring at his slack face in the mirror, put a hand on Peter's shoulder. "Your pal Ben's gotta be a clever fucker."

I knew him by sight from other financial district watering holes, not by name. He was about forty-five, lanky, soft around the chin and eyes, with thinning ginger hair. He looked like he would scrape by as a broker during a bull market, tap friends for lunch money when business got rough.

For some reason as he stared at me, there was sour anger in his watery eyes. "You're Jack Canning's gofer, aren't you? He's a clever fucker too."

I didn't answer.

He nodded at his glass. His courage was good for only a few words.

Peter Bagley tugged the man's sleeve. "Hey, Jimmy, how's the love pile with Trionix going? Jimmy's firm has got a winner, Trionix Technology. His whole office is banging away on the stock, isn't that right, Jimmy?"

Jimmy stared sullenly ahead, thrust himself off the stool and headed toward the men's room.

Peter looked after him. "Those guys are always kiting junk. Real garbage companies. The brokers run 'em up, knock 'em down. Trionix hasn't earned a centime. They make switching gear of some kind, and foreign competition is way out front. I know. I checked into it. Tariffs can't help you with this one. If you buy that stock, you're betting that the Russians will nuke Japan. But Jimmy's boss sells the shares to any widow who walks past the door."

"Who's his boss?"

"Bunny Furbinger. The firm is Furbinger Associates." Peter pinched his nose and wagged his fingers.

"It doesn't ring a bell."

"They weren't much until a couple of years ago. Then Bunny expanded into selling new stock issues. They've got a main office down at the foot of Broadway, a couple of shops up in Westchester, one or two in Florida, something out West. You know how the game is played."

I knew. With the help of a Bunny Furbinger or another sharp

11

stock salesman, a no-luck prospector or renegade gene-splicer could tap the public markets for a couple of million dollars to get his little company rolling. Most of them vanished within a couple of years.

"Furbinger is pushing Trionix for all he's worth," Peter said. "The stock came out last fall at fifty cents a share, negative net worth, no production. Ten million shares, plus twenty million that insiders still own. Jimmy and his friends have goosed the stock up to four and a half—we're talking dollars now, Benj. Nine times your money in four months. Imagine what they could do with a company making money."

"Not as much," I said, and he nodded. Reality never lived up to what could be imagined.

"The music will stop someday," Peter said. "That's what I'm saying in my column this week. Some sucker's going to end up holding an empty bag. Do you realize the market is saying this heap of smoke and mirrors is worth one hundred thirty-five million dollars? What do they think they're buying?"

I asked, "What's Jimmy's last name?"

"Doyle. You should know him. He knows your partner. Sounds like they had a spat." He leaned close to the girl, narrow hand resting on her shoulder. "Ready for supper?"

She nodded.

Peter guided her out, mentioning a steak house in Midtown. At the door he threw me a sportman's thumbs-up, claiming to have bagged another one.

I followed a minute later, before Jimmy Doyle could wobble back to his seat.

3

MY wife had fallen asleep on the couch. She looked satisfied, a sign that the day's work had stretched into the evening. In her red jersey and old corduroys, she also looked a little like a dramatic sculpture, a forearm resting across her eyes, a knee slightly bent. I seldom saw the long lines of her body not in motion or seeming ready for motion. Appreciation was automatic, deep and familiar. It seemed impossible that I would want to live without her.

A log had burned down in the fireplace, and the apartment was cold. I switched off Marty's reading lamp and headed down the hall to the kitchen.

We had owned the apartment for three years. It offered my wife a spacious attic studio with three exposures from a corner turret. Otherwise the ceilings were high and dark, the floors drafty, the paint dingy—and I loved every room. For our top floor we had paid several times as much as the mansion had cost the émigré hook-and-eye tycoon who had built it in the twenties. He had been nostalgic for the old country, and stone relief busts of Romanovs decorated the fireplace openings. Once a year I brushed soot off Anastasia. The long living room looked out across a narrow street at an ancient apartment building, encrusted in mostly dead ivy, where a tenant had thrown open the windows and played endless Schubert last summer. Our mortgage was almost manageable given occasional windfalls from a Seattle Aviation.

When I stuck my nose into the kitchen, a man's face stared back at me from the counter. He was pouty, with a small square chin and pale blue eyes, brows lifted in a world-weary shrug. I recognized him as the artistic director of a public theater, Danton Something, who had come around for sittings. The painting flattered him, somehow dignifying a moue.

It was almost finished, a good piece of work. In two or three years, Martha Norris stood a chance of finding her portraits much and expensively in demand. For the time being, she took the rare commissions as they came and earned less than a broker's messenger. Instead of cultivating bank presidents and their wives, she met a more diverse and interesting crowd. Sometimes she found one of the crowd, usually someone rugged and handsome, too interesting. My problem, I supposed, not hers. The interest never lasted more than a few weeks.

I set the canvas out of harm's way and filled the coffee grinder. While it whirred, a drowsy voice called, "Why so late?"

I went and leaned over the couch. "Somebody ransacked the office."

"Tonight?"

"I was out for a while, came back and found that we'd had company. They made a mess."

"It's a good thing you didn't walk in on them." Propped on an elbow, she could see that I wasn't damaged. She didn't fuss much over things that hadn't happened, but the dangerous possibilities earned me a squeeze on the hand. "The police didn't get them, I'll bet?"

"No."

"If you'd called, I'd have come down."

"There's nothing to do but pick up paper."

"Even so." She leaned across the top of the couch, face half-buried. She had curly dark hair, brown eyes that I couldn't always read, a heavy lower lip that didn't always utter the truth, high cheekbones. Barefoot, she stood eye-to-eye with me, an inch and a half under six feet. My partner's wife, a frail and intense blonde, wore a forgiving smile when she called Marty handsome. In middle age she might be handsome. At twenty-six, lacking any trace of porcelain-princess delicacy, she could hurl herself around a corner and stop an unsuspecting heart.

I had been in love with her from the night a college friend introduced us five years before. At a party of mainly unfamiliar faces, my date from Philadelphia made the blunder of offering practical suggestions on careers in commercial art to the dark-haired girl she'd only met. Martha Norris had drunk enough in the preceding few days that the editing function of her brain was asleep. She had brought back six months of canvases from the Yucatán and was cutting loose, in no mood for consulting with practical people. She suggested my date commercialize a talent that nature in fact hadn't given her. After a moment's silence it was decided that we might find a better class of people up at Doubles. I put my wilted flower in a cab pointed uptown and went back to take a shot at the wandering artist.

Martha Norris was unattached and for weeks indifferent. I didn't pretend to share her passion for painting. But she was twenty-one, gullible in a way, ready to assume that something must be equally important to me. She knew that it wasn't writing, or any of the arts, but there had to be something that made me eager to get out of bed in the morning. From the first evening, getting out of bed was seldom on my mind.

It was several months before she tried the torture cure on the new boyfriend, a weekend in Lexington with Father. At sixty-four, John Norris was a fading, malevolent apparition, meticulously absorbed in dying. Each morning he was driven to the bank to torment the salaried managers who oversaw the family's shrunken estate which, among its other burdens, kept his daughter's mother in a separate fourteen-room subsistence in Edgartown.

In discouraging his daughter's lovers, John Norris introduced them to a gallery of dead grandfathers, portraits of craggy-jawed, beetle-browed Irishmen who haunted the endless heirloom-clogged rooms. He took private delight in the knowledge that anyone who beheld such forebears would shrivel in inadequacy and flee—or

15

betray a predatory urge to price the china. I had remarked, falsely casual, that airing the rooms would be good for the upholstery.

According to Marty, it was Ephraim Norris who bequeathed so many neurotic feelings of not measuring up to later generations. At the age of twenty-six, Ephraim pushed a railroad through Colorado during an Indian war, dealing in a more or less evenhandedly ruthless fashion with the cavalry and the tribes. The army decided not to hang him, and he became wealthy in the mining boom that followed. His grandson became State Justice Norris in New York.

His great-great-great-granddaughter inherited none of his business instinct but a full measure of rebellious determination. It helped her survive her father, who hated the venerated ancestors who had burdened him with wealth that he had mishandled, and hated the daughter who was a throwback.

I went to the cramped kitchen to make the coffee. I called, "Jack came down and shuffled papers."

She came as far as the doorway. "How is the town's best money manager?"

"I'm subdued, thank you."

"I meant Jack."

"He's subdued, too. Business hasn't been fun for the last few days."

"Are your stocks going the wrong way?" She was never really interested in stocks, which were too much like a children's game of marbles.

"Not most of them." I didn't want to think about the firm. Or everything that depended on it. Or about Jack, which was the same thing.

She noticed the clock. "Have you had supper? I got distracted with poor Danton and forgot to."

I followed her glance to the portrait and said, "That's the Danton I've met."

"Thank you, sweetheart. I'll buy supper."

We walked over a block to Bleecker and took a window table. The towers of the World Trade Center glowed over the West Village like a friendly next-door neighbor, prosperous and protective, though in fact they were a couple of miles downtown. The night was clear, and

16

late joggers, drug vendors, trolling hedonists, shopping-baggers and middle-class drudges prowled the frozen sidewalks. The easy flow of vice and respectability got me thinking about Peter Bagley and his circle of broker friends, to no avail. Most of the ones I had met were like tonight's drunk, a little seedy and employed by third-tier firms. Peter wrote occasional blurbs about their favorite stocks and collected favors in private, I supposed. Peter Bagley's game, not Jack's or mine.

I toyed with my pasta and watched a green-haired girl next to a fruit stand palm tiny envelopes to customers. Small change compared to the cash tide that sloshed around the financial district. The forces pulling the money were as powerful as moons, not always visible, not necessarily imaginable.

I thought about the influence of money while Marty told me that her uncle Gil was back in town. She had invited him to dinner. Her brother Sterling was going to work a few blocks from me come summer as a trainee at Goldman Sachs. I ignored that prospect, which implied occasional get-togethers to hear about Sterling's rapid rise, and concentrated on something I could handle: "How is Gil?"

"He says he's fine. He sounds melancholy."

Apart from my wife, he was the only living Norris who believed that wage earners could be social equals. He was the only one who had made money on his own. Eighteen months ago, after selling his interest in a small bond-trading house to a hungry motion-picture-petroleum-insurance conglomerate, Gil and his wife had decided with great enthusiasm that they would spend the rest of their lives traveling. For Dorrie, that meant three months in Greece, several weeks of it at a hospital where the only indicated care was to make her comfortable. I couldn't really guess the impact of her death on Gil. We had gotten along at first because we could talk stocks, later because each of us sensed how much the other loved his niece. His pain was off limits.

"It will be nice to see him," she said.

I nodded. Sterling was another story. Our truce was in constant jeopardy, and at the rare get-togethers his health was at risk more often than he knew. As if reading my thoughts, Marty patted my hand. "Try not to be too mean to Little Brother. You have until summer to practice diplomacy."

I shook my head. "I have until summer to move our office."

I opened the apartment door and caught the telephone. Barbara Canning said, with no hint of sincerity, that she hoped she hadn't disturbed me. It was ten o'clock. "Did you and Jack stop for a drink?" she asked.

"Not together. He said something about dinner guests."

"We have guests but no host." When she was annoyed, her teeth clicked like a shoe tapping. Having to call me looking for Jack must have worn off a week's enamel.

I had a hunch where her husband might be. "Have you tried the office?"

"Of course. There is no answer."

"You probably just missed him."

"I've tried several times."

He may not want interruptions, I thought. "I'll try. He may have forgotten something."

She hung up.

Marty threw her coat over a chair. She tugged back the sleeves of her shirt. The cold had raised color in her face. "If you haven't drunk your limit, I'll find a bottle of wine," she said. She smiled a straightforward proposition. "Maybe some Chopin. We'll work on your subdued look."

I kept my coat on. "I've got to go back to the office."

"What's the matter?"

"Jack wasn't surprised enough by the burglary. Hell, I don't think he was surprised at all. He's back there now."

"Are you sure?"

"No. Just suspicious and feeling guilty about it."

"You should. Jack is your friend." She retrieved her coat, pulled a red knit cap out of a pocket. "I'll come with. Chopin will keep."

4

THE pensioner on guard duty did a double take as we entered the lobby. I could save us a trip upstairs, I thought, by asking if Mr. Canning had come back. The grizzled head would have a quick shake or nod.

If the answer was no, my suspicious nature had done my senior partner an injustice.

I didn't ask.

The mess in the office was the same, and Jack wasn't around. My progress in two years was impressive, from stammering in his presence to trying to outsneak him.

"Are burglars always such pigs?" Marty said.

"There's no telling the percentage."

"You're awfully cool about it. I would want to kill somebody."

"I did, but it's wearing off." Also, it wouldn't clean up the mess. Or answer my questions. I looked around, feeling the dismay again. No point in that.

First, the safe. I opened it and catalogued several boxes of microfilmed records, a handful of odd papers, a lease contract for the office, a general liability policy for the firm—nothing out of place or surprising.

Marty began making stacks of manila file jackets and stray

papers. It would take days to put it all back together. Days to figure out if a few pages were missing.

"What do you think is wrong?" she asked. "I don't know what I'm looking for."

"I don't either."

"Well, you said Jack's had a couple of bad days. Maybe that's all there is to it."

One bad day had come this noon. The director of a pension fund had started the new year by walking out, taking four million dollars of managed money with him. He had been with us a bit more than two years, profitable years for his fund and for us. Stock prices were high and Jack Canning had been reefing in, selling shares, building cash in most of the accounts. The pension fund chief had met a money manager who said prices would keep rising for a least a year and it was time to be aggressive. Jack and I took the pension man to lunch and tried to dissuade him. Our departing client threw a hand wide. "There's a time to be cautious and a time to be bold. Your trouble, Canning, is you don't change with the times." A bull market argument, a bull market decision. Four million gone to chase moonbeams.

The computer diskettes remained in their jackets, apparently undamaged. I set a dozen diskettes on my desk, wondering . . .

Which client's file had Jack asked about?

Wrather. The name didn't mean anything: presumably a new client and a small one. I skimmed through the papers Marty had collected, hoping for a glimpse of something marked Wrather. After a while I stopped skimming and concentrated. Not a single Wrather page came up.

That didn't prove anything. The file might turn up tomorrow.

Unless Jack had had better luck.

I found the computer disk marked T–Z and woke up the system, which had more cheap megabytes than we could figure what to do with. I scanned the directory and there it was: WRATHER. I called the file up and sat back. The electronic system wasn't quite as comprehensive as the paper file. No signature cards could be stored on the disks, no copy of the management contract, no personal notes or letters from the client praising or lambasting us.

Walter and Virginia Wrather, 227 Central Park West, joint account, opened just a month ago. Fifty thousand dollars, delivered in treasury bills.

That surprised me. Our minimum account size was five hundred thousand. Jack relaxed it for friends or their widows now and then, but I had never heard him mention the Wrathers.

I couldn't picture them. There was nothing unusual in that: I had never met a couple dozen of our clients. Most of the investors who lived out of town were just voices on the telephone. Some had grown familiar and evoked mental pictures of the owners that probably bore no relation to reality. Some had done business with Jack for a decade by telephone and mail. He had clients in Honolulu and Mexico City and one retired air force sergeant in Spain.

The Wrathers' account appeared to be normal. The assets were spread in a dozen stocks, the kind of dreary plodders that Jack preferred to every other kind of company. They baked bread or they manufactured industrial fasteners. They didn't cure cancer, and they didn't collapse overnight. About twenty percent of the Wrather account was in cash, which was about average for our people right then.

It looked so normal that I decided I had misread Jack's interest. The Wrathers must have asked him for the kind of second-guessing that Potter had wanted from me.

Except, of course, that their file was missing.

We fussed and straightened for forty minutes, then switched off the light and locked the door.

The streets were empty and could have been abandoned for years except for the mountains of garbage. She took my hand. "I'd forgotten how dead it gets down here."

"The money machine's turned off for the night," I said. *Turned down*, I amended. It never really slept. "Nobody knows what to do with the rooms full of quotation terminals after the markets close. Unless you want to trade Hong Kong or Sydney."

"You could reopen after dark as video-game parlors."

"A possibility," I agreed. In a bad year the quarters would come in handy.

21

"If the money stopped, I don't think anyone would come back here in the morning. It's not a very inviting place."

"You haven't been to the bars," I said.

A small figure turned the corner from Broadway and headed toward us. When he got close I recognized Tom Chin. His topcoat hung open displaying a tight-fitted double-breasted navy silk suit. As sole stockholder of Pan-Orient Commodities, he drove his nephews like a stevedore, trading gold overnight in Hong Kong, tin in London, and currencies from Tokyo to Riyadh. Distorted by amber lenses, his eyes blinked like frantic semaphores: CLICK CLICK, BUY BUY, CLACK CLACK, SELL SELL.

He offered his hand to Marty, who shook it. He said admiringly, "If you're Ben's wife, you're the artist. My buddy Jack says you do cool Yucatán scenes. Are they worth a million?"

"Not yet," she said.

"I'm Tom Chin. If not a million, could I buy one for fifty thou?"

"Sight unseen? No, I don't think so."

"It's all right," I said. "Tom would pay you in Straits dollars."

"Racist," he said. "Seriously, Canning says you are an exceptional realist. That is out of fashion, so probably a bargain. By the way, I may have a client for Canning & McCarthy."

"That's nice of you," I said.

"I try to talk him out if, but he insist on owning equities— stocks, stocks! It's not a big account, ten million pension money. Canning and you are just boring enough to suit him."

Boring was our middle name.

He glanced at his watch. "I needed cold walk to revive brain cells. Now I better go pull Joey's chain. He's idiot nephew," he explained to Marty. "Very expensive to let him run the trading desk for even ten minutes."

"Good night," Marty said.

We went home and took up where we left off. She was good company, friendly and familiar. I had no complaint, I told myself. After five years, the most loyal heart could stray. It was foolish to wish things didn't happen that way.

5

A light snow stalled the Seventh Avenue subway the next morning, and I was late getting to the office. I unlocked the door as Gail Boronson strode down the hall, shaking her umbrella, spilling water drops from her red-dyed hair.

I pushed the door open and she cried, "This is awful! The people who make such work deserve no mercy!"

It was a quarter after nine. I left the mess to her and called our broker to buy a few hundred Seattle Aviation for my account. He phoned back ten minutes after the opening and said we had gotten it a half-point lower than last night's close. "Congratulations," I said.

Waiting for Jack to show, I watched the perfectly bleak January day take shape. Grainy snow drifted onto the window ledge like soot. Airborne trash ripped above the narrow streets where pedestrians bent against walls of wind.

I interrupted Gail, who raised a tolerant eyebrow. Since I had become a partner, she sometimes accompanied her eyebrow lifting with a pleasantry. Not this morning. "Yes?"

"Do we have a card for Walter Wrather?"

Her face was momentarily smooth and forgetful. "You know I don't think Mr. Canning has given me that information."

"Have you spoken to Mr. or Mrs. Wrather?"

"Not that I recall."

I went back and looked up the Wrathers in the Manhattan telephone directory. There were none. I tried the operator for a new listing with no success.

I went back to Gail. "Did you ever meet Mr. or Mrs. Wrather?" I asked.

"If I didn't talk to them, how can I have met them?" Behind thick lenses she squinted. "Why not ask Mr. Canning when he comes in?"

By eleven-thirty he hadn't come in.

For another forty minutes I watched the market to put off calling his apartment. Even in disarray the office was warm and comfortable. After two years I felt I belonged there and hated to think about the tenure ending.

Barbara Canning's voice, when she answered, was slower and deeper than normal. "He hasn't come home. I really . . . really don't understand. You haven't heard?"

"Heard what?"

"From my husband."

"No."

"My brother is checking with the police. . . ."

Her brother, Rudy Thatcher, did occasional legal chores for the firm.

"Benny, I don't want to offend you," she said, "but I can't help thinking something must be wrong at the office. You couldn't have made some awful mistake with a client?"

"No."

"Making you a partner so soon, I wish I understood. The clients all trust my husband so. . . ."

I assured her I hadn't gotten us into trouble. The assurance counted for nothing. She protected herself by assuming the worst of everyone.

Rudy came by the office an hour later. He was short and trim, with a heavy shag of graying blond hair that softened the squareness of his face. His rimless glasses sat on a pug nose, making him look young and scrappy—helpful in litigation when opponents worried that Rudy might throw a punch. Two decades earlier, when he was four

24

years out of Yale, Rudy had jumped from associate to partner at Welden Weir Manges, Etc., Etc., a feat recorded only once before in the firm's long history—by the son of a managing partner. Rudy was nobody's son in particular. Intelligence and ambition had carried him midway up the roster of the firm's senior partners. He took the law seriously, as though it were society's inner glue.

He searched Jack's office in vain for signs of where his brother-in-law might have gone. "Barbara is chewing the rug," he said. "Tame old Jack—but for fifteen years my sister has been waiting for him to run off with a cocktail waitress. Instead he's probably been hit by a fucking bus or mugged."

"You're full of cheer."

"I'm just being realistic. When a solid citizen doesn't come home, you think the worst. Has anyone tried raising him in Connecticut? He could have driven up. I don't know if Barbara thought of it."

They had a rural cottage for summer weekends. Jack wouldn't go there in January. I had Gail get the number anyway, and Rudy and I listened on the speaker phone as it rang.

"Well, a bus is more likely," Rudy said. "On the other hand, it's only eighteen hours. No need to panic."

I nodded.

"But we're going to have to call the auditors in."

I sat up. "The auditors?"

"No reflection on you. And it's my idea, not Barbara's. If we've got a problem, we need to know it."

"We've got one problem," I said. "I'm having trouble making sense of an account. The owners don't have a telephone listing."

"They could just be unlisted. What's the name?"

"Walter and Virginia Wrather."

"Do you have an address?"

"Central Park West."

"How big is the account?"

"Fifty thousand."

He snorted. "If Jack pinched fifty thousand, he's a bigger doofus than I think. Let me get your auditors on the line."

He got them, and two hours later twin giant elves, six-three and almost round, showed up wearing tolerant smiles that forgave

25

whatever indiscretions they would find because they had seen them all. They were dressed identically in black suits, narrow ties, crew cuts and wing tips. They introduced themselves as Fred and Bernard Sosnow and cheerfully repeated their manager's warning that Canning & McCarthy was being billed at twice the normal hourly rate.

Taking over the computer, with Gail at their beck and call, they spent the afternoon comparing numbers with Vince DiMineo, our main broker. I had told Vince that we'd had a burglary and that Jack was under the weather.

My heart shriveled as I imagined the whispers at Vince's office. By tomorrow half the financial district would know that the auditors were working us over. Even if the numbers came up right, a stink would linger. Too many small firms had tumbled over the brink, dragging clients and creditors with them. If any of our customers heard, we would lose some business.

I tried to stay out of the elves' way and do my own work. I talked to Barney Potter and sold about forty thousand dollars worth of his stocks, put half the proceeds into Treasury bills, half into utility bonds.

A broker we had never done business with phoned with a new oil stock he liked. I sat with my head back and listened. He had a low, gruff voice. "Don't blab this all over the place, Ben—it's called Moose Pass Exploration. The president is a geologist, and he has locked up some of the best small leases in the Rockies. Bought real cheap because all the bankrupt guys want to sell. The second well they drilled hit gas on Monday, but nobody knows that yet. This stock could really move. It's two dollars right now."

I gave the line one jerk, to tease him. "How many shares?"

His breathlessness subsided. "Fifty million."

"So on one well and some leases, you've got a hundred-million-dollar company?"

"Well, if you want to look at it that way—"

I told him I did, and he went away to try somebody else. If they had gotten the capitalization up to a hundred million, he and his friends had already spread the story far and wide. There was no point in being disappointed I wasn't the first name on his list.

The market put in a rough final hour, during which the value of corporate America dwindled by a few hundred million dollars without much effect. My Seattle Aviation closed up a quarter-point, which wasn't bad on a weak day.

I heard a commotion and found Gail bawling out one of the Sosnow brothers.

"He was using the *Standard & Poor's* for a foot stool," she complained. "How's this *vildachaya* expect me to find it under those feet?"

The elf and his brother were drifting between rooms with solemn, funeral parlor expressions.

"How are you doing?" I asked.

"It's how *you're* doing that matters. You check out okay so far." He gobbled an ice cream bar.

At five-thirty one of them came in and waved his clipboard at me. "Your broker wants to call it a night. How about if we finish in the morning?"

"How about if you tell me what you've found."

"Here's what we did. We took the balances from your records. A few we need a piece of paper or two but nothing major. We called Mr. DiMineo and had him give the total from each client's account. Everything meshed, give or take fifty dollars. Then we had him tell us any accounts that had cash or securities drawn out in the last month. No securities went out and not much cash. Bernie and I will spot-check specific holdings in the accounts mañana." He spread his hands. "If I can't find dirt, I can't find dirt. What can I tell you?"

"Did you add up Walter and Virginia Wrather?"

He glanced at his notes to be sure. "To the penny. Strictly kosher. Why that one?"

"Bad guess."

Maybe it was something Jack had set up for his mistress, I thought. The cocktail waitress he had spent the night with.

He whistled shrilly. "Quitting time, Brother!"

Gail needed consoling after they lumbered out the door. "Something's wrong here. Why hasn't Mr. Canning been in today?"

"He had business out of town."

She didn't believe it and left for the subway.

There were phone messages on her desk, mostly for Jack. Rudy hadn't called in several hours. Good sign or bad? Christopher Somebody wanted to show us a new software line for financial managers. George Finn, the chairman of Brooker Finn & Company, had tried to reach Jack. They were old friends.

The day's news wire reported that the Dow had tumbled eleven points—far from decisive, but troubling. I read the headlines. The usual cluster of companies had reported earnings for the latest quarter. A handful had raised their dividend payments. A cement producer that most of our clients owned announced it would raise prices by five percent.

The phone rang and I ignored it.

A German bank had been rescued by the government. A pharmaceutical company had rebuffed a merger proposal as unfair to its stockholders. Someone shot a Latin American president. A shipyard sued the navy. Gold closed up a dollar.

The phone started again, broke off.

A small brokerage house collapsed.

That was closer to home—though we were managers rather than brokers. I read on anyway. You never knew when people would pull down their shades. Givonni & Company was the name. They had specialized in institutional business, low profit, high volume, and somehow had gotten caught with inventory that declined and wiped out their capital. The news wire noted that another institutional firm had failed two months ago. The article blamed the failures on sharp seesawing by the market.

When the hall door rattled, I sat up abruptly.

The outer office light was out, and I was using a tightly focused reading lamp. From the hall the dappled glass would look dark.

I reached for anything that would serve as a weapon.

The door opened and the cleaning woman came in fumbling with her keys. Her canvas cart blocked the hall. By the time she raised her eyes, the letter opener I had taken from the desk was back where it belonged. She saw me and gave a start. "Mr. McCar'y, you still here."

"I'll be leaving soon."

"I won't disturb you. I do the next office."

28

I closed the door, packed my briefcase, tried phoning home twice and got no answer. It took ten minutes.

I opened the hall door and came face to face with Jimmy Doyle. He leaned forward, a wing of ginger hair drooping between his eyes. "Where's Jack?"

"He's gone for the day."

"That's no good. I want to talk to him." His tongue was slow, his breath a distiller's reek, his lips pale, his chin stubbled.

"Is it really important?"

He was closer to sober than the previous night, less surly. "Nothing that can't wait for Canning. Tell him I came by."

"Peter Bagley said you know each other."

He raised his chin. "Must be quite a shock for you, huh? We did a stint as trainees at Brooker Finn twenty-some years ago. Canning came in a couple of months after me, and I showed him the ropes."

"It's a good firm," I said, implying he must have been good to have worked there.

"When Canning and I started, it was Brooker Finn Hargrave and Bard, all blue bloods. Hargrave retired, and the Bards sold out. I used to get Christmas cards from Luther Brooker, when they had him in a nursing home upstate. What a life. You drool into a cup and tell some nineteen-year-old nurse's aide you used to corner stocks."

He shrugged, backing away from the door. "I sold stock then, I sell stock now. What's the difference? The clients were from Block Island then; now they're from Queens. They all believe in the same magic. I've sold a dozen companies as the next Xerox, and Furbinger has a dozen more waiting in the hopper."

"I'll tell Jack you came by."

"That's a good fellow."

We didn't ride the elevator down together, but he was pacing and shivering when I got to the Chambers Street IND station. The cold had driven most people out of the island's lower end. We had the station to ourselves until a train squealed to a stop beside the platform and we got aboard different cars.

6

AT Eighty-sixth Street I joined the throng pouring up the stairway at the edge of Central Park. A screen of snow blurred all but the nearest objects. Cars crept on the avenue behind useless headlights, stalling as they joined the traffic coming out of the park. I turned south and looked for the right address. Number 227 was printed on a red awning outside a limestone-faced apartment building that had potted junipers on either side of the entrance. A doorman stood on the top step.

I knocked the snow off my hat. "Could you buzz the Wrathers' apartment?"

"Not in this building, chief." He rushed down to curbside to open a taxicab door.

I waited. When he came back, I said, "Have they moved recently?"

"I've been here two years, and there haven't been any Wrathers."

I tried the buildings on either side, and they didn't have any Wrathers.

It wasn't much of a surprise, but I had been hoping for an easy answer.

7

THE elves came back in the morning but left before noon. "Ben, I wish our fish smelled as clean as yours," Fred Sosnow said. "You've got nothing to worry about."

"You're sure?"

"Here's a man who can't stand good news! I'm telling you, the accounts all add. We went through a half-dozen of them from stem to stern. DiMineo says he has exactly the stocks in the accounts that your computer says he has. Right cash balances, too. Except, ah, you've got an extra five percent of Worthwhile Kitchens, because last week the company paid a stock dividend you hadn't picked up on. Can I do better for you than that?"

The walls crumbled an hour and twenty minutes later. Our broker's assistant, a young Bronx woman named Lisa Merchant, called up bubbling cheer. Gaiety was out of character at Faulkner Wells Rhoades. Vince DiMineo hardly ever bubbled. She said, "Have you heard the news on Dorchester Millinery?"

I barely recognized the name. "No."

"There's a note on the wire. Lance Grendal has offered to buy the company for thirty-six dollars a share."

"Who is Lance Grendal?"

"Some kind of raider, I guess."

31

"Good luck to him," I said, wondering why she had called.

"I thought you'd be excited. Have you been on vacation? You own some Dorchester."

I took a guess. "Five hundred shares?"

"Twenty-three thousand, Ben."

I made her repeat it, asked, "Which account?"

"In your firm's account. Has Jack been keeping you in the dark? He's been buying it for the last month. Your average price is about seventeen. Trading just resumed at twenty-eight. You and Jack are a quarter-million richer. Congratulations."

The firm's trading account held most of our undistributed profits—the money that neither Jack nor I took out in salary and dividends. At last look, we had just under five hundred thousand dollars in it, of which fifteen percent was mine. Jack ran the account, buying and selling rarely. She was telling me that four-fifths of the stake had been riding on a company that I'd scarcely heard of. A company that Jack had never mentioned.

Six weeks earlier, when I browsed through the account, it held more than twenty stocks and about eighty thousand in cash. What had happened to them?

Lisa prodded, "Ben?"

"I'm still here."

"Maybe I should talk to Jack."

"I'll pass the word."

"I didn't know you guys had a pipeline to this Grendal."

"We don't have a pipeline."

"Suit yourself," she said crisply. "You sound surprised at your good luck."

"I didn't know we were into Dorchester Millinery . . . that heavily."

"Yeah? Vince mentioned it the other day, said he wondered what Jack was up to. It wasn't Mr. Canning's usual fare. Naturally I wasn't supposed to ask."

I wish you had asked *me*, I thought. I groped around the desk but couldn't come up with our own account's file. I didn't remember seeing it yesterday either.

"Can you put Vince on?" I asked.

"He's home with the flu."

When I walked out into Gail's fortress, she avoided looking up. I pulled the Standard & Poor's background sheet on Dorchester Millinery and retreated to privacy. The report and accompanying statistics described a dreary history of a corporation's decline. The company was struggling with high labor costs, ancient machinery, fading apparel lines. Dorchester made feeble money in the industry's fat years and lost a bundle in the lean ones. The company's production costs were so far above those of manufacturers in the Far East that sales in the United States were slipping and international markets couldn't be touched. If the pattern continued, Dorchester would slide quietly into oblivion in a few years.

Heaven knew what attracted a raider.

Or Jack.

I shook my head. He would no more buy shares of Dorchester Millinery than take his life savings to the race track.

The papers for our account were nowhere to be found. There was no telling when they would surface from the mess. I went back to the computer. The electronic memory said that we still had our eclectic list of conservative stocks and a heavy cash reserve. Not a share of Dorchester Millinery Corporation.

I checked with Gail. "Have you entered anything in the firm's account lately?"

"Oh, no. It's been more than a month since he changed anything in there."

I phoned Lisa. "Could you send over the copies of the purchase orders on Dorchester? Things are still a mess here."

"No problem."

She was as good as her word. Computer copies of the purchase receipts for the firm's account—and the sales tickets covering most of the rest of our securities—arrived within an hour. I read through them, uneasiness rising. The records from Faulkner Wells's automated files gave the lie to our own computer's recollection. Most of the stocks Jack liked had been sold over the last six weeks. The money that had come in from those sales had been used to buy

33

Dorchester Millinery shares. The buying had been dribs and drabs at first, then persistent in the last two weeks. Eager in recent days. A block of five thousand Dorchester shares had been purchased two days ago. Three thousand the Friday before that.

The trading pattern said plainly that Jack had gotten wind of Grendal's plan. Had bought a little on first hearing of it six weeks ago. Then as the date neared got more aggressive. And in the last days went for broke.

I couldn't believe it and couldn't deny it. More things were wrong than I could count. We didn't speculate on takeover stories. We didn't buy dying companies. Jack Canning never, ever went for broke on anything.

Apart from that, a final problem. What he had done—if he had done it—was illegal.

Dangerously, stupidly, brazenly illegal.

You could buy a takeover target on a rumor, if you didn't really know the rumor was true.

Jack wouldn't buy rumors.

But if you knew, if you had inside information that a raider named Grendal was really going after Dorchester Millinery, it was a violation of the securities laws to buy the stock before the rest of the investing public knew.

Jack's buying had the confidence of someone who knew.

Rudy reacted badly to the news. "You're crazy! Your brokers are crazy!"

I described the signs that Jack had kept the trades out of the computer.

Rudy exploded: "Then my brother-in-law is crazy!"

I called Vince DiMineo at home. He started a coughing fit that finally subsided to dry wheezing. I asked him, "What did Jack say about Dorchester Millinery?"

"Nothing. You know he doesn't tell me why he's buying a stock. I just put the orders through. You—ah, you sound like you haven't talked to Jack.

"He took a few days off."

"I see. I don't blame him. I'm going to be in hot water with Faulkner Wells's compliance supervisors. Jack was buying like he had the stock of the year. They're going to ask me why I wasn't more curious." He tried to clear his throat, which produced more coughing. He got control and said, "If there's an investigation, you know I've got no choice—I'll have to cooperate."

"I know."

"For the time being, I'd better not talk to you. The government will come down on us hard if they think we're getting our story straight. That would really get me fired."

I could imagine the pressure he would get from Faulkner Wells. Jack had dealt with the firm for a decade, but that wouldn't make any difference. Faulkner Wells was a gentlefolk's club that had survived the Crash and numerous other catastrophes by knowing when to cut the other guy adrift.

Vince wheezed, "If I were Canning, I guess I would try to deny everything."

Tom Chin didn't bring his client around. I wondered if he knew someone at Faulkner Wells. Jack's friend George Finn called asking why his earlier calls hadn't been returned. His voice boomed, hinting at the dimensions of the man. "Is everything all right down there?"

"Jack's out of town," I said. "Everything is all right."

Finn was well-connected. Whispers about us were getting around.

8

EXCEPT for a meeting with a suspicious, bad-tempered, damp-eyed and confused Barbara Canning, the weekend was quiet. Jack wasn't in the morgue or any hospital within fifty miles of New York. He hadn't phoned from a Catskills love nest. His bank accounts hadn't been touched, and no charges had been reported against his credit cards. His telephone card hadn't been used. His Mercedes hadn't been found at an airport or any place else. For Rudy, who had put an associate to tracking down the wayward brother-in-law with a certain amount of smug pleasure, Thursday and Friday were days of reporting frustration and insisting he didn't owe any apologies. On Saturday morning Barbara let him know she disagreed. She was truly disappointed that he had failed to find Jack's body. She was certain that the car must be off the road somewhere with her husband frozen at the wheel. It was the only explanation.

She grasped only vaguely the implications of our coup in Dorchester Millinery. She knew the government had taken away the profits of Ivan Boesky and Dennis Levine after finding they had traded on illicit information. She understood that something similar could await Canning & McCarthy. We agreed that the firm's business would carry on as closely to normal as possible. That much was Rudy's accomplishment. Left to Barbara, the partnership would have suspended operations "before Benny does something terrible that ruins us." Rudy explained that closing down would damage the firm worse than I probably would do.

After that restrained endorsement, Rudy took me to lunch at the Gramercy and excused his sister's manners. "She needs your friendship, Ben, and that puts a moral burden on you—because you know she needs you and she doesn't."

He glanced out at the busy lobby. "Too bad you can't sweep that Dorchester Millinery stock under the rug. Then we would just have your senior partner on an overdue sabbatical."

"If he had bought only five thousand shares," I said, "we could get away with it. You don't need a strong excuse for that sort of purchase. We thought it looked cheap. The charts spoke some magic."

Rudy leaned toward me. "All right, this doesn't fit Jack. We don't know how much else doesn't fit. The burglary, that fucking Wrather account—I hate to say it, but God knows what else he's been up to."

I didn't answer.

Rudy said, "You'd better think of practicalities. If the Securities and Exchange Commission can prove that you or Jack bought that stock on inside information, the fines could top a million dollars. They can take everything in the firm's investment account, every dime, and you and Jack will still owe them money."

He buttered a roll and bit off half. "A week ago you and Jack could have sold the firm for a couple million. But if the regulators revoke your license to manage money, your clients will vanish. There will be nothing left to sell."

"That won't happen overnight," I pointed out.

"And maybe we'll get lucky and this will blow over. We haven't heard from the SEC yet. If DiMineo's firm keeps quiet—"

"They can't. If they don't report an apparent violation, their own license can be revoked."

"Well, then. Our best hope is that the regulators have other irons in the fire and won't get to your case for a while."

The next evening, the SEC's chief of enforcement was the guest on *Rich Is Better*, a Sunday night hour of interviews with financial movers and shakers that was watched by a respectable percentage of the nation's stock owners. I was lying on the couch, a beer on my stomach, when a marching ribbon of ticker prices and a familiar fanfare of synthesizer notes introduced the host, Michael Renshaw. A hawk-nosed man with crooked lips, Renshaw smiled like a maître d' who had given the customers a better table than they deserved. He said: "Tonight we have a special guest. He's one of those aggressive fellows in government who keeps you would-be Ivan Boeskys honest. His name is Gordon Trapp, chief of the SEC Division of Enforcement—the cadre known informally as the 'Watchdogs of Wall Street.'"

Renshaw crossed his legs and stared off camera. "Gordon, your office at the Securities and Exchange Commission has a reputation as having a bite to go with its bark. Ivan Boesky, a few lawyers, a stray yuppie and a lot of other people have gone to jail for insider trading. Why are there so many crooks on Wall Street?"

The camera shifted to Gordon Trapp's tousled blond head. His face was boyish, smooth and intense behind tortoise-shell glasses. He leaned into the subject. "We want people to think we bite, Michael. If that perception keeps them from violating the rules, the SEC is doing its job."

"And when that doesn't work?"

"In the last five years, we've brought more than one hundred cases," Trapp said proudly. "A lot of people succumb to greed."

"Correct me if I'm wrong—most of your cases have involved somebody buying a stock before a takeover because of inside information," Renshaw said. "Is there more of that than there used to be?"

"Less, definitely less. We've been having an impact."

Renshaw's grainy face turned to confront the camera. The wrinkled lip rose at one side, exposing a wedge of teeth. I had watched *Rich Is Better* for enough years to suspect that Gordon Trapp was going to be put on the spot. Renshaw said, "I noticed that a little apparel company had a big jump this week on takeover news. But the price had been going up gradually for several weeks before that. Do you think anyone knew something?"

"If they traded on improper knowledge, we want to talk to them," Trapp said.

"Well, look here. Somebody bought five thousand shares two days before the news. The stock normally trades a few hundred shares a day. What does that say to a watchdog?"

"I can't comment on specific situations," Gordon Trapp said.

"For our viewers' enlightenment," Michael Renshaw said, winking at the camera, "the specific situation is named Dorchester Millinery Corporation. If that's a tip, don't tell anyone where you got it. We all know the watchdog never sleeps, or at least hardly ever. . . . Later this evening, we will be talking to—"

I got up and switched off the set as Marty came downstairs. I sat down numbly. How had Renshaw gotten that tidbit to wave under Trapp's nose? And gotten it so fast? I knew that *Rich Is Better* taped on Friday evenings. Somebody who knew about Monday's five thousand shares had gotten the story out in a hurry.

The kind of thing a friend of Renshaw's would do.

Or an enemy of ours.

9

I stopped by *Investor's Week*'s office on Monday afternoon looking for Peter Bagley. It was two-thirty, and he was at lunch. With the weekly deadline four comfortable days away, the lunch hour could stretch to happy hour. My old boss, the magazine's executive editor, Max Dupree, nodded gravely from behind his glass wall but didn't invite me into his office for a chat. He had company, a burly man in crisp blue pinstripes whose mouth was moving rapidly, trying to beat Max's invisible clock. I knew the man, a former broker who ran a small hedge fund from a midtown office and liked to be known as a dangerous short seller. Max Dupree's tiny monkey face was screwed up in a show of concentration, but his eyes were drifting. Sometimes traders brought him good stories that ended up in the magazine, but this fellow's tale apparently wasn't measuring up.

I cupped a hand behind my ear and leaned toward the glass. Max grinned and mouthed an obscenity. The short seller couldn't ignore the distraction and craned around, saw me staring soberly with hands in my pockets and gave Max Dupree a puzzled look as a pile of papers slid from his lap.

Max laughed behind a doll-sized hand.

I wandered back past Peter's office. Nancy Scott, frowning intently, burst out of the neighboring cubicle. She had on a serious navy suit and a black ribbon tie. She carried a file of magazine clippings.

"Is Peter coming back today?" I asked.

"He said he was."

"Will you tell him I stopped by?"

"All right. I've got to go," she said breathlessly, "I'm working on something for Mr. Dupree." Doing legwork for Max was a privilege for a new staff member.

"Should you be telling me that?"

She broke stride and cast me an annoyed look before hustling toward Max's office.

Peter's desk was cluttered with books and clipping files, computer printouts, ashtrays, soda cans, legal pads and an underlayer of dust, erasings and paper clips. The office projected a different image from the expensive suits and handmade shoes. The soft drink cans, four of them, were probably half full. They were lined up beside a precarious stack of *Investor's Week* back issues. When an avalanche occurred once or twice a week, Peter's scream reached the far end of the suite.

I unloaded a chair and read the previous weekend's issue until Peter returned. "Hullo, Benj. Has Max rehired you?"

"He asked me to come in and take over 'Street Smarts,'" I said. "Pep it up, to be specific."

"You're welcome to the column. Don't forget that little Max Dupree comes with it."

"In that case, I'll settle for tapping your memory."

He hung his topcoat and jacket on the back of the door. "In return, tell me your partner's favorite stock."

I felt a chill. "His favorite stock?"

"He must have one. I need an idea for the column."

"Take a look at North American Bakeries. We own a lot of it. Some real estate they've got on the West Side is on the books at nineteen thirties prices."

"Okay. I'll look. Your turn."

"Lance Grendal—what do you know about him?"

"He buys companies; that's about it. Not one of the heavy hitters

41

like Carl Icahn or Kohlberg Kravis. He goes for smaller companies. Didn't he just announce something?"

"Another takeover. Could I look at the clipping file?"

He punched a telephone number. "It's Peter, dearest. Get me the file on Grendal, G-R-E-N-D-A-L, Lance. Right away, darling."

A clerk delivered a legal-sized manila folder a few minutes later. Peter led me back to a row of tiny conference rooms, left me in one with a round table and cushioned chairs. The magazine's file on Grendal was thin. When he wasn't chasing companies he kept his name out of the papers. I spread the dozen clippings out on the table, not hoping for much—some link between my world and Lance Grendal's. The articles went back about ten years, to a couple of one-paragraph notes that a Bahamian investor had bought a quarter of the shares of a small steel company. Five years ago *Business Week* had noticed that Lance Grendal was a big boy and had run a profile accompanied by a paparazzo's photograph of a man in white ducks standing at the bow of a yacht. The man was middle-aged, with black hair, a Vandyke beard and a streetwise smirk.

The article described Grendal as an expatriate barefoot boy from the Bronx who liked boats, teenaged mistresses and bruising financial battles. In journalism, everything fit series sentences. His father had sold yard goods north of Gun Hill Road, and a brother still ran the family business from a peeling storefront. Lance was the youngest son. After a tour with the army in Korea, he had turned his back on the woolens counter and spent a government-paid year at Columbia. Nominally he studied accounting. In practice, according to the magazine, he shagged espresso waitresses. After a year he set up housekeeping with a beautiful Thai potter, cut his studies to a few hours, and let the bisexual potter recruit bedmates for both their accounts.

When he inherited a little money from an uncle, friends expected him to restock his dope chest and retire until the money ran out. Instead he bought into the yard goods business, leapfrogging his father and brother's experience on his first foray. For two generations the family had bought wholesale and sold at retail, suffering the usual setbacks of small merchants that kept prosperity always a year away. Lance plunged straight into the salvage market, buying the inventory of a bankrupt manufacturer and peddling the goods to small retailers from the back of a borrowed station wagon.

He tripled the inheritance. Then he talked himself into a bank loan that raised his capital sixfold. His next move took four months. He liquidated a Massachusetts shoe manufacturer's inventory. The goods were worth millions, but Grendal stretched his capital like a gossamer thread and acted as a wholesaler's wholesaler. He earned about ten percent on the job, the article guessed, and may have tripled his capital.

All the story until that point was pieced together from unattributed sources and the Thai potter. But Grendal's first banker described the next maneuver. "He came back to me and said he could repay the loan right then. Or if the bank was interested, we could give him a credit line for several times the original amount and he would go pick through the bankruptcy courts in the Deep South to see what was being given away. I knew those first deals could have been beginner's luck. But you've got to trust your nose, so we backed him." By the end of the year Grendal had made himself several times a millionaire, operating with an instinct for making money that the banker likened to a musician's perfect pitch. "The only thing that will ever bring Lance down is if he gets bored," the banker said.

The Thai potter had vanished by the time a Southern news magazine labeled Lance Grendal one of the business world's brightest young comers. He was a dozen times a millionaire, owned two medium-sized private companies and pieces of a half-dozen others, and he had married a little Georgia peach whose daddy was lieutenant governor. Lance could be counted on for contributions to almost any charity as well as to the New York and Georgia Democratic parties. His operations appeared to be legal if not white-glove clean.

Then the Internal Revenue Service came knocking. For years Grendal had been claiming tax deductions for a hunting lodge in the Great Smokies, a condominium on Paradise Island, a Trumped-up ocean-going yacht, bills from a Park Avenue gourmet shop. The tax agents decreed that those luxuries were undeclared personal income and billed Lance Grendal for just over $2 million including interest and penalties.

Grendal was used to success, and adversity was a shock.

He reacted as unpredictably as ever, throwing what looked from the outside like a six-month-long temper tantrum. During that time he broke, or at least dismantled, much of what he had spent the previous decade acquiring. He booted the little Georgia peach, who had ripened to 170 pounds, back to Savannah. He settled with her by signing over a tire-retreading company that had made money for each of the last dozen years but in the next two years, for reasons that no one could pinpoint, wheezed and faded like a tubercular patient.

He paid the government with a cashier's check written on the dismemberment of a paperboard mill that had employed half of a South Carolina town. He fired his old law firm and brought his legal work in-house, hiring a tax attorney who had been disbarred in New York and an elderly general counsel from a bankrupt grocery chain. Other Grendal companies were sold to an array of small-time buyers with seemingly nothing in common but their obscurity. Grendal bought a new yacht that he named *Reprisal* and drifted from port to port as far south as Venezuela. His lawyers stayed behind and continued the liquidation.

Nobody guessed what Lance Grendal was up to. When the paper storm subsided, his empire remained largely intact. But control of the companies had migrated offshore, vanishing behind a screen of Bahamian banks and holding companies, cross-controlled through corporations based in the Cayman Islands and Panama. None was immune from U.S. taxation. But none was in the slightest way accessible to tax examiners.

A Senate subcommittee, chaired by a South Carolinian, found Grendal's defection a national affront. Two staff lawyers headed south to trace the labyrinth of corporate shells that Grendal and his attorneys had woven. After six weeks in the sun, the lawyers came back tanned and smiling and bearing an organizational chart that would have been simpler if it had tracked the intermarriages of European nobility. The main corporations were Grendal Offshore Ltd., Grendal Hotel Enterprises, and Paradise Assets. Grendal's attorneys had been exceptionally cooperative, the senators' agents reported. The subcommittee pondered the lines descending from the three corporate headings like a tangle of mangrove roots, congratulated the lawyers on their diligence, and went on to something else.

From the Bahamas Grendal launched a raid on a small specialty steel company. He acquired thirty percent of the mill at the bottom of the business cycle, waited eighteen months and found a Japanese conglomerate willing to pay four times his cost.

He spent most of his days sailing and his sleepless nights, according to a former associate, prowling the top two floors of the Caribbean Princess Hotel—owned by an untraceable subsidiary of Paradise Assets—devouring financial reports prepared by his cadre of accountants on potential takeover targets.

Most of the reading led nowhere. Now and then he bought a few million dollars worth of a company and let the word out that he was on the move. If a rush of other buyers pushed up the stock price, Grendal silently sold out at a profit.

A dozen actual forays had won him control of a fertilizer company, a Florida railroad, a department store chain and a couple of manufacturing companies. All were small operations, especially by the standards of Wall Street deal-makers whose names made headlines. But the total of assets that Grendal controlled from his hideaway had to be impressive.

The article ended with a vague suggestion that Grendal might have trouble digesting all the odd-fitting pieces he had devoured in the preceding decade.

There was nothing more in the clips for a couple of years. The latest article, more than a year old, reported that Grendal Hotel Enterprises had sold its interest in an offshore drilling fleet. No price was mentioned.

I shuffled the clippings back into the file jacket. They added up to a vague portrait of a smart, volatile man who enjoyed taking risks. Many of the risks seemed to be with money borrowed from other people. His track record was excellent. Boredom might be his worst enemy.

Peter Bagley was on the telephone. As I laid the clipping file on

45

his desk, he put the receiver against his chest. "Hang around for a minute, Benj."

He murmured noncommittally a couple of times, hung up, and asked me, "So why do you care about this guy?"

"Our portfolios overlap a bit. I'm interested in who else owns our stocks."

"What's the story on Grendal?"

I gave him the gist of the *Business Week* article. "I'd heard that he was small-time," I said. "He's not really, but he keeps his head down. He seems to play a lone hand."

I thought about it and realized how strongly that impression had come through what I had read. There was no mention of truly close advisers—just employees who could be replaced. No reference to fellow sharks with whom he swam. A hint that he liked to bite the pilot fish who tried to wiggle close to him.

Never a suggestion that friends or brokers heard tips on his raids. Let alone money managers he didn't know.

Peter tossed the file on a shelf behind him. "Maybe I'll do an update on him someday. Why don't you and Marty hit a couple of clubs with me one of these nights?"

I said we might.

"She can come alone if she wants. Tell her." He held off the intimacies of friendship with brash and rude asides. His relationships with women were similarly brusque, and so short-lived.

"Jimmy Doyle came by the office the other night," I said. "He wanted to talk to Jack."

Peter scratched a slack cheek. "That sounds like the Jimmy I know. He probably wants to let his old friend in on Trionix. He wasn't always such a jerk. Working for Bunny Furbinger must have been the finishing touch. Speaking of jerks, Furbinger has a great stock deal you and Jack may want to buy." He scratched around his desk like a man drowning, panic rising. He found a glossy, magazine-sized brochure that described a company called Smoke-Less Wonder International. Peter said, "It's not international—just a guy operating out of his basement on Staten Island. He wants to market a new filtration system to cut down on tar in cigarettes. There's a diagram in the prospectus."

The diagram showed a kettle-shaped object with tubes going to and from it.

"You fill that little pot with water and hang it from your belt," Peter said. "The tubes run the smoke through the water and it comes out clean. Isn't that creative? When I was in school we called them *bongs*. Furbinger offered his customers fifty million shares at a dime each, and they've sold out."

"That's five million dollars," I said.

"Well, the guy on Staten Island doesn't get all that to play with. Furbinger keeps fifteen percent off the top, plus expenses like a thirty-thousand-dollar bash at Windows on the World to introduce the company to Wall Street. I think I'm in the wrong business."

I gave him the prospectus. "Didn't you say his game will end sometime?"

"He hasn't run out of suckers yet," Peter said.

10

IT was a long afternoon. The head of the Division of Enforcement of the SEC, Gordon Trapp, announced after lunch that his office would investigate recent trading in the stock of Dorchester Millinery Corporation.

He said that a respected brokerage firm had volunteered information about irregularities in one of its accounts.

They were hanging us out.

I called Rudy Thatcher, who was sympathetic. "Be glad that the SEC hasn't made your name public yet. That's when your best friend won't take your call."

I told him about my research on Grendal, adding, "I can't buy the idea that Jack heard anything from Lance Grendal's camp."

"Well, Jack heard something somewhere—unless you did the trading. What is the next most likely source if not Grendal? Why not somebody at Dorchester? Have you thought of that? They might have gotten wind they were being stalked."

I went home early and annoyed Marty by hanging out in her studio. She had turned on the electric lights, which made the cluttered room so bright that it seemed barren. She was working on a bluish-gray study of the buildings across the street. The downsloping perspective compressed people on the sidewalk into figures shrunken by dreadful weight.

She looked around now and then, hoping I would disappear. Finally she said, "If worse comes to worst, we won't starve. And we won't lose this place—if that's what you're worried about."

It was, but I didn't remember mentioning it to her. If the government got properly riled about somebody breaking the rules in the stock market, they could strip every asset from the suspect. The only bargaining chip was to have someone bigger to turn in. I couldn't think of anyone to throw to the wolves.

"Mother wouldn't offer to help, and I wouldn't accept," she went on, "but Uncle Gil would be good for mortgage payments."

When she was twenty, Gil Norris had paid her way in Mexico for a year. His room at the Knickerbocker held a few of the disturbing jungle paintings that he had gotten in exchange.

"Also, he's got broker friends he could tap to take you aboard," she said.

Hiring someone in trouble with the SEC was asking a lot. If the government barred me from the business, it would be asking the impossible. But I nodded.

She wiped a brush, threw it into a turpentine jar. "We've got savings. We could prepay the mortgage for a few months, hunker down."

I glanced around the room. It never occurred to her to be afraid. Seldom occurred to her that anyone else would be afraid.

She asked gently, "Are you planning on spending a lot of time at home?"

"I don't know."

"Your clients still need attention."

"True." They might not for long. Or might not get it from me, if Barbara Canning and Rudy put their heads together. A sense of inevitable failure crept close like a cold tide. If I gave in, accepted the wintry embrace, disappointment would gradually become something that felt natural. Without Jack, the firm was dead. My role in it was finished.

If the taint from the SEC's inquiry wasn't too great, there might be another job on Wall Street, several steps down the ladder. Not likely another partnership. With practice could I fit in at the kind of firm that hired slightly damaged talent? At a firm that shuffled clients' accounts three times a year, feeding heavy brokerage commissions to anyone who referred a customer?

"I'll go in for a full day tomorrow," I said and left the studio.

So I went back to the office at nine A.M. and before noon the mail arrived. The airmail envelope bore a stamp of the British West Indies, and the message in Jack Canning's tidy script was succinct:

> *My dear Ben,*
>   *Never trust a friend.*

11

A commuter flight took me up to Connecticut on Wednesday morning. An icy rain made Dorchester Millinery's headquarters look shabby and forlorn. At the edge of the roof a broken gutter sent a sooty torrent cascading onto a parking lot that was a moonscape of craters and pebbled blacktop. Wet patches crawled down the main building's brick walls like spreading rot. The plant testified to too many lean years when maintenance had been put off for better times that never arrived.

In the lobby a female mannequin wearing scarlet pants and a sailor shirt held the hand of a toddler dressed in a green jumper. Next to them a living room set displayed Dorchester Millinery's best chintz upholstery fabrics. The colors were faded, the fabric wilted.

The company's president, Roscoe Tullman, hadn't wasted any of his failing resources on the office. The carpet was thin, the desk wore old scuff marks, and the walls were as dingy as parchment. Tullman looked like a Yankee farmer who had worn himself out plowing rocky pastures. He was in his late fifties, according to the annual report, but could have passed for ten years older. His bony face had picket-fence teeth and a prominent nose, hairless brows, a few bands of white hair combed straight forward. Instead of breaking under the dying company's weight, his shoulders under the gray worsted jacket had curled into a gentle wishbone. His desk was clear, as if all

51

the corporate problems had been swept into Lance Grendal's arms.

He didn't ask his secretary to bring me coffee. "You implied on the phone, Mr. McCarthy, that you are not certain we're being offered a fair price for the company. Is that the sum of it?"

The price was generous, but I had needed an excuse for visiting. On the flight I had entertained a slim hope. If Grendal walked away—or was pushed away—and the stock fell back into the teens, the transgression by Canning & McCarthy might seem less pressing to Gordon Trapp at the SEC.

I told Tullman, "We've got thousands of shares, so the price is important to us. Grendal is offering barely the stated book value."

He rubbed his naked brow with a large finger. He was patient but not infinitely so. He would suffer shareholders until he knew they couldn't hurt him. He raised his lips away from the teeth. "We haven't been robustly profitable, as you must know. Assets are worth little if they don't earn a profit."

"On the other hand, Grendal isn't known for paying top dollar."

"I reckon he's an astute businessman. I don't expect him to pay a penny more than he has to. Our directors will consider the offer tomorrow. I've already recommended that we accept. It's in the best interests of our people."

"Have you looked for a buyer who might pay more than Grendal?"

"There's a time limit on Mr. Grendal's bid," Tullman said. His voice was tighter, and his long fingers drummed on his cheek. "It wouldn't make much sense, would it, to risk the deal in hand to chase some wild hope of finding a better one? Grendal's offer equals twice the stock's previous price. Frankly, that seems hard to beat."

Whatever mixture of loyalty and inertia had kept him in this office, he must have sensed the company's bleak future. Grendal's deal was the last exit before bankruptcy.

I said, "What do you think Grendal has in mind for the company? Will he try to turn the operations around?"

"I would guess he will give it a quick, painless death. Our tax credits are worth more to him than the plants and inventory. We have a couple of fashion lines that turn a profit. I suppose Mr.

Grendal will retain those and merge something similar from his other companies."

"Grendal doesn't usually keep prior management around."

"It looks as though I will be retiring."

"Do you mind if I look the plant over?"

"Not at all." He cleared his throat. "Some of our biggest shareholders have been itching to sell out for ten years. Now they can do it. If someone caused the deal to fall through—for whatever reason—he could expect to be buried in lawsuits."

I nodded, properly intimidated. "Thank you for being so candid."

"One of my newfound pleasures is saying what I mean."

I hesitated at the door. "Just curiosity, but how did Grendal zero in on Dorchester Millinery?"

"I wouldn't know. He has analysts looking for vulnerable companies, wouldn't you expect?"

"What tone has he taken with you?"

"I would call him polite but firm." The corner of Tullman's mouth twisted again. "He called me at my home eight days ago and named his price."

"When did you notify the board of directors?"

"That same evening, of course, by telephone. Now—I still have a business to run. I'll get someone to show you around."

He left me at his secretary's desk and told her, "Call Jerry Symms up here."

Jerry Symms was the production vice president, a wiry, rough-skinned man of forty who had gone to work for Dorchester Millinery right out of high school. He gave me a twenty-minute tour of the decaying plant, which he seemed to love and mourn. "We're a decade behind on technology, which means high labor costs. In Hong Kong they can make corduroy and ship it halfway around the world and still beat our prices. A couple of machines back in the dyeing section are older than me."

When Symms escorted me back to the executive wing, a man stood in the glass-walled anteroom beside Tullman's door. He leaned sinuously over the young secretary's desk. He was heavy-boned, six-two or -three and wore a khaki summer suit and a pale blue shirt that showed off a deep tan.

53

"New team stakes out its turf," Jerry Symms said. "That's Chet Demming, one of Mr. Grendal's people."

"Is Grendal in town?"

"Not that I've seen. His financial wizards have been scurrying around. From their looks, a lot of us are going to have to pack our bags."

"Is Demming an accountant?"

"I don't think so. I haven't figured out his job."

"Introduce me."

He opened the door to the anteroom. "Mr. Demming? This is Benjamin McCarthy; his firm owns some of our stock."

Demming had been chatting with Tullman's secretary. He swiveled from the waist, baby blue eyes fixing me from under sun-bleached brows. He held out a hand. "McCarthy? I don't recall your name from the shareholder list—but it's a pleasure all the same."

"We're probably too small to show up," I said.

"Well, you've made yourself money on this baby. Our people say the stock is trading at thirty and change."

"Has Grendal come to town?"

"Well, now, Lance likes to keep his whereabouts secret. Security, you know. You gotta excuse me."

I collected my hat and coat from Tullman's secretary, who followed Chet Demming with big dreamy eyes.

The pending sale of Dorchester Millinery was the lead story in the afternoon's local *Tribune*. I read the account over lunch at the Airport Holiday Inn. Grendal Offshore was offering to pay twelve dollars in cash plus an unsecured note with a face value of twenty-four dollars for each share of Dorchester Millinery common stock. All the company's directors and officers who were quoted found the deal a godsend for stockholders. Hundreds of the shareholders were former mill employees who lived in the area. The sale also promised benefits to the rest of the community, Roscoe Tullman insisted, because Lance Grendal would bring to town the financial muscle to revitalize the company. So much for his candor.

One director, Edgar H. Parsons III, called Grendal's price

adequate given the company's dismal outlook. A smaller article, bylined by the *Tribune* business editor, described Grendal's past successes in rescuing small companies.

I went up to my room, unpacked an attaché case and spent an hour reading Dorchester Millinery's annual report to shareholders. On the next to last page, a color photograph showed the board of directors staring glumly down the length of a polished table. I glanced over their names and affiliations. Two were outsiders, retired officers of a railroad and a pet food company, who lived in Florida and Maine. The five other directors were Tullman, two vice-presidents, and two somber-faced older men, Edgar Parsons and a skeletal figure named Philippe Nicodemus. Parsons had a bald head, hard eyes and a prominent chin. The accompanying proxy material said that Nicodemus owned about 1.8 million shares, or ten percent of the company. Parsons held more than two million shares, including a half-million owned jointly with his wife, Emily Lloyd Parsons. On paper they were wealthy people. Getting cashed out by Grendal must be tempting.

None of the names clicked as somebody Canning & McCarthy had done business with. None was the kind of friend who would pass along a tip that Grendal was circling.

After the market closed I checked in with Gail for prices. She gave me messages from several clients who needed consoling about one thing or another. "Also," she said, "George Finn called again. I told him you would call back. He's been talking to Mrs. Canning." She inflected *Mrs.* just right to indicate suffering.

Only one of the clients had his ear near enough to the ground to catch anything about the firm's troubles. He had heard that the SEC had hauled Jack in for questioning. I told him we hadn't heard from the SEC.

12

CHET Demming was staying over. When I went downstairs for supper, Demming and Tullman's secretary had their golden heads together over plates of spaghetti.

The hostess let me sit two tables away, under crossed spears and a buckskin shield. A college-aged girl took my order. She came back quickly with a dark beer and spinach salad.

I tried to guess whether Demming's date was pleasure or business. If he wasn't an accountant, what was his job description—troubleshooter, general factotum? Getting friendly with Tullman's secretary could have opened locked drawers and closed books for Grendal. He would know the company's weak spots and its fortified points before going in.

A minute after my steak arrived, Demming felt me staring at the back of his head. He turned, draped an elbow over the back of his chair and searched for the source of the neck hairs' tickle. When he saw me he nodded briefly and turned back to the girl. They worked their way through another bottle of wine in the next forty minutes. During that time he glanced my way only once.

As I finished my coffee, he got up and loped over. Towering above the table, he smiled amiably. "How 'bout joining us for a drink, Mr.—it is McCarthy?"

Demming introduced Tullman's secretary as Miss Wegner. She

56

wore a white, long-sleeved jersey dress that accented her tiny breasts. Between swan wings of yellow hair, her face was a petite pink heart with dimpled chin. The dark lashes were long and curled, the cheeks flushed. Her green eyes were glazed under sagging lids.

Demming said, "What would you like—brandy? Sorry we couldn't talk this afternoon. Lance wants this baby wrapped up."

"You seem to be moving quickly."

"Never quick enough, friend." He reached out a big-knuckled hand and patted Miss Wegner's arm. "Y'know, Mr. McCarthy, we didn't get much chance to compare notes. I reckon if you've been a shareholder for a while, you could give me a few pointers on Dorchester Mill'nry. We've just come aboard."

Working for Grendal, he would have to be smarter than the beach bum looks and talk suggested. He had decided the young money manager would respond to flattery.

I delivered the smug confidence he expected. "We do look our investments over pretty carefully."

"I figured that. How much money do you manage?"

I told him a third of the real figure and he acted impressed, though it wouldn't have made a splash in Grendal's pool. "So what's your bottom line on Dorchester?"

"Some assets, a bit of real estate, a bundle of tax losses." I recited what I remembered from the annual report. Tullman hadn't mentioned the real estate, which included raw land and highway frontage.

"Yeah—that's a prime piece of land they got tied up with that old mill. Eighty acres, y'know, only ten of it built. With a couple of the directors' connections, no reason the city couldn't decide the site would make a smart industrial park."

I nodded solemnly. "Isn't Grendal worried that somebody else might see the potential and cut him out?"

Demming laughed. "Not a chance. For the deal to work, the pieces gotta fit. That takes Lance's moxie. We're buyers of last resort. Our numbers boys say Dorchester Millinery won't last another eighteen months truckin' on its own."

"So why the rush?"

"Lance's got other skillets heatin'. He hates it when things ain't movin'. We don't make money during the time-outs." He raised his brandy. "Well—cheers, McCarthy . . . Miss Wegner."

Miss Wegner banged a snifter against her nose.

I left mine untouched. "If the deal goes down, Grendal makes four or five times his money—is that about right?"

He watched me with the clarity of a man who hadn't had a drink in his life. "Well, now how d'you get them numbers, buddy?"

"Grendal is offering thirty-six a share. He's paying twelve in cash, the rest in Chinese paper that he says is worth twenty-four. The value might be less if someone else were pricing it, depending on how good they think Grendal Offshore's credit is. He hasn't said yet—but I suppose the paper could be zero coupon notes?"

He didn't react.

"Or it could be paper that pays its interest in more paper? That's the low-cost way of doing it. So Grendal's out-of-pocket cost is twelve in cash, let's say three-quarters of it borrowed. That means he's putting up three dollars a share of his own capital. If he can extract, say, twenty-four dollars a share in total value from Dorchester Millinery—by selling real estate, using the tax losses, later selling off the profitable lines—he repays his own debt of nine dollars a share and has fifteen left. Five times his investment."

He grinned. "You just pulled them numbers out of the air."

"Pretty much. But it would have to be something like that for the deal to attract Grendal."

"Well—I'm not saying you're right, buddy. But if you was, that would be big leverage for Lance, ain't that the truth."

He hadn't mentioned the twenty-four dollars a share worth of Grendal paper that would be left outstanding. I hadn't either. If two years down the road, Lance Grendal had stripped away all Dorchester Millinery's valuable assets, he would offer the leftovers to the people holding the notes. It would be a take-this-or-nothing offer.

If Grendal made a twelve-dollar profit on eighteen million shares, it would work out to a little more than two hundred million dollars. A decent couple years' work for a medium-sized player.

"It's great leverage," I said, "if the deal closes."

"We got the bare bones settled. Tomorrow we'll tie it all up with pink ribbons."

"The board of directors votes tomorrow?"

"Yep."

"When is the meeting scheduled?"

"That's confidential, you understand."

Miss Wegner had her chin propped on her palm and was trying to bat her eyes at Demming's shoulder. Her sleeve had gotten into the spaghetti sauce.

"Of course, you never know what you've bought, not for sure, till you see the package from the inside," Demming reflected. "Heck, Kathy's boss could be hiding the really bad news from us. Right, Miss Wegner?"

"He's sneaky," she confirmed, slurring a little. "Alwaysh looking down my dress." She lifted her chin off her palm and pointed.

Demming took her hand. "You can't trust a guy who does that."

13

ACCORDING to the front desk, Grendal Offshore Ltd. had booked a half-dozen rooms, but the night clerk didn't remember anyone in the entourage who might have been Grendal. "We've had a dozen reporters asking if Lance Grendal is staying here," he said. "Who the devil is this guy?"

"The savior of Dorchester Millinery."

"Of what? I live up in Westerly."

After breakfast, a small pack of severe gray suits bearing black attaché cases shared two cars that took the highway leading to the plant. Chet Demming didn't show until after nine. He gulped a glass of orange juice, stopped at the lobby phone bank for a couple of minutes, and headed out to the parking lot.

It looked like the directors might be meeting before lunch. I decided to tag along after Demming and meet my board. Instead of heading for the plant, his red Thunderbird glided off in the opposite direction. A stop light slowed him down and I caught sight of the car turning down Route 12 toward town.

He sped through the business district and onto a shore road fronting Long Island Sound. The houses got further apart and began looking like they had stood there since Great-Grandpa went whaling. The nicer ones were high-shouldered with widow's walks, iron ornamentation on the roofs, and forests of chimneys. Low stone walls ran along the road.

Two miles into mansion territory, Demming's brake lights flared and he swung between iron posts into a driveway. I glanced at the mailbox, saw PARSONS, and drove past as he parked under a porte cochere.

If Grendal was visiting old Edgar H. Parsons, my first choice was to meet them without the beach boy on hand. A hundred yards down the road, I turned around and sat with the heater on. On my left a guard rail separated the road from a broken slate shore. The water was gray and seemed to buckle under windy blows from the sky.

Demming took his time. If he, Parsons and Grendal all left together, I would have gotten my feet cold for nothing. After forty minutes the T-bird emerged from the driveway and sped back toward town.

I took his parking space and rang a buzzer at the side door. The response was immediate. A woman opened the door. She was in her thirties, with rumpled coppery hair and a lush figure. Her pale lipstick was smeared, her blue wool dress twisted here and there as if it didn't fit, and she was smiling. "Did you forget—"

Her smile vanished. She said, "Who are you?"

I remembered a name from Dorchester's proxy statement. "Are you Emily? I was supposed to meet Chet here."

"Here?" She inched the door toward me and peered around it. Her pretty hazel eyes were close to panic. "Oh, no—no, he wouldn't have . . ."

"Perhaps I misunderstood. Is Mr. Parsons available?"

She closed the door firmly.

I chased the cleaning lady out of my hotel room and phoned Dorchester Millinery's office. The switchboard confirmed that the board meeting had begun at nine-thirty. Mr. Tullman couldn't be disturbed. She didn't know when he would be out of the meeting.

I wondered how old E. H. Parsons III planned to vote. And

61

how long had Chet Demming been working on the director's young wife?

And how many other bases had Grendal's team covered? Enough that he wouldn't be in doubt about the outcome of the directors' meeting?

14

BEFORE noon the directors of Dorchester Millinery Corporation voted to accept the terms of Grendal Offshore's takeover proposal.

I read the two-hour-old news wire back in my office. The two days in Connecticut hadn't been a total waste. Nobody up there had a connection to Jack that leaped out at me. If E. H. Parsons or old Nicodemus had been our clients, the SEC would have had the rope for a ritual public hanging. But I hadn't found a link, and Gordon Trapp might not either.

The government could send out a dozen eager young lawyers with old shirts bearing our scent. With Jack residing abroad—whatever his reason—the legal presumption of innocence was remote. I had phoned Rudy Thatcher hoping he had tracked down his brother-in-law at a beach hotel. The envelope had been postmarked St. Kitts. Rudy didn't think Jack knew anybody down there, but admitted he couldn't be sure. "Jack has surprised us all," he said. An associate had been phoning island hotels for two days without success.

"St. Kitts could have been just a stopover," I said.

"He can't get too far. His credit cards haven't been used. Can you imagine Jack living in a hammock? He needs a French restaurant twice a week to feel the world hasn't gone to pot."

Gail had performed heroically in restoring order in the office. Most of the printouts and contracts had found their way back to the correct file jackets. She had set up a special stack marked HEADACHES that contained the fragments she couldn't make sense of. On top was a notecard on which Jack or I—the scrawl was unidentifiable—had penned a reminder PORCELAIN ODDS 3½. God knew what it meant or where it belonged. The cryptic sample discouraged further delving.

No trace of anything related to Walter or Virginia Wrather had turned up, Gail insisted. Her anxiety came bubbling over as anger. "The goddamn file isn't here, all right? Stop asking."

Later she said she had to go home before it snowed again. I wished her a good evening and wondered if she was rushing to a job interview. She knew the end was coming. The office was open because bureaucracies ground ahead at their own pace. Our broker's records had been demanded by the government, Lisa said. She would be dealing with me in the future because Vince—through whom Jack had placed the Dorchester Millinery orders—had been quarantined by the managing partners. Or Canning & McCarthy Investment Counsel had been quarantined.

In a week or two the bureaucratic wheel would roll over us. It wasn't a major case, and Gordon Trapp didn't have to rush.

In my hotel room I had looked up the local Dorchester Millinery directors' telephone numbers. When the market closed I got on the phone. The only director I was interested in was the knobby-chinned old man, Edgar Parsons. When a woman answered, I dropped my voice half an octave, identified myself and asked for Mr. Parsons.

His bark fitted the photograph, clipped and hard. He said, "Roscoe Tullman mentioned you this morning, McCarthy. What could we have to talk about?"

"Stock values, I hope."

His snort burst in my ear. "I can imagine. You'll tell me your stock is worth more than I think. You're wasting my time. If you plan to oppose the merger, do your best. I doubt you've got enough stock to make a difference."

"If I wanted to oppose the deal, I would sue in court to block it," I said. "That isn't on my mind."

"Dare I ask what is?"

"Grendal plans to pay part cash, part paper. The debt won't be secured by the company's assets. It sounds like we could be left holding an empty bag."

"There are always risks in business, Mr. McCarthy. May I remind you that I and my family own more than eleven percent of the company. If I am willing to accept Grendal's IOU, why shouldn't you?"

I made a conciliatory noise and kept him chatting for a few minutes. There was no sign he had ever heard of Canning & McCarthy before that morning. No sign at all he knew us well enough to tip Jack on the deal.

Another line rang as I hung up. Jimmy Doyle spoke softly. "I want to talk to Canning."

"He's not available."

He sounded absolutely sober. "Okay, tell him something. Tell him nobody's so pure he can't be got to."

"I'll relay the message," I said.

"No you won't. You're just a little gofer; you don't talk that way to the boss. I'll tell him myself."

"Suit yourself," I said, but he had hung up.

The answering service took care of the incoming phone for the next hour as I used my private line to reach a couple of clients whose business needed attention. Between clients, Marty called. "You sound grouchy, darling. Danton's not happy with something about the portrait. I've got to go over to the theater and talk him out of demanding changes."

"I'm sorry," I said, without caring.

"The point is, I won't be home for supper and I don't want you worrying."

"I won't," I said. But she had gotten my attention.

"Okay. Bye-bye."

"Bye."

If something was going on, it wouldn't be with a fancy item like Danton. I dreaded to imagine a face, hard and purposeful, across a table or a pillow from my wife. Yet it would have to be someone serious and tough-minded, someone I might like apart from our little conflict of interests.

Life would be hopelessly dull if she left. An apartment with high ceilings and drafty rooms needed an extraordinary source of energy. Martha Norris provided the passionate heat and light. I didn't have enough of my own.

Glancing down Broadway, I watched a truck edge over the sidewalk onto Maiden Lane, honking furiously at the empty street.

It was too late to return George Finn's call. I didn't want to, anyway. I had lied to too many friends, my own and Jack's.

I tapped out the symbol for Seattle Aviation and felt better. The shares were up three dollars from where I had bought, justifying a fleeting thought that I was not only prosperous, but smart.

I shut the machines off, locked the office. The building had largely emptied out.

When I rounded the corner toward the elevators, I was surprised to see somebody standing at the end of the hall. He turned. It was Jimmy Doyle. He looked tired, his head tilted back, lank ginger hair spilling across his forehead. He was leaning against the wall between the elevator doors, hands holding the belly of his crimson shirt.

I stepped closer.

His stubbled chin had sunk, his lips were white. Fast short breaths clicked in the back of his throat.

I hurried.

"I'm bleeding," he said.

His hands were red. The top of his gray slacks had turned black. His eyes swiveled, offering a plaintive look as though the effort hurt. "Jumped me . . . right off the elevator."

He tried to lick his lips. His tongue stuck and his legs buckled.

15

THE police found me holding his hand, and an officer suggested we go down the hall to my office. Later a mustached black man with deeply pitted cheeks and an air of indifference asked questions. He took less than fifteen minutes. I said I didn't know anyone who had a grudge against Mr. Doyle. He said, "The kids come down here to steal computers. We can't keep them out of these buildings."

"Was he shot?" I asked.

"It looks like stab wounds. You may as well go home. My name is Sergeant Teeger. If you think of anything, you can call."

I went down the hall alone. There were two uniformed policemen near the elevators, along with a zippered bag on an ambulance gurney that they ignored like a witness who had ceased being helpful.

Marty was in her studio under bright electric lights. Danton had cancelled. A sienna sketch was taking shape on a large canvas, a scene of a man sitting on a park bench with his back to the viewer. In front of him lay a stretch of concrete, an iron fence, empty water and sky.

It looked like Battery Park. I had seen enough to know that the water would be a cold gray reflection of the sky.

She smiled at me and looked back to the canvas, ignoring the dark windows. She had never seemed more valuable.

16

A woman called two days later and identified herself as Julia Doyle. She said, "I'll see that you and Mr. Canning don't have any trouble about the money."

"What money?" I said.

"The money that Mr. Canning lent us—lent my husband, really," she corrected.

The empty cadence in her voice was for the husband, I assumed, not for a few hundred dollars. I said, "Whatever's convenient for you. I'll tell Jack you called. I'm sorry about Mr. Doyle."

"Jim said it wasn't quite proper. But you know, Mr. Furbinger expected his brokers to buy his awful stocks in their own accounts. Most of them didn't do very well."

That I could understand.

"Jim was losing money," she went on, "and we didn't have much savings with Janet in college. Mr. Canning is an old friend and I guess he could afford what he did for Jim."

"How much did he give your husband?"

"Well, we had twenty thousand that my mother left us. Mr. Furbinger didn't know about it. And Mr. Canning lent us another thirty thousand. He didn't actually give it to Jim, of course. He used the whole amount—ours plus the loan—to buy the kind of stocks that Mr. Furbinger didn't like. Old plodders, Jim called them."

It was Jack's term too. I thought I understood. "How did he buy those stocks?"

"I thought you knew—he kept an account for us with your firm. I guess I should discuss this with Mr. Canning."

"It's okay. Was the account under a different name?"

"We used my mother's maiden name, Wrather."

The scheme fit Jack's idea of charity. The capital remained under his control. In a good market, he knew his old plodders would make money. After two years, his crony from the Brooker Finn days might have an extra thirty thousand of his own and Jack would have his capital back, along with a two-percent management fee to make it all businesslike.

It was like making a gift of a partnership.

Rudy had other ideas when I told him. "Maybe my brother-in-law has been getting something back from Doyle, like tips about takeovers."

"Doyle wasn't in Lance Grendal's league," I said. "Certainly not among his confidants."

"Jack got something," he insisted.

17

BUNNY Furbinger's main office stood at the bottom of Manhattan, where Broadway, Battery Place, Whitehall and Beaver Street fanned out as granite-walled spokes. The fifth-floor windows overlooked a tiny triangular park at Bowling Green. Pale beech desks lined the front office. Fuchsia carpeting, black tubular chairs and hanging rattan planters gave the brokers' bull pen the look of a Beverly Hills restaurant.

Bunny had blond hair that was combed back in a damp bird's wing. His pink cherub's face smiled and pouted at the same time, as if suspecting that not everybody he met loved him. A barely noticeable overbite must have inspired the nickname Bunny, which would have been a burden for a child but seemed to be worn proudly by the fifty year old. It was BUNNY on his business card, BF on the cuffs of his silk shirt. There weren't many Bunnys running around the financial district.

I had waited a day before calling. He came bounding across the sales room, red bow tie bobbing, hands outstretched. "What a tragedy about Jimmy!"

There was an air of tension and excitement in the low-ceilinged room where ranks of young brokers worked telephones and quotation machines. Most of the salesmen wore telephone headsets, the quicker to cut off one prospective customer and get on to the next one.

"Is this a layout?" Bunny demanded. "I've got seventy registered reps working for me, new offices opening in Sarasota and Los Angeles, and my own research department. The public's crying for aggressive stock ideas. Today we're selling a new preferred stock issue for a wonderful little company, Tex-Mex Condiments."

"It's good of you to see me," I said.

"Heavens! Any friend of Doyle's." He led me back to an office that was a contrast to the modern sales pen. Here he surrounded himself with wing chairs covered in red leather, a carved desk larger than a pool table, antique bric-a-brac in a display case, cherry wainscoting and yellowing prints of steeplechasers and schooners. He didn't fit well into the comfortable scene he had set. Everything about him—crisp gray suit, candy-striped shirt, cuff links, gold watch—looked brand new. His prosperity was too recent to bear scuff marks or creases.

"Furbinger is low rent," Peter Bagley had said at lunch. "He took a fall ten years ago that put him out of business, but he's come back."

"What happened?"

"Usual trifle, he was manipulating a tiny stock." He dredged up the details as well as he remembered. Furbinger and a friend had opened accounts at several brokerage firms and began buying shares of a small company called Presto Box, which manufactured cardboard shipping containers. At the same time they leaked word that Presto Box was going to be taken over by a European consortium. As the price shot up, Furbinger and his collaborator sold their stock and began feeding out short sales. A few days later Presto Box's eighty-year-old chairman returned from Alsace and declared that the company wasn't for sale at any price and never would be. And just for the record, earnings looked pretty poor for the next six months in the box business. The stock's price fell like a sack of concrete, and Furbinger and his co-conspirator covered their short sales at nice profits.

Somebody got suspicious at the sudden and flamboyant prosperity of the Presto Box chairman's idiot grandson, who had been left in

71

charge while the old man took a European cure. Why hadn't the grandson knocked down the takeover rumor right away instead of delivering straight-faced "no comments"? When the idiot grandson's stock trading records surfaced, he rolled over quickly and pointed to an old prep-school chum named Bunny who had suggested that Grandpop's annual vacation was a good time to run a game with the stock.

Furbinger denied everything. He had merely been speculating that Presto Box's young heir apparent could convince his grandfather to merge the company. When word got around somehow—who could imagine how?—and the stock ran up, Bunny sold. He understood that the grandson had been talking to a lot of traders. Personally, Bunny Furbinger liked to keep his mouth shut. Gossip was dangerous. The government's investigators checked around. Nobody had heard anything from Bunny.

Circumstantial evidence, plus his confederate's testimony, might have convicted him. He couldn't be sure. The securities commissioners couldn't be sure either. So they struck a deal, whereby Bunny Furbinger admitted nothing but agreed to be barred from the securities business for two years.

He had come a long way back. The door burst open and a young woman with fluffy gold hair and a taut skirt interrupted us. "Provost has someone on the line with ten thousand Trionix. Do we want it? The last bid was four and a half."

She waited almost on tiptoes, swaying forward, breathing lightly. Her cheeks and earlobes were rosy.

Bunny lifted his upper lip. "Tell him we'll take it at four."

She nodded. "Four, yessir."

"'Bye, Susie," he said. As she dashed out, he watched her rump. He shook his head and smiled at me. "She's not big on brains, but it's personality that counts."

"That was quite a haircut you offered on Trionix," I said.

"Paying four? Anyone's a fool to sell Trionix. Why give a fool a break? The stock's going to ten."

I got down to business, inventing as I went. "Doyle had wanted to talk to Jack about joining us."

"Oh really! Employee loyalty isn't strong these days, is it?"

72

"He said he could bring us good takeover ideas."

Furbinger covered his laughter with a pudgy hand. "That's wild—pathetic, but wild all the same. Takeover ideas? Dear God, Doyle was seldom sober enough to remember which of our stocks he was supposed to be pushing, let alone to pick up—and remember—takeover stories. I liked the poor jerk, but he wasn't producing. You can't carry someone forever."

"Were you going to fire him?"

"I hadn't decided." He pushed a button on his computer and the screen shifted a couple of times, dense columns of stock symbols and numbers. He sat back and folded his fingers across his belly. "It's a tough break for Doyle. But for Christ's sake, if you go wobbling around the streets after dark, you're asking to get jumped. The police were on the phone the other day for all of five minutes. The guy asked if Doyle had any unhappy clients who held a grudge. I told him if clients held a grudge brokers would be buried six deep in front of the stock exchange."

"If he had heard a takeover story, somebody might have wanted to keep him quiet," I said.

"You're back to takeovers, huh? There are better ideas around and I've got them. If you want to do your clients a favor, take a look at Trionix. I could probably get you twenty thousand shares at four and a half. If you look down the road eighteen months, it's a fireball, earning a buck a share. Give it an average multiple for a high-tech company and you'll have a twenty-dollar stock." His eyes and his heart weren't in the pitch. He watched me quietly.

"I thought Trionix was only going to ten."

Dimples flashed. "That's in the next six months. Stick around longer and you'll really make out. You're buying the founder's brains. Dylan O'Keefe is a technical genius." He dug around in his desk and sailed a pewter-colored card at me. "We're having a little get-together for clients. Here's an invitation. O'Keefe will be there and so will Susie. No brains, like I said, but an easy pickup if you buy stock from her."

18

JIMMY Doyle's brown-shuttered bungalow was a half mile from the South Norwalk commuter station. His widow sat me in a brocaded armchair and brought a sheaf of papers. On top was a photocopy of a management contract between Canning & McCarthy Investment Counsel and James K. Doyle. There was nothing on paper about logging the account as Walter and Virginia Wrather, but judging by date Jack had done exactly that.

"Is this what you wanted?" Julia Doyle asked. She was a stout blonde with deep creases around the mouth and grainy skin. Her manner was businesslike.

"I would like to take this with me," I said. "I'll mail you a copy."

"Whatever you say. Jimmy was very fond of Mr. Canning. It was almost hero worship."

"I'm sorry about what happened."

She glanced at a silver-framed photograph of herself, her husband and a plump-faced girl who had her features. "The police aren't trying very hard. They said they've questioned everyone who was leaving the building. I don't think they did."

Burglars who killed only one person might not be prize catches. "Did your husband talk about stocks?"

"What else?" She released a sigh. "Most of the ones we bought lost money."

"Which ones?"

"I never paid much attention. What did it matter? There was one, Trisonics, I think, that was all he talked about lately."

"Trionix."

"That's it. He was trying to sell it for Mr. Furbinger, but he didn't like the company."

"Did he ever mention one called Dorchester Millinery? It may have been some time ago."

She looked up in surprise. "It wasn't some time ago. It was last week. I'm sure. He was stomping around here saying how could they get away with using Dorchester Millinery. He said nobody in his right mind would buy the stock. Do you know what it was all about?"

I asked her if she was sure that was what he had said. Nobody would buy the stock. She nodded. "He meant Mr. Canning wouldn't have bought the stock," I said.

I got a ticket back to Manhattan in the overheated South Norwalk waiting room and went outside to the platform. There was no counting the mornings that Jimmy Doyle had performed the same ritual. It would take him ninety minutes to reach the office and get on the phone to sell Furbinger's wonderful little companies. One day uranium mines, the next satellite dishes, the next molecular biology. All with promises like bright balloons: scientific break-throughs, world-beating products, soaring profits. By the time the promises deflated, Bunny and Jimmy would have found other customers.

Jack took a Darwinian view that the market redistributes capital from the hands of the gullible to the hands of the wise, or at least the crafty, who are fittest and survive.

Hard-nosed Jack, who lent a rarely seen old chum thirty thousand dollars, but kept the money under his own control. Sentimental charity from a cautious man.

I walked down the platform. It was four o'clock, and no one was heading into the city and no one had started arriving back. A trace of winter light clung to the sky above the concrete pier.

Two other travelers came out of the waiting room. They were

75

both tall and both wore short tan topcoats. They craned to look down the empty track. One shrugged and they walked down to my end.

"What time's the train?" He was young, with regular features and dark hair, neatly turned out. His coat hung open over a striped gray suit and a red foulard necktie. His cordovan loafers had tassels and a deep shine. He could have been a salesman or an accountant.

"Four-ten," I said.

He nodded and his friend, half out of sight on my left, hit me. The blow landed under the ribs, on my right side.

It was paralyzing. I tried to breathe and couldn't. Tried to curl up, but hands grabbed my elbows and dragged me backward, across the platform. When my heels left the concrete the hands let go.

The fall was joltingly short, broken as my shoulder struck something, the fender of a parked car. I landed on my back near the front wheels.

A pair of loafers jumped down to the frozen ground. One foot kicked a whiskey bottle away. He stepped closer and the foot lashed at my knee.

I gasped.

Tan bluchers, soles fresh and hardly scuffed, joined the loafers. I tried to retreat between cars. The bluchers kicked at my forehead and scored. "You're a fucking nuisance," one of them said.

As I pulled my arms up, another shoe found my ribs. I tried to double up, didn't see what happened next. He must have planted a hand on each car, swung up and brought his heels down. A bomb went off in my side.

"He's an asshole, no fight. Turn him over."

The bluchers knelt. He was wearing chinos, a baby blue turtleneck and a brown plaid sport coat. He pulled my arms away from my face. He had red hair and a blotchy, pocked face. He said, "Come on, do it."

"Mark him up a little more first."

He drew back a heavy-knuckled hand and obliged.

"Okay, that's enough."

I looked through pink haze at the voice. He held a camera, aimed at my face. A flash exploded, and the camera whirred. A moment

76

later he took another shot. He said, "Okay, asshole, smile and show how pretty we made you." The shutter clicked.

Red let my shoulders drop. He shouted down from a great height: "You can go home now. Go see what we left you."

"Do you think he understands?" The dark-haired one leaned close. He smelled of cologne.

Red shouted. "You un'erstand, asshole?"

The handsome one said, "How'd an asshole like this have such a pretty cunt at home?"

They hoisted themselves onto the platform. An odd thought struck me in the midst of blacking out.

Wall Streeters don't do this.

The clump of car doors and a starter's screech brought me back. A rising clack-clack-clack on the other side of the pier told me that a train was pulling out. It was almost dark. I stared at the gravel my face lay against. The black smear could be blood or oil.

Several cars over, an engine caught and revved strongly. Lights snapped on.

The cold had sunk into me. As I took inventory, a piece at a time, my mind screamed its urgency. Cracked ribs, a yard of raw skin, perhaps bruised spleen or kidneys, possible concussion. None of them meant that I couldn't stand up, if I could ignore the complaint of nerves that preferred I stay put.

Rolling onto my belly, I pulled my knees up, aware of something grinding in my side.

Nearby a Mercedes began backing out, and its headlights swept across what must have been a ghastly apparition rising from the ground. The driver had a pleasantly long face and a confident mouth that stretched in shock. He spun the wheel and the tires fired gravel as he slewed away.

Five minutes or so later I shuffled into the station. It was an instructive five minutes that proved there was no absolute connection between discomfort and the ability to move.

I eased into a telephone booth, fumbled out my credit card and tried the apartment. It was half past five. She would be there. Working, not thinking yet of going to the Lion's Head. . . .

The phone rang twenty times before I gave up.

I got the worst of the blood off in the men's room. The face that was left looked human if not widely presentable. It promised to look worse as the swelling of lips, cheek and forehead darkened. Nothing to be done about it. Or about the ripped pant knee or spattered shirt. People got on the train in worse shape.

A crew-cut young man asked if I needed help. I shook my head. "Just fell on the steps," I said. The police would take time.

I tried home again, tried our downstairs neighbors.

The five-thirty train rolled in, and I crept aboard. An hour to Grand Central.

She was resilient, sure of herself, no match for the likes of Handsome and Red. Too sure of herself to realize that.

I was first off the train, fighting a tide rushing under the iron archway. I stopped at the first island of telephones, leaned under the bubble, punched the number with clumsy fingers.

Wall Streeters don't do this.

I lost count of the rings.

19

THE apartment lights were on. I pulled my keys out as the taxi hissed away.

The first-floor neighbors were arriving home with friends, one of the wives boasting that Oscar had pumped a stomach that morning and gotten a frog. They laughed and I slipped by Oscar and Rhoda without having to pass inspection.

I pounded up two flights of stairs, opened the door and let it swing wide. Bile rushed into my throat.

The living room was in its usual mild disorder. Magazines and books were stacked everywhere. Wine glasses stood on the coffee table like sentinels over a friendly but undisciplined camp. A painter's smock hung over the back of a chair. Compact discs out of their cases, coffee mugs nearby. Nothing that looked like trouble.

I called out, not loudly. Not expecting an answer.

Turning on a light in her studio took an act of will. She had made progress on the park-bench sitter. I had been right about the bleakness of the sky and water. A palette lay on the cluttered oak work bench, the paints mixed in gaudy islands bleeding into one another. Before quitting for the day she always covered the palette with plastic to keep the colors moist. Tonight she hadn't. Half a dozen unwashed brushes lay on the table.

The phone began ringing and I ignored it.

79

Downstairs, I checked the bathroom and the bedroom. The braided rug in the bedroom told me nothing, but I kept staring at it. Like an overheated engine, my mind had seized up. I walked into the kitchen and looked down at the barren city garden.

The phone rang again. I picked it up. Handsome and Red might have more to say.

A woman's voice, instead, cried out. "Ben, Ben—"

She was incapable of hysteria.

"Where are you?" I said.

"At the hospital."

My heart choked. "Are you okay?"

"He said that you—that you weren't expected to live. I got here and they said you hadn't been admitted."

"Where are you?"

"St. Vincent's." It was several blocks away.

"Wait there. I'll come over."

The knowledge had caught up with me that I needed a doctor.

She was standing in her long shearling coat outside the glass doors of the emergency room. She had come out in a rush, very businesslike. "I saw how you got out of the cab. How bad?"

"Just kicked around."

She looked as good as she ever had—almost as intent as when she was working on her park-bench scene, and much angrier. "You've been kicked in the face."

"True."

"Where else?"

"A couple of places. I'm glad you're all right. They said to go home and see . . ." I couldn't say more without risking tears, which would have embarrassed both of us. Until the taxi brought me into sight of the hospital door with the familiar figure in the light, the fear had been held under tight control. Now my grip on her arm was half for support, half in case the sidewalk opened and tried to take her.

She patted my hand. "Poor Ben. Where were you?"

"South Norwalk."

"In Connecticut? For God's sake, you needed a doctor."

She got the attention of the emergency room staff with the firm insistence that would have pleased old Ephraim Norris. In remarkably little time I was on my back in an examination room with a young intern ooh-ahing as she uncovered my abdomen. "You will need X-rays, Mr. McCarthy. And that bruise on your forehead could be a problem. Are you having any double vision? Have you spit up blood? Urinated any?"

"Haven't had time."

"You will, I'll bet. Let me give you some advice. Next time let them boys have your wallet. We had a man in here yesterday, good-looking young lawyer, who put up a fight in Roosevelt Park. He had nine stab wounds." She raised an eyebrow.

Her chatter on street crime went on, as she tried to keep me awake. I wondered what she had to say about white-collar crime. Did she know that it could get down and dirty?

When the intern left, Marty said, "Why did they do it?"

"Something about Jimmy Doyle. The two bruisers took pictures to show someone they'd done a professional job."

"Do you know who hired them?"

I shook my head and then said, "Bunny Furbinger." I was sure, but didn't know why. Equally certain, with an awful feeling, about Jimmy Doyle.

"What has Bunny Furbinger got against you?"

"Later." I wanted to sleep. Not easy. Instead of following me, they could have visited her at home. That was part of the message. It had sunk in.

She bent over and put her lips against my cheek. "Does that feel okay? There isn't much unbruised space."

"It's fine."

"You look dreadful. You're reasonably handsome most of the time."

"Thanks."

"Mother thinks I married you for your looks." She shook her head.

The next day the medical tally was short: two cracked ribs, a bruised kidney, miscellaneous bumps and bruises unworthy of documentation. No concussion. Mrs. McCarthy had raised hardheaded boys. I was home before noon and took advantage of my convalescent status by parking on the sofa and soaking up tea. My luck held to sending Marty out for a copy of the new *Investor's Week*. The glossy cover painting showed the Treasury secretary of the United States grimacing with an arrow, emblazoned with a rising sun, shot through his head. Irreverence was *Investor's Week*'s strong suit. Being a couple of years late on a story had never bothered Max.

She had tossed me the magazine with a disgusted look. "You should be ashamed you ever worked there."

She went upstairs, where I could hear her singing. Her confidence was awesome. One battered husband, one clear threat to her—but Norrises didn't intimidate. Admirable enough, but her toughness also was a closed door that rejected sympathy or small assurances before they could be offered. If she ever felt a chill coming past the door, she attributed it to hours away from her work or a touch of the flu or a physical yearning. Her uncle called her a self-contained spirit—rough on nearby bourgeois pups. Always hard to keep up with.

I checked Peter Bagley's column, "Street Smarts," found it was devoted to a coming glut in pulmonary catheters, and thumbed my way to the stock tables at the back of the magazine. Seattle Aviation had made me four points. Dorchester Millinery had closed at 30½.

I dozed and walked down a path left by Bunny Furbinger's thugs. Jimmy Doyle lurched out of an elevator with a bloody shirt front. Except that this time it was Marty, who looked down at her shirt front and clucked like the intern. "Next time, don't be a busybody."

Gil Norris came by at six, made appropriate noises about my face. Marty hung up his coat, a bulky old chesterfield. "I offered to make it another evening," he said.

"I'm glad you didn't."

"My niece said you were unfit company for her to suffer alone."

"That's not true," Marty said. "You said he would be tiresome and I would need a distraction. So far he hasn't been."

Gil snorted in disbelief. "So how do you feel?"

"Mending."

"You're not Irish if you don't moan and groan a little. But you'll recover. I suppose there's no point in wasting sympathy then." He made a pass at smoothing his tweed jacket, which gaped across a bulging argyle sweater. He was overweight and disheveled, with a spray of fine red hair showing a pale, spotted scalp. He had retired from his tiny trading firm but still dabbled in distressed bonds. He lived alone in fits of boyish enthusiasm and melancholy. In his way he was tough and unsentimental. He disliked deliberately sweet people and was bored by children, who imagined that every fat old man yearned to play grandpa. He had thought Marty useless until she was fifteen and her interest in art took on adult seriousness. Then he fell in love with her with such doltish intensity that he mended fences with her father to regain a family standing.

Marty kissed his cheek, asked, "And what have you been up to?"

"Apart from raising money for Juilliard? Not a blessèd thing, sweet. The stock market doesn't interest me. Prices are ludicrous. Every money management firm seems to be run by a twenty-five-year-old bent on suicide. Present company excepted."

"It sounds like prosperity is getting you down," I said.

"Other people's prosperity. Somebody actually told me the other day—actually said it—that the only mistake you can make is not buying stocks. People worry too much about overpaying, he told me."

"Were you talking to a broker?"

"A good guess, but no—it was a portfolio manager for a big bank." He harrumphed. "A young fool bent on redistributing his clients' capital."

"How old is he?"

"About your age. Not old enough to know any better. I told him I would sell him the few stocks I still own if he would pay me twice their current market price. If he truly believes his thesis that price is no object, he should have jumped at the opportunity. He believes it, of course, only when he sees other fools in the market paying the same price, verifying his folly. If I had offered him my stocks at half the prevailing levels, he would have balked at that too. He needs the comfort of a crowd."

We had a drink in the warm kitchen while I sliced broccoli.

"Your wife told me what happened," he said. "Most people hire lawyers to beat up their enemies. Is this connected to your other problem?"

"I assume so."

He looked at me in disappointment. "If I were you, I would be trying to find out for certain."

"I am."

"If you count success in cracked ribs, you've made progress. But I would be trying to find out who tipped your partner that Lance Grendal was closing in on Dorchester Millinery. Was it Doyle or Furbinger?"

"Not Furbinger."

"So—Doyle?"

"I don't think Jack was tipped. At least I don't think he was told that Dorchester was going to get a takeover offer. He may have been told something else that made him buy the stock, but not about a takeover."

"Why not?"

"Jack doesn't buy takeover stories. If they're wrong—and most of them are—you lose money. If one is right, the government assumes you knew something you shouldn't have."

He grunted. "I always distrust pillars of rectitude. Preachers, public moralists, I assume they're all diddling the choirboys. I have never been as taken as you have with your partner."

"I've never thought of him as a pillar of rectitude," I said.

"How did you and Canning meet?"

We took our plates into the dining nook, and I told him. A trader named de Veigh had introduced us. I had been working for *Investor's Week* when Arnaud de Veigh, who was known to hundreds of financial district regulars as Old Turkeyneck, was advertising Jack as the smartest man on Wall Street. It was a title that de Veigh passed around twice a month, but its newest holder had scored a coup of some kind and was fair game for journalists looking for easy stories. Jackson Canning and I met for lunch a few days before Thanksgiving and traded comments so inane they barely qualified as small talk. The market was cheap, we agreed, but a lot depended on what the Federal Reserve did in the next few months. I waited for him to tell me, subtly or directly, what an infallible investor he was—waited in vain. The war stories that finally came out weren't about his successes but about a couple of blunders that had cost him dearly. He had drawn a general lesson from the disasters that I heard only later. Jack Canning would not bet a dime on the future. He bought only assets that already existed, not those that might develop if a new product clicked or a drill bit found gold. He bought companies that had fabricating plants selling for half the cost of building them new, companies selling for less than their cash in the bank. He was a scrap dealer, I supposed, a gentleman's Lance Grendal.

Jack said a successful investor was driven by controlled greed. He took a fussy pride in how well he regulated his own greed. That November everyone in town, including Old Turkeyneck, was ballyhooing the stock of a property insurance company called Southeast Equity of Atlanta, known as SEA for short. Arnaud de Veigh dug in his heels next to me at the Union Club's urinal and whispered about SEA's growth rate, which was being whispered, shouted and telexed in half the men's rooms on both coasts.

When I mentioned Southeast Equity to Canning, he shrugged and said, "Where does the music stop? The stock is selling at twenty times its net worth."

Gil nodded aggressively. "They never learn, do they?"

"The buyers knew it was overpriced," I said. "But it was moving up and they hoped they could sell it to somebody else ten points higher."

"And the somebody else," Gil said, "would buy solely because it was moving up. The worst risk a fellow like that runs is to get stuck owning his last stupid decision."

Gil knew the rest of the story. Southeast Equity was worth less than anyone had imagined. Its phenomenal growth in sales was created out of whole cloth by the chairman and his treasurer. When the company collapsed, it buried a lot of traders besides Old Turkeyneck. A week later I bought Jack Canning lunch at the Portfolio Club and asked if he had stayed away because he had heard rumors of trouble. He stared down his long nose at the table. "No, no rumors. . . . I didn't see anything wrong in the financial

85

statements either. Did you ever meet the chairman? He was a young Jimmy Stewart, with a faint twang in his voice, so you expected him to come out with 'aw-shucks-mom.' He broadcast common sense. I sat through one of his presentations to securities analysts. He said that Southeast Equity's profits would double in two years. It seemed likely they would."

"So why didn't you buy the stock?"

"It was already expensive. I asked myself where would it sell in six months if everything kept going great. Twenty percent higher? Fifty percent? And what would happen if profits didn't live up to Jimmy Stewart's promises? The price could fall fifty percent—or eighty percent. So there was no contest. My first job is to protect clients' capital."

Gil Norris peeled cellophane off a cigar. "I never doubted Canning's prudence," he said.

I plugged the coffee pot in on the server. Pulling out our London bottle of duty-free Napoleon, knowing Gil never refused, Marty said, "Jack is my friend too."

"You've never been a great judge of men, my dear," he said. "Hasn't your mother told you?"

Nodding, she looked at me. "Fairly often."

Conversation lagged. I poured coffee and Gil leaned back, cognac in one hand, coffee in the other, cigar in his mouth. He could keep them moving like a rotating guard. He said, "Humor me a bit. What would you do if you came across good inside information? Suppose you knew that Dorchester Millinery was going to be taken over. You wanted to buy the thing"—he blocked my objection with a raised palm—"unlikely as that sounds. How would you go about it?"

I considered. "Under those circumstances, I wouldn't buy it. It would be too late to take the right steps—that's if the idea is to buy without being caught."

"Yes, or with a minimum of risk."

"Well, the two most important questions would be how much stock I wanted to buy—and whether I could be connected to the information."

He puffed on his cigar. "You know the source slightly, not in a way that somebody else could easily prove."

"That's important. If the SEC couldn't prove a connection, then they couldn't prove what I knew. My word would be as good as anyone's, provided I hadn't thrown every dollar I could find into the stock. For a money manager like me to buy a few thousand shares of Dorchester Millinery wouldn't be incriminating by itself."

"But Canning bought how many shares—twenty-some thousand, did Martha say?—without telling you," Gil pointed out. "That's bound to look suspicious."

"Right. His timing is one problem. Buying so close to Grendal's offer looks bad. If he had put together a position several months ago, that wouldn't be so damning. They might suspect, but proving anything would be difficult." I shrugged, felt the twinge of bruised muscles that had stiffened during the evening.

We had laid a small fire across from the table. I went into the kitchen and came back with a couple of thicker logs.

Gil Norris stared distractedly at the lighted apartments across the street. Snow had melted during the afternoon, dimming the street's luminescence. He said, "If the SEC merely suspected something, that wouldn't be enough to put Canning or you in jail. But as federal bureaucrats, they still could destroy your business with a protracted investigation accompanied by innuendos and leaks."

That was true. If an alleged infraction of the rules was minor, people on the Street usually accepted a penalty rather than fight. The penalty wouldn't ruin you, but arm-wrestling the government might.

Sitting down, I caught a glimpse of myself in the mirror. The forehead bruise was black and yellow. I wondered who had looked at the picture Handsome snapped.

"If you wanted to break the rules," I said, "there would be a way. Not that hard, either. It would have to be set up in advance so you didn't leave a trail. Then if you had the arrangements made and the right situation came along, you could go for it."

Marty stared at me over a glass of sambuca. "You haven't mentioned this before."

"Criminals rarely tell their wives," Gil said.

I smiled. "What got me thinking was the way the Wall Street grapevine telegraphs so many takeover deals. People have made a lot of money by finding out what raiders like Carl Icahn and Lance Grendal are up to. Even since the government cracked down, the information still makes the rounds. Gossip on whether Icahn is buying an airline. Whether one drug company wants another. If a raider zeroes in on a company that has stock options trading, and you find out early, the payoff can be fifty times your money. So for someone tied in with the right investment banker or lawyer or secretary who knew a story was true, it would look pretty tempting. Ten thousand gets you five hundred thousand, fifty thousand gets you two and a half million. One hit and you retire to the South of France in relative comfort."

"Provided the regulators don't catch you like they did Ivan Boesky," Gil said.

"Boesky was arrogant and careless. He kept playing, deal after deal. So did Dennis Levine. The first ten million wasn't enough."

"So they went to jail," Gil said.

"If you didn't want to go to jail," I said, "you might invent a cutout, a person who exists only on paper. You create a person named Mr. Hall. Mr. Hall opens several brokerage accounts at firms where you're not known. He uses a mail drop down in the financial district—one of those places that provide telephone answering and mail collection."

"These things exist?" Marty asked.

"They're all over town, and most are legitimate. If a small businessman wants a Manhattan office, these services provide an address, sometimes with pay-by-the-hour secretarial help. Some rent desk space. It helps establish your image to get mail on Wall Street or Park Avenue. They must vary in how closely they scrutinize their clients. Mr. Hall would want one that doesn't mind payment by money order from a client they never meet.

"As for a broker, the perfect choice would be a small discount house that deals with clients by telephone and mail. That is even more common. Jack and I have out-of-town clients who are just names and voices. I couldn't swear they're all who they say they are."

"It's not only discounters," Gil said. "I keep a small account at

Merrill, mostly for playing with bankrupts' bonds. The young woman I have been assigned knows only a voice on the telephone. She is so inexperienced in everything except merchandising Merrill's own packaged funds that she understands nothing of my transactions. Mr. Norris is a little old and most eccentric. Last year I did a hedge on Manville Corporation, buying the preferred and shorting the common, that locked in about thirty points on the preferred. When I closed it out, she voiced regret that it hadn't been successful. For all Merrill knows, I could be Manville's chairman of the board."

I nodded. "So Mr. Hall calls a brokerage firm or two and has new account forms sent out to his office. He sends in a bank check, drawn for cash at a bank where he is not known, and establishes the account. He trades it for small amounts, always by phone. The broker's confirmation call goes to the office number, where the 'secretary' takes a message. Mr. Hall calls in from time to time to collect the messages. Nobody at the mail drop knows how to reach him, and nobody really cares. If he wants to create an appearance of an outside existence, he sets up two offices and has them forward messages to each other. It doesn't matter, because he doesn't get much mail or many calls. For the office service, he is a no-problem, high-margin client. He obviously isn't duping people in Kansas to send him money for herbal cures. He says he's on the road a lot and that's fine with the mail drop. Once in a while, a messenger comes at odd hours and collects his mail. After a few months, Mr. Hall has built his brokerage account up to twenty or thirty thousand dollars, by sending in small checks. He likes to trade options, take large positions and sell them quickly. He doesn't make much money or lose much. Then one morning he buys call options on forty thousand shares of Biscuit Inc., and two days later Biscuit gets a takeover bid and rises fifteen points. Mr. Hall has made about six hundred thousand dollars. He sells the options and a day or two later asks for a check for most of the amount. The broker sends the check to his office. A messenger picks up Mr. Hall's mail, walks out. Mr. Hall is never heard from by his broker or the mail drop again.

"He has opened a bank account by largely the same means. He signs as Mr. Hall and deposits the check, then a few days later draws out cash. The bank never sees Mr. Hall again. If the SEC ever suspects that Mr. Hall's option buying was illegal, the trail stops cold at the bank. Mr. Hall no longer exists."

Gil raised an eyebrow at Marty. "Your husband has a felonious mind. But it wouldn't be quite that simple, would it? Banks and brokers require identification, references, Social Security numbers."

"Parts of that would be more complicated," I said. "How far is a Long Island savings bank going to check West Coast references on a thousand-dollar new account? What's your risk if the bank checks and draws a zero? You take your thousand dollars and go down the road to a place that's offering two toasters for new accounts. When you bring people money, it isn't in their interest to ask too many questions."

"Yes, a lot of Florida bankers proved that point—some in New York and Boston too. I suppose the same would apply to discount stock brokers."

"If you wanted you could be your own reference," I said. "Willow Real Estate Associates, based at another mail drop, confirms that Mr. Hall is a stand-up guy."

"Social Security numbers could be collected from the obituary column," Gil said. "The widow gets a call from a totally unsympathetic bureaucrat to check the deceased's number. If you made a dozen such calls, how many people would give up the information? The better your bureaucratic manner became, the higher the compliance."

"I was thinking of another way," I said. "Your cutout could be created from a living person. Say a Mr. Hall living in Connecticut. Just get his Social Security number and the name of his bank—or use the identity of somebody you already know. Right away you've got checkable references."

Gil's heavy lips formed a sour smile. "For purposes of your illicit trading, you become Mr. Hall. Let's see, what would be the risks? One, it behooves you to make certain that the real Mr. Hall receives no mail or telephone calls from his new bank and new broker. If they have only the mail drop address and number, you've eliminated that danger. An infinitesimal risk would exist that his real banker might mention to Mr. Hall that a broker has been checking references. Can you imagine that scene? Mr. Hall, who hates the stock market, cries, 'What broker?' But that danger isn't really worth considering. A person who believes random events will foil him doesn't embark on this sort of venture. Um . . . I notice that using a real person solves one problem that we hadn't considered. The real Mr. Hall will be a known quantity to all those private bureaus that compile credit and spending histories. So he will withstand more than cursory inspection. A cutout created from thin air will vanish the first time a bank officer takes a hard look."

Getting up, I brought the coffee pot over to the table, set it on a cork trivet. I moved the brandy and sambuca closer as well. Marty poured refills and asked, "What about the danger that someone at the new brokerage or bank will know the real Mr. Hall? Or just by chance, a secretary at the mail drop?"

"Those risks would exist," Gil agreed. "But they would be minute, unquantifiable. Our person would tell himself, 'I could also get hit by lightning while walking to the mail drop. So why worry about the long shots?' He would feel he had covered the manageable risk pretty well. He wouldn't keep any of the accounts open for more than a year. The first that the real Mr. Hall hears of the scheme might be two years later, when the Internal Revenue Service tells him he forgot to pay taxes on his stock profits."

Gil celebrated our brainstorming with another cognac. "If you and I could manage this much, imagine what someone with resources—access, say, to forged driver's licenses—could carry off."

"So why do it the clumsy way Jack did—when he was certain to be caught?" I said.

"Why did Levine keep at it? He knew regulators were sniffing around. It was time to close his operation and run. But he stayed to get caught. That might be your answer."

"Wanting to get caught? It doesn't fit the man I know. People who want punishment ask for it in other ways too. Jack isn't a guilty neurotic."

"Well, then—as you said, maybe he bought for other reasons."

I said, "Can you think of a reason to buy twenty thousand shares of Dorchester Millinery?"

"If somebody wanted to hurt Canning, they may have found an

incentive he couldn't ignore. Your friends have proved they are violent."

"A threat?" Marty said.

"It would be quite a threat that got a man to ruin himself," Gil said.

"If he did," I said.

"Is there any doubt about that?" Gil asked.

"We've sat here and figured out how to trade in Mr. Hall's name without his knowing. Maybe somebody did the same for Jack and me."

"But we had to use a broker who didn't know Mr. Hall," Gil said. "I assume your broker would recognize Jack's voice."

"What about having a woman pretend to be your secretary?" Marty said.

"Our secretary doesn't phone in orders. We do that. Besides, the thing would blow up as soon as any of us got the first call back from the broker confirming a trade."

Remarkable, I thought, that I hadn't stumbled across any of the printed receipts. More evidence of Jack's culpability; he must have intercepted them all.

Gil roused himself and helped Marty carry dishes out to the kitchen. It was late and he moved heavily, showing his age. He called over his shoulder, "Perhaps your broker never sent the reports."

"He says he did."

He stopped in the doorway. "Strange, isn't it, how much of this depends on your broker's word? Suppose that instead of Jack, it was your broker who was threatened?"

20

I phoned Faulkner Wells's office before the opening on Monday and talked to Lisa. Vince DiMineo was taking time off. She passed the information reluctantly.

I called him in Scarsdale.

"Ben! We shouldn't be talking. The SEC gets crazy about collusion."

"I won't keep you long."

He cleared his throat. "You don't understand. I can't talk to you at all. Is—is it true that Jack has gone?"

"It's true."

He was silent for a moment and I thought he might have hung up. He said, "That doesn't look too good. The SEC, I mean, will read it as a sign of guilt."

I listened to another silence, then broke it. "Vince, is there any chance that someone other than Jack made those trades?"

"What do you mean?"

"Could it have been somebody else?"

"I don't know what you're—"

"Somebody else on the phone, pretending to be Jack."

I heard a faint exhalation. "That's nonsense. I know Jack's voice and his style. Never 'Good morning, Vinnie, have you heard about the ten stages of drunkenness?' Always formal, 'Let's buy five hundred Peltz Imperial for the Turney account, two hundred for Potter.' When he wants to socialize he asks if the phones are ringing."

"You'll have to admit, Dorchester Millinery isn't our style," I said.

"Canning takes a flier now and then. Look, I'm sorry, Ben. You're ready to jump on anything to get your firm off the hook. I understand—I respect loyalty. But this isn't good, us talking. You won't help yourself if you get in the way of this investigation."

He hung up, and I stared out the window. Details were crisp and vivid even in distance. Columns of steam venting from rooftops rose like pale granite pillars. Skyscrapers looked close and bulky. Reality was intense when you were in trouble.

For two hours I placed small orders to lighten portfolios. It was more from caution than any deep worry about the market. The few thousand shares disappeared quickly without slowing the ascent of prices. If there was ever a time to sell, it was while twenty-eight-year-old portfolio managers were still brave in their buying. Once they ran for cover, the great long party would end.

Each time Lisa called back with a confirmation she sounded uncomfortable. I couldn't think of anything to say that would put her at ease.

How much did she know, I wondered, about Vince?

Trading slowed just after noon and I risked a call to Sol Lehrman. He answered brusquely with his last name, discouraging interruptions. The background noise sounded like a civil disturbance. For a moment Sol didn't recognize my voice. Then he shouted, "Oh, sure! What do you want?"

I told him part of it, and he said to come around.

That left me several hours to make up a list of names for Sol to work with. It turned out to be a short list.

From the visitors' gallery of the stock exchange, I watched the final minutes of trading. The action was frantic as big plungers made their portfolios comfortable for overnight. That brought a lot of selling on the one hand, because you didn't want to carry a chancy stock on margin for seventeen and a half hours when God only knew what would happen in the Middle East. Buying poured in, on the other hand, because there was no sense being short when so many companies were getting taken over.

Brokers scrambled across the paper-strewn floor clutching order slips, waving for attention. The yammering voices rose in a wave, subsided, came back roaring like a breaking surf. The Dow Jones Industrial Average, according to the electronic boards over the floor, was up more than fifteen points. A strong finish would buoy everyone's spirits into tomorrow. A really bang-up close would bring back to the market the retired auto salesman in Moline who hadn't bought stocks since the sixties. Everyone on the floor was waiting for him.

Five minutes before the closing bell, a twenty-thousand-share block of General Motors crossed the lighted board twelve and a half cents higher than GM had traded a minute earlier, and the Dow climbed another fraction.

I scanned the swarming heads for Solomon Lehrman and eventually spotted him at the center of a crush of brokers and blue-jacketed clerks who looked ready to lynch somebody. Sol was the specialist who handled orders for a half-dozen sleepy stocks. Today it looked like one of the sleepers had begun turning cartwheels. As orders flooded in, Sol would be trying to match buyers and sellers to keep the trading more or less orderly. When he couldn't make a match, he would have to buy or sell stock from his firm's own account, like an auctioneer who had to buy an occasional baby carriage nobody wanted just to keep the market moving.

He could tack twelve and a half cents a share on to some of the trades, according to exchange rules, and those fractions added up in most years to a six-figure income for Sol.

Somebody behind me in the gallery hissed, "They're just all crooks!"

It was a widely held sentiment. He was hissing in my direction, a crater-faced old timer with a string necktie and black suit. A blond exchange employee was escorting a group through, reminding them of the busiest day on record, the best day, overlooking the worst day, and singing cheerfully, "Today we're having an average day" as the Dow notched up another point.

"It's all rigged," the old boy announced. "The Rockefellers and foreign bankers suck the working people's blood." An icy blue eye assailed me. He chewed the inside of his lip as if he wanted to spit over the railing.

On the floor, the final bell rang. A whoop of relief burst above the mob, and eyes darted to the tote board which showed the Dow up seventeen and a half points. Nice day's work, everybody agreed. Directly below, a wilted Sol Lehrman staggered from the floor.

He met me twenty minutes later in a pub around the corner, looking as though he had been mugged.

"I watched from the gallery," I said. "You got popular."

"You should have thrown me a whip and chair." He pushed his fingers through dense steel-wool hair, glanced at himself in the mirror behind the booth. His long face was exhausted but strong. He preened some more, grimaced in satisfaction. "Half-hour before the close, everybody decides they want to own Troubadour Industries. They were ready to kill me for stock. God knows why."

The name meant nothing to me. "What do they do?"

"Make computers in Hong Kong."

"Maybe there's a takeover in the wind."

"And maybe not. There's nothing special about the boxes they build, except they read backasswards maybe. It's all rumors, stupid rumors. I shorted more than twenty thousand shares today, as high as eleven and a half. This one's going to put Bridget in a Ferrari." His Manhattan came and he swallowed half of it, rolled back his eyes. We had secured a rustic wooden booth with the logos of nineteenth-century stocks burned into the table top. The clamor around us was growing as brokers poured out of surrounding buildings and made a beeline for emergency stations. He flicked his glass with a diamond-laden pinky. "So what's new with you?"

"One of our stocks has been trading funny. I thought you might help me find out why."

"So you want help from the friend you don't call twice a year. Very interesting. Listen, was that girl with you at Christmas your wife? If I get the information you want, I get to sleep with her. If she's your wife, I figure you won't mind. You can sleep with my wife. Do you like ponies?"

"Have you changed the subject?"

"No. Bridget is a young palomino, all hips and hair."

Another Manhattan landed, and midway through it he began to wind down. He sighed. "So what is it? You want to know who's buying?"

"And selling."

"I can check around. What's the stock?"

"Dorchester Millinery. Who handles the book on it?"

He told me the name of a well-regarded specialist firm. "You know there's a takeover offer for Dorchester Millinery?"

"I know."

"You know both the exchange's surveillance department and the SEC are looking at the stock's trades."

"I know."

"So is this going to come back at me if I help you?"

"It could."

"And would you have told me if I hadn't asked?"

"I might have mentioned it."

"Working on the floor doesn't improve my view of human nature. Let's assume you wouldn't have. What do you want?"

"Can you get me copies of the trading records the specialist gave the SEC?"

"No way."

"Can you get a look at the stuff?"

"That's a maybe. You guys are involved in this one?"

"It looks that way."

He leaned back, eyes staying with me, but uneasy at what they saw. "You're involved and you ask me to screw around in an SEC investigation."

"Would it help if I say I think we've been set up? And I don't want you to get into trouble."

"It wouldn't help enough. If somebody in the government leans on the stock exchange, Sol Lehrman loses his book. Look, I can say a friend of mine sold some Dorchester just before the news and wants to know who was buying that day."

"Can you say during that week or two? You've forgotten the exact day. There are a couple of names I want you to look for."

"All right. All I'll be able to get is the brokerage firm's name. It would take a subpoena to find out who the customer was."

"That's okay." A sophisticated person would buy through a girl friend or a cousin or a lawyer anyway, depending on how careful he was. "Keep an eye peeled for anything from Furbinger Associates. It's a new-issues house. Or Faulkner Wells Rhoades."

"Very blue-blooded," he said. "I'll see what I can do."

21

ON Tuesday Rudy Thatcher and I had lunch with George Finn, a registered bulwark of the establishment. On Wednesday the firm of Canning & McCarthy officially became a pariah.

Brooker Finn & Co. occupied a stone building on Broad Street that had been fortified with brass doors to hold off generations of unworthy money. Today there was a guard near the entrance and an elegantly tailored mannequin in the middle of the lobby at a Louis Quinze reception desk. In George Finn's father's day a dollar had to have passed across a couple of generations, giving up any taint of sweat, to nest in the Finn vault. An industrial fortune, like a vulgar painting, looked better under a patina of age. Ten years ago George Finn had recognized that the old bloodlines were thinning and might no longer sustain the business. Opening the door to nouveaux bucks if they came in large quantities, he had saved Brooker Finn from the oblivion that swept away so many silk-stockinged brokerage houses. He had preserved the firm's stodgy independence. While many Wall Street partnerships had sold stock to the public or merged into conglomerates promising access to capital, Brooker Finn still got by on its aging partners' wherewithal. The firm had the feel of an old smoking room full of comfortable chairs and seat-sprung traditions.

The board room, where the public could gather to watch price changes, was a long high-ceilinged gallery decorated in mahogany panels and burgundy armchairs. Most of Wall Street had given up the public rooms as uneconomical. Brooker Finn had recently refurbished its own with a new electronic board that showed stocks' symbols and prices in foot-high characters.

George Finn looked like a bald polar bear. Oblivious of the commanding presence his six-foot-three frame had among his customers, he hunched forward, one white manicured paw propping up his chin as he watched the quote board. His features were small and sharp, like an elf's, easy to overlook on the massive face. He wore thick bifocals that made his eyes shrunken and timid.

His most obvious affectation was the role of country sportsman, for which he dressed in tweeds—today a dark butterscotch with red plaid overlay—that set him apart in streets where navy, charcoal and pinstripes held sway.

Beside Finn stood an elderly, lantern-jawed man with shoulder-length white hair who had been Labor secretary a few years earlier. The former secretary wore a black suit with a white carnation in a lapel and was stretching, trying to grow a couple of inches to gain Finn's attention. Finn pointed to the quotation board and spared a few words that set the old man nodding and cackling as Finn snatched a telephone from the ledge behind him and gave one of his brokers an order. He was setting a good example for the men in the score of leather armchairs that sat shoulder-to-shoulder the length of the room. The telephones that invited spectators to place orders weren't getting much use.

Finn waved to Rudy and me, and his voice boomed, "Good to see you, gentlemen! I've done my duty today by the retail trade. Let's go upstairs."

On the way to the elevator, he called to the mannequin, "Tell everyone we're having a special on Telephone. It's down three-quarters for no good reason."

"Yes, Mr. Finn."

"Have you heard more from Jack?" he asked.

Rudy shook his head.

"Tell me more about your thinking on Faulkner Wells, Ben."

The elevator stopped and a white-jacketed waiter greeted us. My theory on Faulkner Wells got put on hold.

The twenty-first-floor dining room was another page out of an older world: plush carpets, heavy damask, an age-darkened mural of Manhattan in the 1800s. The corner windows presented a vista of the harbor, where gusts of sleet made the Statue of Liberty shimmy and sway. From another oak-fretted window you could peer down a crooked street to the columned entrance of the New York Stock Exchange. The combination was stirring: liberty and wealth, virtue and its reward.

"The grapevine must be breaking down," Finn complained as a waiter brought in drinks, a dry martini for him, Bloody Marys for Rudy and me. "I heard an odd whisper and called to invite Jack to dinner. Barbara was hysterical." He set down his drink. "Bloody hell! My friends come to me when they're in trouble. Why didn't Jack call?"

"He may have wanted to spare you the embarrassment," Rudy said.

"I don't embarrass easily," Finn said. "And my reputation is pretty durable." He had gained his prominence by repairing the financial district's reputation five years earlier, when it was in tatters. In its periodic siege, Congress had complained that three events were causing doubt about Wall Street's dedication to fair play. The first was a national publicity tour by the exchange's president, a retired general named DeCoursey, who told after-dinner crowds from Boston to Seattle that stocks were both a patriot's investment and a shrewd businessman's. The second event, a few months later, was a severe business recession that deflated stock prices by an average of forty percent. The third was the discovery that as DeCoursey made the rounds praising stock ownership, the exchange's member firms had been selling short millions of shares.

A Senate committee chairman dropped a few words about nationalizing the stock exchanges, and Wall Street panicked. George Finn, whose firm had been buying stocks on the brink of the recession, was invited to join the exchange's board of governors. Immediately he was tapped as chairman of a new housecleaning committee. Two firms that had violated exchange rules were

101

suspended. Finn encouraged closer liaison with regulatory committees. The threat to the Street passed.

Finn's rise to prominence wasn't universally welcomed. His management at Brooker Finn raised suspicions of democratic sympathies. But eventually even his critics recognized that George Finn had been the ideal choice, a man secure enough on the establishment's upper decks to rock the boat, sensible enough not to capsize it.

He pressed Rudy. "I talked to some people over at the exchange. I have trouble believing what I've heard about Jack."

Rudy jumped at the opening. "I know you can't get involved in the investigation. But Ben already has a friend checking for whoever else might have been buying Dorchester Millinery stock before the news."

"That's a sensible line of inquiry. What else?"

"He—we—are especially interested in whether anyone at Faulkner Wells Rhoades bought except in Jack's account."

"Do you think it's possible?" Finn asked.

"We'll have to see. But if you assume Jack didn't buy the shares, that leaves only his broker, Vince DiMineo, or somebody else at Faulkner Wells. What you could do is encourage the official inquiry to ask the right questions."

"I can do better than that," Finn said. "I can ask the questions myself. If we've got a rotten apple at a member firm, it's my duty to find out. I'll have Andy Meadows—he's surveillance chief at the exchange—make certain that all bases are covered."

Lunch came, thin strips of veal with apple slices, and the talk turned random. The state of the market. The state of Barbara Canning. The weakness of exports. The implausible cowardice of Jack in not staying to fight. Finn told me regretfully, "I'm afraid his departure is one hole in your premise."

"Maybe he welcomed the excuse," Rudy countered. "There are weeks I would pay good money for a scandal that drove me out of Manhattan."

Finn chuckled. Behind Rudy, frozen rain lashed the windows. Plumes of cloud drifted between the taller buildings. I thought it was a good day for running away. Finn said, "My respect for Jack

Canning is hard to overstate. Not many people on Wall Street truly think for themselves. Jack follows his own inner voice."

"Maybe that's what got him into trouble," I said.

"How do you mean, Ben?"

I wasn't sure. "If somebody tried to buy Jack—or pressure him—I don't think it would work."

Finn's smile was gentle, a counterpoint to his buoyant manner. "You're quite right. But why would anybody try to do either to Jack? He's never been involved in takeovers, has he? He doesn't engage in the riskier trading strategies. He doesn't handle funny South American money. Rudy, can you think of a reason?"

Rudy shook his head.

"Neither can I." Finn stared pensively at my discolored forehead. My appearance had been distracting him. He finally couldn't resist asking what had happened, and I told him.

22

I got into the office on Wednesday just in time for Rudy's call. He read me the government's press release announcing that the SEC was investigating Canning & McCarthy Investment Counsel for illegal trading.

The statement reviewed the details of Grendal's bid for Dorchester Millinery. It noted that the firm under investigation had bought Dorchester's stock heavily in the days before Grendal's offer. One principal of the firm had not made his current whereabouts known. The facts were being referred to the United States Attorney for possible criminal prosecution. An audit had been completed of the advisory firm's accounts.

"How did they find out about the audit?" I asked Rudy.

"From me. Why do you think you're still open for business?" His voice was tinny, broken by background noise picked up by his speaker phone. "If I hadn't been able to show them a clean bill of health, they'd have gone for an injunction a week ago to padlock your door and freeze every dime."

"I don't remember your mentioning it to me."

"I told you they had asked for the firm's records. Regardless of the bitch they've got with you, I wanted everybody to feel comfortable that the investors were okay. Too bad they didn't give the results of the audit."

It was a lose-lose situation, I thought. Mentioning the audit, the SEC had tacked the equivalent of a diphtheria warning on our door. We would be closed down by clients jumping from the windows rather than by court edict.

Not much difference, unless you had to be on hand for the slow death.

"You didn't have much choice," I said.

"Where can I reach you when the next round of official crap hits?"

I thought about following Jack to a sunny island. "At the office if it hits by late afternoon."

"Then home? We may have to respond quickly."

"I may be out of touch for a while."

"Out of touch where?"

"I'm going to drop in on Vince DiMineo." Shake him till he rattles, I thought.

"You're out of your goddamn mind! Forget it. DiMineo's a witness."

"He's a liar too."

"You don't know that. And if he is a liar, let your buddies Sol and George Finn collect some evidence."

"I was planning to collect the evidence from DiMineo."

"You may be Irish, but you can't be that stupid. All you would do is get yourself in deeper trouble. If DiMineo's got anything to hide, you'll spook him to bury it. Sit this one out."

"I'll think about it."

"Don't think. Obey."

A lawyer I had never heard of called and said Faulkner Wells Rhoades would not be able to do further business with us. Could we have our clients transfer their accounts elsewhere? If we couldn't arrange it overnight, any trades would have to go through a third party.

Gail began phoning clients, and I came on and told them about the charges and about Faulkner Wells's position. The sticky part was why Mr. Canning was absent. The lines got quiet.

"Do I have a loss?" a widow asked.

"No, you're up twenty-two percent since this time last year."

"You can't expect me to stay, can you?"

An hour after I got off the phone with the chief investment officer of a chemical company's pension fund, which was a fifth of our business, the fund's lawyer showed up with a notarized letter canceling our trading authority. Even Professor Potter, who had been worried about his oil stocks, jumped ship. "I'm retired and this is all the money I've got. I just can't take a chance."

"No." I wouldn't have.

"If everything works out, I would like to bring the account back. You and Canning did well by me."

One curmudgeon said he never believed anything the SEC said so we could keep his money. The son of another client threatened to sue if I obstructed his father's departure.

It took all day.

I sat and surveyed the wreckage. The walls hadn't cracked. Drawers hadn't been turned inside out this time. But one official press release had worked like a wrecking ball. Our credibility was rubble and dust. The firm had life and value only as long as it had clients.

We had lost more than half our business in five hours. We would lose more as soon as I reached other clients.

I put my head down on the desk and lifted it an hour later, phoned Rudy with the numbers. He was back to being a smooth, civil barrister. "We're going to have to take the firm into bankruptcy," he said. "You might want to file personally too."

"I don't think so."

"You're going to be broke. Your legal bills can wait. But anyone else you owe money to is going to come after you."

"I'll pay them," I said, with no idea how I could follow through on the boast.

George Finn called in on Jack's line. "Good afternoon, Ben. Do you feel you have the plague?"

"Several kinds. Faulkner Wells doesn't want our business."

"I'm an opportunist. Bring it here."

"Are you sure? There may not be much."

"We have a young fellow named Fletcher who will take over your accounts. I'll have him start the paperwork and arrange things with Faulkner Wells first thing in the morning."

"It's kind of you."

He brushed the idea off. "Kind nothing. It's good business. You'll be with us twenty years from now. This nonsense will blow over. Now—this is strictly social. I thought you and your wife—her name is Martha?—might want to come out to the farm for the weekend. We could shoot a bird or two, maybe draw a bead on the SEC's case. I've invited Barbara Canning and her brother."

"Have you learned something?"

"Andy Meadows has just gotten started."

"You're taking a chance," I said. "We could be guilty."

He gave an explosive laugh. "In that case, I will say I was gathering fuel to cook your goose."

Peter Bagley met me at the Gramercy Park's bar. The rendezvous was well away from Wall Street and chance encounters with friends. "If Max heard about this, he would demand a story," Peter said.

I got a glass of Madeira and felt better. I asked him, "When did you ever interview people before writing about them?"

"There isn't time, usually, so I invent." He let his straight face crack a little. "Does the SEC have a case?"

"No."

"Are you sure?" There was more reporter than friend behind the question, and he was embarrassed.

"Ninety-five percent," I said.

He scooped up his beer and half-emptied the glass. "I'm glad to hear that, Benj. So what's on your mind?"

"Did you hear any talk about Dorchester Millinery before Grendal announced his offer?"

"Not a word. None of the top hedge funds was putting a story out. The arbitrage desks either. It was a quiet deal."

"That's what I was afraid of."

"Sorry." He wrinkled his high forehead. "Was that all you wanted to know?"

"Are you still buddies with Michael Renshaw?"

Peter shrugged. "We still live in the same building, so we're

107

neighbors. On the other hand, he's never invited me to be a panelist on *Rich Is Better*. We can't be great friends."

"Renshaw waved the Dorchester Millinery buying under Gordon Trapp's nose. Somebody must have told him that the trading wasn't kosher."

"He won't tell you who. Or me. Renshaw is jealous of sources."

"Can you try?"

He sighed and went off to the lobby pay phones. He was gone a long time. He came back looking smug. "We're friends after all. One of Renshaw's staff people got an anonymous call on Friday afternoon. It was close to taping time."

"That's all? Someone makes a telephone call and Michael Renshaw puts the spurs to the SEC chief?"

"Not quite. This call had the ring of authority. So she taped it and told the man they would call him back. That was no go, of course. The caller said he would call back. When he did, Renshaw asked enough questions and got enough details on the size of the trading in Dorchester that he concluded somebody probably had gotten a leak on Grendal's plan."

"Does Renshaw know the caller?"

"I don't think so. He wouldn't care, if the story was good."

"What kind of man called? Young, old? Educated?"

He propped his chin on his fists. "Rich, poor? Do you really need this? Okay. Then give me a quarter."

Peter came back in five minutes. "Sorry, Benj. White adult male who probably worked on the Street, or at least knew the jargon. Not at all distinctive or recognizable."

Peter caught the waitress and ordered two more. "If I were trying to track him down, I would look for someone with a grudge against you and Jack. Or maybe against your broker. Most people blow the whistle out of spite." He switched to a confidential tone. "The Street gossips too much. It makes my job easy; everybody wants to tell me something. But reputations get rough treatment. Like Markey Wahl & Company, with all those whispers of something irregular, how they had gotten killed trading index futures."

"I remember. It was a plausible story."

"Right. Other firms had gotten wiped out, so why not Markey

Wahl? Once the story got started it was all over the place. Their regular accounts ran for cover, and Gordon Trapp and the SEC froze every asset in sight. Everybody thought the government had stepped in just in time to prevent an exact replay of the Cornelius Trust blowout. Remember that one? Those two jerks in the bond and bill department lost the bank about a hundred million in unauthorized trades."

Wondering what his point was, I nodded. Cornelius Trust's name had made headlines for weeks after the bank failed.

"What's different about Cornelius and Markey Wahl is that the old man, Noble Wahl, denied doing anything wrong at his firm," Peter said. "No losses surfaced. The government had put his business in the toilet. Wahl was still screaming his innocence last fall when he had his stroke. A couple of people that I talked to who knew him thought he was telling the truth. Somebody started a story that wrecked him."

"Bad luck," I said.

"Once Noble was gone, there was no one to push for investigating how the rumors got going." Peter stretched around and peered through the haze. We were a dozen feet from the door, and sometimes a draft blew in.

"We're pushing," I said.

"Good luck. It would be easier if you hadn't got left holding the bag alone." He cleared his throat. "Have I told you I'm thinking of leaving *Investor's Week*?"

"You know you haven't."

The idea seemed unlikely. The magazine was Peter's job, hobby and vacation. Most of his social contacts flowed from his role as columnist. I didn't know how he would get along.

"I've had an offer from the Street, a pretty good one," he said. "You're trustworthy. This shouldn't get back to the office."

"It won't from me," I said.

"Morgan Stanley wants someone to help them dig into special situations, size up the investment potential. See if things are what they appear."

"Right up your alley."

109

"I know. The pay's about twice what Max has to offer. Plus a percentage—a tiny one, but a percentage—of the action."

"It sounds good."

"The Street is where the money is. If you can bank two really fat years in this business, in a crazy bull market, you're fixed for life." He saw dollar signs dancing in the smoke and laughed them away. "Of course, your living costs must go up as you discover new necessities. I would find I couldn't live without a summer place on Block Island."

"And an apartment in London. But if you decide to go for it, good luck."

"Thank you, Benj."

I left him for a minute and took my turn at the telephone bank. I tried the apartment and got no answer. In a sour temper I went back to Peter and suggested another drink.

He shook his head. "I've got a dinner date if she hasn't given me up."

"If you're going downtown, I'll drop you."

We got a cab at the Gramercy's front door. Peter leaned back, fished for a cigarette. "I'll tell you something funny about Lance Grendal. You've got to wonder how some of these guys run their empires. I found out he's got an office in town he uses sometimes. It's owned by a shipping subsidiary of Grendal Offshore Ltd. on Fifth up around Seventy-second. *Very* classy. I went up a few days ago just on the chance I would get an interview. He wasn't in town, this Chinese girl tells me. She volunteers to brief me about his current life interests. Life interests! But she meant it. Lance has given up smoking and violence toward animals, she tells me, and he's taking high colonics to reduce body toxicity. He meditates to understand the interstices of finance better. Now where can I print that?"

I shook my head. "I didn't know you were working on a story about Grendal."

"Minor diversion until a good subject comes along. I sort of wanted to know where Grendal is investing. So I ran his name through the computer bases of corporate filings. Remember Bunny

110

Furbinger's Trionix? Lance Grendal owns a piece of it. The price is up another dollar and a half."

I tried to make sense of that. "Furbinger isn't one of Grendal's brokers."

"And Trionix isn't Grendal's kind of stock. He likes things he can liquidate. Trionix would turn to dust in a strong light." The cab slowed and Peter glanced out. "Well, this is it. Are you going home?"

"No."

He got out at his restaurant. I stayed with the cab down to Chambers Street.

A green-eyed girl with springy curls greeted me as I got off the World Trade Center's elevator at the 107th floor. She wore Dayglo-pink harem pants and a silky blue blouse slit to her navel. When I said I had forgotten my invitation, she waved me on. "Bunny is two rooms back, with the president of ConCom."

ConCom was the client company on whose behalf Bunny had the good times rolling. A crowd of brokers, pin-striped fund managers, salesman, clients and gate-crashers bounced between high-stacked buffet tables and a platform where a Dixieland combo was braying "Sweet Georgia Brown." On the refrain, the trombonist stepped to the microphone and rasped, "ConCom's *bound* to climb!"

Near the door a pair of shaggy-haired young men in European suits sipped milky drinks, over which one asked the other, "Just what does ConCom do, John?" His accent had originated north of London.

"I've been telling customers they make multiplexers," John answered, "whatever they are. If we'd got the fucking prospectus printed, I could sound more convincing as I sold it."

The other man said, "I sold an unbelievable amount without knowing what I was talking about. Information is a handicap."

As I stepped out of eavesdropping range, I spotted Bunny Furbinger. The round body was backed up against the Dixieland group, hemmed in by admirers. As he shouted over the music, his gestures were grand, as if he were tossing out hundred-dollar bills. Beside him stood an ascetic-looking man who presumably was

111

ConCom's president. Judging from his expression, he had just found a worm wiggling in his whiskey.

Before I could move, a hand grabbed my sleeve. Meg Silverman batted her lashes. "Ben?" She backed away a step to give me the full effect of the gypsy eyes and coal black hair. "I tried to reach you when I heard the news. It's dreadful, Ben."

"Bad," I agreed.

"I wanted to take you out for a cheering-up lunch. We should do that anyway. We haven't seen each other in too long. Since fall?"

I had run into her at a Goldman party a few months before that. She was beautiful and smart. I hadn't inquired too closely whether she was attached. By the second meeting she clearly was.

"It's good to see you, Meg."

She tucked an arm under mine. "Now that I've got you, I promise to testify to what a reliable character you are. Socrates has gone back to Athens to help the Socialists steal things."

His real name was Ilias, an exiled Greek banker who had moved in with her a few months after a husband moved out. Meg called him Socrates.

"Sorry to hear it," I said.

"Oh, don't be. His mama's there and he missed her." She turned away, gazing fondly at a man in a chef's hat who was slicing pink ribbons of roast lamb. "Let's mosey that way, Ben dear. I haven't had a chance to tell you that I got promoted. Roger left the bank and little Meg's now chief investment strategist. So you should return her phone calls."

"Haven't I always?"

"You became remiss last fall, when you suspected the calls weren't about business." We reached the buffet table. She winked at the chef's hat and told the weary face beneath it, "Give me something with skin on it."

We elbowed away with loaded plates, finding a sheltered corner behind a champagne fountain. A life-sized ice sculpture of a naked Diana, caught in the middle of the hunt, posed on one toe above the terraced cascade.

I said, "Why are you gracing Furbinger's bash?"

"Good Scotch, adequate food, intriguing people if you're seeking

112

a cross-section of prevailing opinion. That big hairy man over there runs trust money and wouldn't buy an automobile stock if his life depended on it. That's because, he told me without meaning to, he lost a bundle of his clients' inheritances in auto stocks eighteen months ago. If I sample the wisdom a bit more and find one or two other people who loathe auto stocks, I'll make a mental note of it for our next strategy meeting. It won't mean that we should buy Detroit, but it will tell me that a lot of idiots think they shouldn't. Then a few minutes ago I eavesdropped as this boy who I happen to know works at the New York Federal Reserve was trying to make points by telling someone he expects a discount rate cut pretty soon. That stuff I listen to because he may know. Bunny attracts a diverse crowd."

"Does your bank do business with him?"

"With Bunny? Oh, please!" She choked on her drink. "You're trying to hurt my feelings. Bunny invited me because the fat little darling entertains an insane hope that someday, if Meg is at loose ends as usual, he might get incredibly lucky. Which dear Ben could do if he only returned phone calls. But of course Bunny isn't true blue to anyone like my friend Ben is." She gave me a look of exaggerated patience. "And how is the Lady Vermeer?"

Mentally I sighed, realizing just how much of a handful Meg would be. "She's fine."

"All right. Mr. McCarthy doesn't stray. So why are you here?"

"I've got business with Bunny."

Her round-eyed disbelief lasted only a moment. "I know you don't mean that."

"It's half true. Is there anything I should know about Furbinger Associates?"

"Like what? Like that ConCom and these other companies he promotes are nine-tenths imaginary. You already know that. About his sexual kinks? I've never stayed late enough to tell you."

"More mundane stuff, Meg."

"Well, he has come a long way in a couple of years."

"It's been a giddy market."

She set down her Scotch glass, picked up a champagne flute and held it under the fountain. She drew back with a sodden sleeve, sipped, wrinkled her nose. "No bubbles left. Haven't you heard the rumors about Bunny? He got some start-up capital somewhere, a lot of it. Envious people say it was Colombian or Atlantic City money looking to get scrubbed clean."

A lean man in gray tweeds came over and said hello to Meg. "I worried this was going to be a dull party," he confessed. "Then I saw my favorite market strategist."

She gave him a restrained flash of the eyes. "You're sweet, Richard. Richard Lamprey, Ben McCarthy."

He nodded. "Pleasure. Could I pry Meg away to buy her a drink?"

"Meg's engaged," she said sweetly, "but only for another moment. What I told you, Ben, is just hearsay, so don't quote me."

Richard inspected the ice figure of Diana, which turned slowly on a motorized platform. "You know, she reminds me of someone," he said.

"Nesbitt?" I suggested.

Meg snorted. "More like the big-titted bimbo by the elevators."

Richard sucked in his lips. "Yeah, the cheekbones and curly hair. You're right." He watched a backthrust leg swing by, noticed the considerable anatomical detail, and clucked.

Meg looped an arm through his and headed for a bar. I headed for Bunny. The fan club had thinned, and he was chatting with his client beside a glass wall that looked uptown. Against the spray of lights, any two men in dark suits and clean shirts could look substantial and respectable.

I worked my way in close. "Is the genius behind Trionix here tonight?"

Bunny's mouth sagged. "Oh . . . McCarthy. I'm glad you made it." He looked more startled than glad. Startled that a felon would show his face. Or—if he knew two thugs who rode commuter trains—startled that I was in one piece. He squinted, concentrating. "Trionix, you said? Sure, Dylan O'Keefe is somewhere around. He and ConCom's president, Herb Butler here, were discussing the telecommunications market. It's a privilege to listen in. Change is coming too fast for the weak players. Today's revolution is tomorrow's outmoded thinking."

Herb Butler's wrinkled mouth wiggled until it smiled. "Excellent

114

point, Mr. Furbinger. Are you an admirer of Mr. O'Keefe, sir?" he asked me.

"I've never met him. I'm relying on Furbinger's recommendation."

"That would be good enough for me," he said. The sale of ConCom stock must be filling his pockets to earn Bunny such a tribute.

"Actually, Trionix has other fans," I said.

"I'm certain the admiration is deserved," Butler said. His long desiccated face could have hung on a headshrinker's bedpost. Money wouldn't make him happier, I thought, but neither would good health or a loving family. He found life sour-tasting, even the sweet parts.

The band had taken a rest, and we had to compete with only the din of self-congratulating liars, backslappers and freeloaders. Bunny was looking away. The withered head was picking at its cuffs.

"I was going to ask Mr. O'Keefe about Lance Grendal's interest in his company," I said.

Bunny's attention suddenly was all mine. Herb Butler squinted above my head, but listened. He said, "Grendal is a takeover artist, I believe. Is Trionix vulnerable to a raid?"

Bunny Furbinger had the good manners not to laugh. He shot his client a quieting glance. "Ignore him, Mr. Butler. He doesn't know what he's talking about."

"What don't I know?" I said.

Bunny drew back his round shoulders. "Nothing about dynamic companies, for starters. And nothing about good social behavior, for finishers. Coming to a gathering of honest investors after what you and your partner have done is inexcusable."

ConCom's president looked perplexed.

Bunny amplified quickly. "Today the SEC accused McCarthy of insider trading connected to one of Grendal's deals."

"How—ghastly."

"That entitles me," I said mildly, "to claim to know a lot about Grendal's business. His stake in Trionix is a matter of public record. What I'm curious about, Bunny, is why he would get involved in one of your phony companies."

He looked tempted not to respond. But Butler's squint had transferred to Bunny. Furbinger raised his hands. "How would I know how Grendal gets his stock ideas? He must have a half-dozen people looking out for him."

"Whoever gave him the Trionix story got something in return— early word on Dorchester Millinery."

"Are you implying—" He sputtered, unwilling to accuse himself. His bow tie bounced like an angry pink bird.

"I'm just curious who put Grendal into Trionix," I said.

Bunny's flush deepened. "It's news to me, if it's true at all. I would consider it a courtesy if you left."

23

WE walked several blocks north the next evening and had an early dinner. A few people Marty recognized stopped into the restaurant. They interrupted us with hellos and have-you-been-next-doors. As we settled the check, Paul Christian, the chef and owner, bundled an armful of champagne bottles to the neighboring building. I held the door for him.

The Likeness, a portrait gallery that represented Martha Norris, was celebrating its renovation with an open house. Janie and Peaches had bought the building behind them, knocked a hole in the rear wall and given the Likeness double its old floor space plus a second front door on the next block. Now the gallery had two faces, Janie explained, like the town's art critics. Smells of varnish, paint and dust lingered over the crowd that had filled the long building.

As I hung up our coats, Peaches swept down on us like a strafing jet, blowing obstacles aside. She was a cute blonde of miniature proportions except for weight-lifter shoulders and forearms. She wrapped an arm around Marty's waist and almost unbalanced her.

"Why, Mizz Norris! So nice to see you! And you brung along Mr. Norris. Don't see him too often." Both Peaches and Janie had operated small galleries in Arkansas tourist traps before moving to New York. She whispered, "We got so many celebrities here tonight you wouldn't believe. I even invited the competition from the other

117

galleries and they came, bless 'em, to wish us well and steal our talent."

She grabbed Paul Christian on his way out and kissed him.

She came back to us, telling Marty, "Your stuff's getting a lot of attention, sweet. Who'd you tell me was that puckered-up dude you painted?"

"A friend."

"We're all your friends, honey. Come on." A pine balcony stretched most of the length of the building. We took drinks upstairs. Several of Marty's works occupied an alcove of white-painted brick. Until I saw the portrait, a study in gray and blue, I had forgotten that the model had been Jack. He wasn't puckered-up. The long waxy features held more good humor than he usually let anyone glimpse. Marty had started the canvas during a weekend at the Cannings' country home. Once he had been badgered into sitting, Jack was a conscientious subject. He had settled into a weathered bench with a novel to read and a martini to keep him quiet.

"Not the life of the party," Peaches said. "I would charge a lot to paint that puss."

"He's not paying," Marty said. "It's a birthday present."

"This next dude looks like Red Skelton. He's sad too."

"That's Uncle Gil. His wife died last year." Marty leaned close to the portrait. She seemed satisfied. There were a couple of others, built like most of her work with underpainting and thin overlays of color that gave even Jack's pale flesh an inner glow. Peaches left us to work our way along the balcony. There wasn't much to admire. Near the back stairway was a series of portraits done mostly in primary colors with a palette knife, a red wedge of nose, blue cheeks, yellow eyes, yellow hair. Pieces of broken white dinner plate supplied the ears. A card below the frame identified one work as MY FRIEND ANDY.

Marty stepped back. "Do you know this genius's work sells for five times what I get? He said in a magazine article that he does a portrait in an afternoon. There's a painting of a checkerboard. The artist says she's satirizing the literal."

It wasn't a very good checkerboard. The squares were pinched at

118

the top, and the lines were wavy. I put an arm on her shoulder. "Refresh your husband's art knowledge. A well-drawn checkerboard is just a checkerboard, right? A badly drawn one is a statement."

"Basically that's it."

"So from that perspective, you draw too well."

"I also paint too well," she said cheerfully.

Downstairs we settled onto a bench near the door shared by a man with a white ponytail and a black cape, who poked a walking stick at anyone who wandered too close. Eventually Janie caught up with us, dodging a jab, and accepted congratulations on the renovation. She was blue-haired, fashion-model sleek. In a loud whisper she asked Marty, "Do you figure that old dog next to you is a critic?"

Marty glanced at the man. "Is he?"

"He said he was, so I let him in. Now he's poking the cane at everyone's heinie. If he's a critic, I guess it's okay. I seen that bitch Mary Bonemeal here gropin' my artists. Maybe she'll get poked."

We drank champagne and toured the ground floor, where most of the crowd had congealed. I saw a handful of paintings that looked as though the artist had seen or felt something that ended up on the canvas.

Peaches broke through the mob an hour later, when we were near the back door. Her petite features were set like stone. "Martha, I don't know how to tell you this, so you'd better come and look."

Marty's portraits were the center of a small circle of onlookers on the balcony. Peaches bowled through them. Uncle Gil hung undisturbed. The portrait of Jack had been pushed askew by the pressure of a blade that had sliced two long diagonal cuts through the canvas.

"There was nobody around, and no one could see into this little nook," Peaches said. She squeezed Marty's arm. "I can't believe some crazy got in here. I've got to check that he didn't get any others."

"You'd better take these down," I told her.

"Of course. Where's Janie? I want to call the police. Someone

119

might remember who was up here in the last ten minutes. Are you okay, honey?"

"Yes." Marty nodded, looking oddly at me. We got downstairs and I said, "I'm sorry. I pressed Bunny Furbinger last night. I should have seen something like this coming."

"It's just a painting," she said. "I can repair it . . . or do another."

As we rode a taxi home, I imagined the cherubic stock promoter hanging by an ankle from a 107th-floor window at his next debutante ball. It was implausible revenge. If I got Bunny through a window, he would be too heavy to hold.

I paid the cab and followed Marty upstairs. She was a dozen steps ahead of me, and she opened the door before I reached the landing.

She turned on the light. Her back stiffened.

I was being slow and stupid that night.

"Ben!"

She said that much.

Nothing more.

I caught up with her. The apartment had gotten something like the attention I'd received at the commuter station. Batting spilled from the sofa. The telephone dangled from the leaded glass doors, thoroughly smashed, of an antique hutch we had bought somewhere south of Wilkes-Barre and portaged back on the roof of a rented car. Shattered wine bottles, spattered walls—I stopped cataloguing as I heard her feet on the stairs to the cupola.

She stopped at the doorway to her studio. I went up and looked over her shoulder. Paintings had been hammered into ruin against the workbench. Others had the familiar shredded look from the gallery.

She picked a canvas off the floor. The wet center had been stabbed to tatters. Around the edges fragments remained of the park scene. She held it with one hand. She recovered a lightweight tripod easel she used for sketching, jerked it upright and set the painting on the ledge.

She looked around with an expression I had never seen on her strong face: wounded, helpless, despairing.

120

I got her down the stairs. I found Gil's brandy in the hutch and poured enough to kill a stevedore. She drank, coughed, brushed my hand away. "I don't need mothering. You'd better call the police."

And ask them to bring a net big enough to hold the intruder's rage.

I had felt it at the office after the break-in. Then on the South Norwalk train platform. Twice tonight. More than anger. Rage that vented itself in mindless smashing, kicking, slashing.

Too intense for Bunny Furbinger.

An image from the studio jumped into my mind's focus. I went upstairs and found a spilled can of turpentine. I mopped up, tossed the sodden rag onto the workbench, then looked around for a metal can for safer storage. A junk closet behind the stairway held such essentials.

I opened the closet's louvered door and faced my friend Handsome. Sweat clung to the black hair streaking his forehead. His weight was on his heels, which put him off balance for lunging. He brought an arm up stiffly and jabbed his knife at my eyes.

I threw my weight against the door. It closed with a clatter of feet, mops and spare canvas rolls. His breath rasped between the slats. The knife blade slid through, snicked back and forth, grazing my cheek.

He hit the door with his shoulder, and the frame holding the louvers cracked loudly. He kicked and split a slat. He was coming out.

Backing away, I grabbed the legs of the sketching easel. As the door banged open, I swung. The wooden crown struck him under the hairline, and he side stepped past, wobbled, clasped his forehead. I hit him again, shattering a wooden leg.

He fell on his face.

As Marty appeared at the top of the stairs, I collected Handsome's knife. It was a long, narrow device with a blade that had locked in place. I raised a finger to my lips.

Where was Red?

There weren't many places to check in the apartment. I covered

121

them, knowing it was foolhardy because Red could have a more dangerous toy than a knife.

He wasn't with us.

I bolted the hall door and went to peer from a living room window. A red-haired man in a tan coat leaned into a telephone bubble, an arm waving in agitation.

Somebody was getting bad news.

24

HANDSOME'S breath wheezed. He was on his belly, one arm under him, the other limp at his side. His fingers were large and flat, with immaculately tended nails. Holding a ball of twine, I came up behind him. I put a shoe tip on the ball of his little finger and stepped hard. His breathing quickened but he didn't move.

He was dressed for the art gallery in a tweed topcoat that had gotten smeared with cerulean blue. He had a fawn corduroy jacket, a black turtleneck shirt, natty gray slacks with buttoning pocket flaps, blue wool socks, tasseled loafers.

I wrapped a half-dozen turns of cord around one heavy wrist, cinched it, pulled his other arm around and bound the wrists together. I cut the twine and tied his ankles. He gave no sign of coming around.

Marty ran upstairs. "The other one left. Are these the two who beat you?"

"They're the ones."

"I'll call the police." Handsome moaned, scraped his feet on the floor. "And an ambulance."

"Wait a minute," I said.

She stayed in the doorway, eyes wandering from ruin to ruin.

My adrenaline was still pumping. Kneeling, I pulled Handsome's head around. A gash at the top of his forehead had made a mess. I

123

was worrying about how deep the wound might be when his eyelids suddenly lifted. The eyes were brownish gold, as warm as a small furry animal's, full of friendly interest. So much for my reading the truth in a man's eyes. He had killed Jimmy Doyle with the knife that lay at my feet. If I had missed him with the easel, he would have enjoyed taking his time with Marty and me.

The knife was black-handled, with brass rivets and a nickel inlay like a dragon's head. He looked at it and looked at me and hissed an obscene and precise threat.

Hands trembling, I took a paint rag off the bench, folded it into a small square and forced it between his teeth. He snapped at my fingers, then tried to push the rag out with his tongue. I cut a couple yards of twine and tied the gag in place. Grabbing his collar, I trundled him down the stairs, not gently. The bathroom was just around the corner. I flicked on the light and hoisted him over the edge of the bathtub, lowered him so his shoulders and forehead rested on the worn enamel. I closed the drain and twisted the cold water tap.

He jerked his head away from the flow.

As the bottom of the tub filled, he rolled his face to the side. Then he struggled onto his back. The water rose and flowed over his cheeks. Raising his head, he tried to sit up. I pushed him back.

He surfaced with eyes clenched, choking water from his nose.

Before he could get a full breath, I pushed his forehead down and held it as he thrashed. After ten seconds I let go. He came up eyes bulging, face red, chest racked by convulsions that couldn't fully expel the water. If you wanted to drown a man, gagging him speeded the job and made it relatively quiet.

I put my face close to his and said over the faucet's roar, "The people who hired you didn't tell you some things they should have. Like what happened to the guy they sent around in December."

I pushed him back down, held him for a while, then turned off the faucet and pulled loose the gag. "You get one chance on this. I want to know who paid you."

He slumped, hacking. I started lowering him and he stopped coughing long enough to scream a curse and complain, in perfect fairness, "I never did this to you!"

124

I sat on the edge of the tub and told him, without a quaver in my voice, that if he didn't give me what I wanted I was going to hold his head down for ten minutes, then drop his body off a West Side pier like his predecessor's. He was a television child. On television people could do anything. A bespectacled office clerk could suddenly operate a machine gun as if he had been born holding one. A tame money manager could drown a tough stud who never said uncle to anybody. He believed me.

I got him started on names.

His was Danny Natoli. His friend was Bongo Harris. They worked together, had been together since elementary school, and sometimes even dated the same girl. They were best friends. They never knew who hired them. A longshoreman named Phil in Brooklyn, who had contacts, had said that someone named Jesse would call and they could do something for him.

"How did Phil know Jesse?" I asked.

"He doesn't. People hear about Phil, that he's got people like me to get jobs done. You can call this guy and get somebody's knees broken or a warehouse emptied."

You got hold of Phil by calling a hardware store in Red Hook and leaving a message. You sent money to a post office box. You paid before the work was done. Phil had a reputation.

They heard from Jesse. Mr. Jesse. For breaking into the office, Danny Natoli and Bongo each got five hundred dollars. Mr. Jesse had been very specific about what had to be taken in the burglary. The file with Canning & McCarthy's name—or it might be labeled OFFICE ACCOUNT or HOUSE ACCOUNT or something similar—would contain flimsy receipts with a brokerage firm's name on them. They had to collect all those slips and remove similar documents from several other files at random. "He called them confirmation slips, like in church," Handsome said.

The receipts confirmed our stock purchases and sales, a separate report for each transaction. The slips listed the stock, along with the date, price, commission charge and total cost.

"He used those words, *confirmation slips?*" I asked.

"Yeah, that's what I said." He was sitting chest-deep in cold water, his teeth beginning to click. He was starting to suspect I was the kind of sissy who wouldn't drown a guy like him.

"How much did Mr. Jesse pay you to kick me around?"

"Five hundred."

It seemed to be the standard rate.

"You weren't supposed to kill me?"

"He just said you were a busybody and had to get hurt bad. Bongo and me decided since he didn't say kill you, we wouldn't."

The Polaroids they took had been sent to Mr. Jesse by messenger. The messenger had been met at Queens Plaza by another messenger. You could check all over the five boroughs for a month and not trace the other service. Danny also reported to Mr. Jesse by telephone. Sometimes he was there. Most of the time it didn't answer. I made him repeat the number. The first digits—608—belonged to a financial district exchange. He couldn't tell me much about Mr. Jesse's voice, his probable age, or anything else helpful. "He was snooty, like he was better than me. Kept calling me 'young man.' Smart ass."

"How much did he pay you to kill the stockbroker?"

His lips tightened. I could hold him under water for a week before he admitted a murder.

An hour later the police came. I gave them Mr. Jesse's phone number, the name of the Red Hook hardware store, a summary of Phil's business, a description of Bongo Harris. I gave them Handsome's knife and referred them to a Sergeant Teeger who was handling the Doyle case. A uniformed officer suggested mildly that I shouldn't have questioned Danny Natoli.

I nodded contritely. I was kicking myself for questions not asked that might have given me a better picture of Jesse.

Gil came over and helped restore order to the apartment. We turned on as many lights as we could, put a high-spirited Liszt on the CD player and tried to distract his niece from the graver damage upstairs.

Sol Lehrman phoned, apologizing for calling so late. "I did as much checking as I could, pal. Your brokers, Faulkner Wells, did the only concentrated buying of Dorchester Millinery, except for guys putting together Grendal's piece."

"You're certain?"

"The rest was dribs and drabs, a few hundred shares here and there that don't add up to anything. There has been a lot of money on the other side, though, betting the merger won't go through. If Grendal backs away, what's Dorchester worth? Ten, twelve, fifteen?"

"If they stay out of bankruptcy."

"Either way, it's a big drop from thirty-four this afternoon. One firm has been shorting the hell out of the stock. It's the one you asked about, Furbinger Associates."

"Furbinger—are you certain?"

"Sorry if I've shot down a theory you were working on. Furbinger Associates didn't show up at all as a buyer. But they've got heavy money saying the deal isn't going to hold."

The phone rang again, long after we had gone to bed. Three A.M.

I rolled from a sleepless paralysis, picked up the receiver, listened to a silent line.

There was a hiss of slow breath. Then the voice, like a scream from the bottom of a far-off drain.

"How dare you defy me!"

Silence. The fury came over the line like an electric shock.

"How dare you!"

I said softly, "I dare."

As I hung up, Marty stirred restlessly. I lay awake wondering who was up at this hour, stalking around a bright room in one of the city's towers, shouting his rage at the walls until he finally had to pick up the phone and scream at me.

25

I woke up late and heard Marty moving in the cupola. I climbed the cold stairs. She was cutting sheets of canvas from a roll and tacking them to 18-by-24-inch stretchers. On the easel, her drawing pad held a hasty charcoal sketch of a man on a park bench.

"You're not wasting any time," I said. The ruined paintings were stacked facing the wall.

"Last night I was sick. Today I see things I'll change."

My feet were freezing. I sat on her stool and rubbed them. From the row of windows the day looked bright and windy. The sky was strips of cold pastels. It was nearly eleven o'clock, and I wasn't at the office. Plenty of work awaited. The remaining accounts expected professional attention. I felt indifferent to their cares and to my own. Indifferent to the market, which normally filled my hours.

"Will the police keep that boy?" Marty said.

I thought I had dreamt about him, something horrible about a confrontation ending with a black-haired primitive animal in charge. He would be a blushing bride, I hoped, for someone at Riker's Island. I said, "If his knife matches Jimmy Doyle's wounds, he won't get bail. Meanwhile they've got us to support an attempted murder case. And there's an assault in Connecticut. He won't be going anywhere. His friend Bongo is the one we've got to watch out for."

She put her nose close to the frosted glass and looked down at the street. Snow-topped cars and rushing pedestrians were equally anonymous. She folded her arms inside her cardigan.

"I was thinking about something that Handsome told me," I said. "I'd wondered if it was by chance the burglar took our firm's trading records. It wasn't. Mr. Jesse told him to make certain he got all our confirmation slips."

"That's interesting. Could Mr. Jesse be Vince DiMineo?"

"It would make sense. If Vince loaded our account with Dorchester Millinery that Jack never bought, he would want our records destroyed."

"Why?"

"Because our records don't show the Dorchester purchases."

"But why would he load the account?"

"I don't know. He has a good arrangement with us. He gets a lot of business. Jack likes him." It didn't add up. But Vince knew that Marty was an artist. And Mr. Jesse had known exactly where and how to strike.

I went downstairs and showered. I bagged the things we were throwing out, left them in the back of the building, and walked slowly around the block. There were the inevitable dented delivery vans and station wagons, double-parked outside restaurants, boutiques and flower shops. But no sign of Bongo.

I lured Marty downstairs for sandwiches, cleaned the plates and walked ten blocks uptown before flagging a cab to the Knickerbocker Club. Gil's rooms were snug, with shelves full of potboiler novels and a hearth enclosing a gas log. I had drunk with him there once in a while, avoided his card games.

He sorted through his mail, giving me a quarter of his attention.

"How is Martha?"

"All right."

He nodded. "She is resilient. You are lucky to have her."

"I agree."

"But you're not always comfortable with your good fortune."

"Right again—but that's not what I came to talk about."

He ignored the hint to mind his business. "My niece believes she has noticed time accelerating. That is an unusually keen perception for someone still in her twenties. Sharp fellow that I am, I was too busy carousing around Europe to detect the phenomenon until I was past forty. The fear of time makes her a little too eager for a tame soul like you. I would expect her to be chasing around the Virgin Islands and drinking too much, the promiscuous dilettante wasting every talent except the easy one. Instead she stays in her studio and works. And fortunately, she seems to love you."

He tossed the mail aside, fumbled for a cigar. "Do you want her blubbering on your shoulder? That's the one thing you don't get with Martha. I loved my brother John, but he was a weak, cold man. My niece learned emotional self-reliance at an early age."

"She's neither weak nor cold," I said.

"Remarkably strong and passionate," he agreed. "That can be a problem too, can't it? Personally—and this is from a faltering memory—I've never regretted any of the time I spent in bed, even when I was young and reckless and had to leave quickly. It's not as clinically wise these days, but I can't see why a woman would feel different. But it seems my niece is prudishly restrained."

It depended on your definitions, I thought, and said, "You're not much help."

"Not if you're looking for sympathy. But you must have something else on your mind."

I did. I told him, "I want to get a look at Furbinger Associates' internal records. Customer accounts, trading activity."

"What do you hope to find?"

"Anything that ties Furbinger to Lance Grendal or Dorchester Millinery." I hesitated. "There is a way you might be able to help. What I want to do is illegal."

He wasn't shocked. A small laugh rolled through his body. "It's kind of you to mention that aspect ahead of time."

26

GIL hadn't gotten back to me by Saturday morning when Rudy drove us out to the country.

George Finn met the car at the edge of a snow-pocked field. He wore baggy wool trousers, a heavy tweed jacket and an Irish cap. A shotgun was broken open across his arm. A gloved hand held several fat pheasant carcasses. Around his legs a pair of yapping spaniels danced in a trail of blood.

George hoisted the birds. "I've foraged dinner."

The spaniels barked approval.

He leaned against the car, cheeks flushed, an elfin grin flickering on. He said hello to Barbara Canning, then to Rudy Thatcher. His eyes fastened on Marty, who was dressed for the cold in a pea jacket and chinos. "Martha, I'm glad you could make it. Jack is a fast fan of yours. Ben, do you do any shooting?"

I shook my head. "City boy."

"I was thinking we might do our shooting in the city. Down around the stock exchange. Maybe I will bring Ginnie and Freddie here to flush game."

The spaniels heard their names and sniffed the driveway for a new scent.

"I'll show you the house first. Then a walking tour of the farm to get us ready for lunch. I've got two hundred acres, mostly fallow."

George led the way to the house. The main structure was colonial with massive bare brick chimneys at either end. A frame addition on the south ended the symmetry. The L-shape helped define a square that—judging from the bare stakes poking from the snow—served as a summer garden. Across the road a barn and other outbuildings hunched on a ridge. A quarter mile down toward the valley was a small brick building that George told us he used as a tenant house.

The dogs followed us in the front door, feinting at the game, and raced down a hallway. The house had a bachelor's comfortable clutter, outdoor prints, overflowing bookcases, leather and print furniture in earthy colors, a feel of easy, long-established habits. George laid the shotgun across a mantel and hung our overcoats on an ancient peg rack.

Barbara looked the room over with a patient smile. She wasn't dressed for the outdoors. She had chosen a navy silk suit, a white wing-collar blouse, a pearl necklace and pearl earrings, a long fox coat. For most of the two-hour drive from Manhattan she had been aloof, nursing a grievance with Rudy. She sat in front with her brother, who tried to talk to us over his shoulder. "We could slap a civil suit against Vince DiMineo right now," he said. "Get discovery, deposition everybody at Faulkner Wells so they know I'm serious. But you haven't got a thing on Furbinger."

"We haven't really got a thing on Vince," I said.

"Enough to scare the shit out of him. That's a start."

George Finn's housekeeper, Mrs. Gibson, served us tea and biscuits before going off to dress the birds. George talked about stock exchange politics without conviction. He confessed he was becoming more of a Connecticut recluse. "The firm is very profitable—and faintly boring," he said.

Rudy Thatcher said, "From what passes my ear, you're damn lucky to be bored. A lot of your competitors have been losing money in this market. Commissions are too low, costs too high, the public too inactive, the market too choppy."

"True, all true," George said. "I didn't intend to sound ungrateful for prosperity. Our costs are as difficult to restrain as anybody's. Every graduate we hire as a junior analyst expects to start at a hundred thousand. And commissions are ridiculously low for large clients. Little old ladies from the East Eighties are beating my brokers down on rates like bank trust managers. But we're doing well. The trading desk is a reliable source of profits. I spend part of every day there. The Finn instinct for the market's mood seldom fails." He tapped his nose.

"I could use that instinct," I said.

"I lend it out," he said. "Call anytime. Has Fletcher gotten your accounts transferred?"

"He's done fine," I said.

Rudy broke in. "Except for the firm's own account. That's frozen by court order until the government can plunder it."

"Are there any clients left?" Barbara asked.

"Of course," Rudy said. "Canning & McCarthy is going to make it. It gets better from here."

She shook her head. "If I can't trust my brother, who then?"

"Rudy is right," George said.

"He and Ben want to hang everything on the broker, poor Vince," she complained. "If you ask them what proof they have, it all comes out sighs and mumbles."

"We know that the punks who hammered on Ben know things that poor Vince would know," Rudy said.

She waved him away.

We went outside again and crossed the road. Barbara had borrowed boots but still found the going rough. While my wife and George Finn strode ahead over frozen ruts, I hung back and lent an arm. Without letting go, Barbara smiled stiffly. "Very gallant of you, Benny."

"Nothing of the kind."

She surveyed the track to the barn, cheeks bunching in dismay. "Oh, no. I know gallant when I see it."

Rudy called ahead, "This is quite a retreat."

"One can take only so much of the city bastards," George said.

Rudy hurried to catch up with him. Barbara sighed. "Tell me, Benny. Is your wife still painting? There can't be much money in it—unless you're successful."

133

I tried to think of a response short of tripping her.

"Well, I'm certain she's doing very well," Barbara said. She smiled to show she either meant it or didn't, I could take my pick. Her meanness was automatic, almost impersonal. At dinner last summer, the last time Marty had agreed to her company, Barbara had dissected the charity circles of which she was part with all the compassion of Handsome and his knife. There was a dress-wholesaler-turned-eminento who mispronounced French words. The ambassador who doted on male dancers. The Russian émigré writer who couldn't find a publisher for his plagiarized stories of repression. In their presence she admired them all, savoring the danger, I thought, that her insincerity would be discovered.

I wondered what Jack had seen and adored in her, whether he had been fooled or had fooled himself, or whether years of prosperity had tricked both of them.

"Before we picked you up," Barbara said, "Rudy hinted that you had learned something about our situation."

"Nothing useful, or Rudy would have told you." Thirty yards ahead, Rudy and George walked together.

She looked at me for more. I pointed. "Let's see the horses." I was learning to be mean myself.

In a stabling section of the barn, a couple of mild-eyed old mares that George had picked up at an estate sale greeted us with snorts. A grizzled man who lived in the house down the road, Mr. Gibson, was rewiring an electric heater that kept the stable from freezing. "This is Kate," George said, rubbing the nose of a fat blond, who rolled her eyes, "and this sweet chestnut is Gigi. She used to be popular with the neighbor boys."

Marty was charmed. "They both look sad."

From a distance, Barbara said, "You would be despondent too, if your destiny lay in a glue bottle."

George chuckled. "Fortunately utilitarianism has its limits."

His hired man found sugar in his pocket, and George parceled it out between Rudy and Marty. George said, "I have a nephew who adores these old girls. Sad to say his mother spends the winters in the Caribbean. So the mares feel orphaned." His tone was wistful, as if he also felt orphaned. Despite his prominence, I guessed he might be lonely as only bachelors could be. It explained his protective interest in friends, a substitute family, and his time for visitors he hardly knew.

He came over to me and said softly, "Rudy told me you think someone besides your broker may be involved. He also says you need help sleuthing."

"Do you know a firm called Furbinger Associates?"

He shook his head. "Let's go outside."

We walked through a pasture gate and down to a frozen pond. George's big hands were thrust deep in his pockets. "So many brokers have sprung up over the last few years. They come and they disappear before I hear of them."

"Furbinger's big move has been within the last eighteen months. He went bankrupt a few years ago after a brush with the government. Somehow he got the capital for a comeback. It would be worth knowing who his backer is."

George squinted, studying the perimeter of the pond. It was shaped like a lopsided egg, about fifty yards across at the widest point. Tufts of dead grass thrust from the thinner ice along the edges. It was a bitter day, overcast and windy.

"Furbinger would not be the only broker on the Street with a silent partner," George said. "There is no shortage of tainted money looking to cleanse itself, and unfortunately, controlling a brokerage firm seems to be one of the more popular methods. I'll have Andy Meadows look for Furbinger's connections."

I described Bunny's short sales of Dorchester Millinery.

"That argues against a connection, doesn't it?" George said.

"Or for a very intricate tie," I said.

He stared at me thoughtfully. "If Furbinger and Lance Grendal are partners," George said, "this is a major case of stock manipulation. Grendal announces a takeover bid for Dorchester Millinery. The price levitates. Furbinger sells short at the inflated price. Grendal quietly sells his own shares. What would you imagine is the next step?"

"Grendal cancels his takeover plans?"

"Yes. The stock plummets. Furbinger makes money on his short

135

sales. Grendal makes money on his stock. Do you believe it is Furbinger or Grendal who is your Mr. Jesse?"

"Rudy told you about that too?"

"And more. I'm dreadfully sorry about your wife's work."

"Grendal doesn't know Jack or me from Adam. Also, everything I've found out about Grendal points to a loner. Why would he get involved in something illegal with a third-tier player like Furbinger?"

"You can't have it both ways," George said. "Either they're in cahoots or they aren't."

"Here's another chore for Andy Meadows. You could ask him to watch for signs of Grendal unloading his Dorchester Millinery shares."

Behind us Rudy and Barbara were quarreling. Marty came up and dug both arms under mine. "Your face is turning red." She said to George, "This is a lovely place. It feels a little bit wild."

"That is much nicer than saying it looks untended. The soil doesn't support much beyond a few grazing head. I don't fancy myself milking at five A.M., and Gibson would rebel."

Rudy and Barbara caught up, wearing looks of resentment.

"Let's take a quick turn around the pond," George said. "Then we'll thaw out for lunch. There's something here you might enjoy."

A shoulder of trees and brambles thrust out from the woods, almost touching the west end of the pond. George stomped a few yards into the thicket and paused. He pointed. "Just ahead. Those bushes are wild raspberry, full of thorns, so we can't get much closer."

Several pale headstones tilted from the thicket. The thin slabs were pockmarked by age, the inscriptions illegible.

"The family plot," Rudy said.

"A family named Wye," George said. "The oldest stones date to the eighteen thirties. Further into the brush are a few bits of foundation from a farmhouse."

"Finn's folly," Marty piped up.

George gave a jolly rumble. He walked ahead of us, circling the pond, close to the edge of the bank that sloped to the ice. The wind was in his eyes, and his foot missed a node of ground. He stumbled.

136

There was an air of silly improbability about it.

He fell heavily and silently. A lighter man or a younger one could have halted his slide down the bank. It was slow and almost stately. George's hands pawed at the ground without gaining a hold. His feet and then his knees reached the ice where it was too thin to support him. He plunged into the water up to his waist.

For the slightest instant it was comical.

But he was in mortal danger. The water was freezing, and he was already half-soaked. His arms waved for balance. He stepped backward, ponderous and awkward.

I scrambled down the slope, warning, "Don't move." By stretching I could touch his shoulder but couldn't get a grip. He was too heavy in any case to be pulled out like a child.

He balanced precariously, breathing rapidly, eyes wide and shocked behind glasses that had gotten knocked a bit askew. He barked at me, "This is a little absurd, isn't it?"

"Can you take a step forward?"

"The, uh, water gets deep around here."

"How deep?"

"Six or eight feet."

More than enough.

I heard a high-pitched bleat as Rudy and Barbara caught up. Barbara Canning clapped both hands over her mouth. Her eyes were slits.

Rudy slid down near me. He extended a hand. "You pull George, I'll pull you."

Rudy's heels were slipping without anybody pulling on him. The only way George would get out was by climbing out, and his legs must be losing their feeling. If he tumbled into deeper water, his coat would make him next to immobile.

I stepped into calf-deep water that flowed over my boot tops and brought almost instant numbness. I meant to steady George. As I took his arm, he wobbled and grinned nervously. His fingers bit into my arm. His teeth made a sound like a scolding squirrel.

He edged in half-steps toward the bank. His balance went a little at a time. First a wobble. Then his left shoulder dipped. He waved an arm in a cartwheel, the one that wasn't linked to me, and cried

137

"Whoa!" He turned as he fell. His forehead hit my chin, and we went down.

I didn't feel us go underwater. Blinking, I was there. The light was remote and gray. Sound was cut off except for blood rumbling in my ears and a squeak as my throat tightened. The water was a gentle pressure, not really that cold after the first shock.

I reached for the fuzzy light and met resistance. My knuckles bumped a rippled bottom of unbroken ice.

I couldn't be far from the hole we had made. But in what direction? My arms stretched wide and found no opening. No sign of George Finn either. The light was brighter on my left, but it was deceptive, diffused by ice and water. I pressed upward. The bottom of the ice was harder to identify.

The water seemed darker. There was no sense in panic, no need. I congratulated myself on recognizing that I had time, that this was a problem that could be dealt with. I could do it rationally, patiently, because there was plenty of time. The cold was tolerable, almost warm, and the darkness helped me concentrate.

The faltering brain said to push against the ice, so I did. But it held. It held my feet too. That was the problem. Couldn't feel them, and the legs wouldn't move when I tried to kick.

The grip tightened. Somebody yelled in the distant surface world.

"Quit struggling goddamn you!"

There was light, and the voice was familiar. So I quit struggling.

Rudy Thatcher pulled me out. Then he pulled out Marty, who was holding my legs. The grizzled man from down the road brought horse blankets and wrapped us. George Finn was sprawled on the bank, eyeglasses missing, gasping. "Get Ben up to the house," he ordered. "He needs heat. You too, Martha."

"I wasn't in there for five minutes." I recognized the voice. She had screamed at me like a parent administering medicine.

"I wasn't either," I said.

"Close enough," she said.

They hoisted me, encouraged me to use the stiltlike logs that had been legs. "You saved George's life," Rudy told me. "But for a while I thought we'd lost you."

27

MR. and Mrs. Gibson took care of George with much fond cooing from the old woman. Rudy and Marty got me up the stairs and into a cold white room: white claw-footed tub, white-painted high walls, old-fashioned wainscoting buried under more shiny paint. I shivered uncontrollably. Rudy tugged off my jacket and pants, an odd expression in his wide blue eyes. He said, "You should see yourself. You've got icicles in your hair." He got me into the steaming tub and then disappeared.

After a moment Marty came back. Her teeth were rattling. She had gotten off the sodden boots and stood barefoot in a heavy black wool sweater and chinos. Dipping a hand into the water, she held her teeth together and managed to say, "You seem to need a lot of taking care of."

She kicked off the chinos and climbed in with me. After a while she pulled off the sweater and settled back with a groan.

It was dark when I woke up. Voices had been chattering through my dreams. A shrill bleat—Barbara Canning's—at the sight of George Finn waist-deep in the pond. A bleat, I recognized, of laughter. He *had* looked silly. George's voice, from miles off, *"Get Ben up to the house!"* Lucky Ben. The house was nearby.

I rolled over in sleepy contentment and found warm shoulders beside me. She woke up and said, "How do you feel?"

"Fuzzy. Not remembering everything."

"Your head hit awfully hard. I could hear it. We should have driven to a doctor."

"I think it's okay. I don't hurt especially. I just don't remember it all. Being underwater I remember."

She rolled sidewise. "We got George out, but you'd gone under. He nearly drowned trying to reach you. And he was in my way."

"Neither of us—George nor I—was much of a rescuer."

"We saw your foot through the ice. You were kicking further under. Do you remember that?"

"I thought it was the right direction."

"Yes, you were quite insistent about it."

How do you thank someone for overcoming your insistence like that? I asked and she laughed. "How much thanking are you up to?"

The next time I woke up my watch dial said seven-thirty. Evening or morning? Marty was sitting in a chair, feet under the bed covers, reading a paperback by a dim light. She wore a white terry cloth robe. Her expression was free of worry. When she felt me watching, she closed the book.

"It's warmer under the covers," I said.

She nudged me with a foot. "Really?"

"Yes."

Smiling, she turned off the light, shed the robe and came back to bed. In the darkness she said, "When I woke up, it seemed I hadn't told you everything I needed to. I know that what I've done hurts you, but I don't know how much. You're so damned quiet about what you feel. I'm afraid that someday you'll get fed up with an unreliable wife and leave. That's not what I want."

No point in asking what she did want. No shop sold a lifetime elixir against boredom.

"It doesn't have to happen that way," I said.

"It usually does, you know."

We went downstairs finally. A fire was roaring in the huge living room hearth. George Finn was wearing two layers of sweaters along with wool pants and a brightly knit scarf. His eyes were again safe behind heavy lenses, shy and concerned. He said, "If you hadn't been there, I would be at the bottom of the pond. Thank you, Ben."

"Except for us you wouldn't have gone near the pond."

He chafed his hands. "Nonsense. People at the stock exchange, a few of them, think George Finn walks on water, never mind ice. We have disproved the notion. You probably should have let me call my doctor."

"If I feel shaky I can see one back in town."

"All the same," George said. "You return favors with a certain flair. You and Martha must have a drink."

At a big mahogany secretary he folded down a scarred lid and picked out a bottle. It had no label but was half-full of something a little darker than lemon water. He poured three sparing measures. "This comes with a story. I have exactly sixteen bottles left. Thirty-two years ago, while I was still at Princeton, I had an opportunity to buy some rye whiskey. Two barrels were sold to me as an investment. The whiskey was made with Lithuanian hops. I don't suppose anyone has done that for forty years."

It had mellowed into something like a rye liqueur, all warmth with no bite. "It's wonderful," I said.

George beamed. "What I've been drinking all these years is from one barrel. A couple of months after making the purchase, I became nervous and sold the other barrel. I took a loss and congratulated myself it wasn't worse. I kept this batch because I couldn't find a buyer. It took me twenty years to realize what a splendid investment I had made."

His smile was small and self-conscious. "I've had similar lapses once or twice in the stock market. What about you, Ben?"

"At least once or twice."

We sipped his rye and he showed us some of his books in a case beside the fireplace. A number were old classics about financial speculation by people like Richard D. Wyckoff and Edwin Lefevre. "I have read every one of them," George said. "It is interesting how little the markets have changed since the twenties and thirties. The technology has evolved, but human psychology hasn't. When I'm perplexed by the stock market, I often ask myself what one of the

141

great speculators of the twenties would have done in a similar situation. The answer isn't always profitable, but it bolsters my confidence."

Rudy Thatcher came down before dinner, but his sister was complaining of a migraine and didn't appear. "She's embarrassed— she wouldn't have laughed if she had realized George was in danger," Rudy said.

"Of course not."

"But she wouldn't come down now and face George Finn if her room were on fire."

"I doubt that he noticed her laughing," I said. "George was pretty busy."

Mrs. Gibson set out a late dinner, assured herself that George wasn't running a fever and bundled up for the trek down to the tenant house. Marty and George served the four of us on a table close to the fireplace.

Conversation wandered. Our combined lore on hypothermia filled a couple of minutes. The economics of unproductive farms took longer. George insisted that every acre he kept idle lightened the burden on the region's governments. "Hay prices are higher throughout Connecticut because of our nonproduction. Marginal operators stay in business, pay taxes; the owners and their employees remain off the welfare rolls. Their children go to college. Their barbers buy new automobiles. The ripples of prosperity spread endlessly from my sleeping land."

I picked up the theme. "If every farm in the state were inactive, the ripples would become a tide of wealth lifting all of New England."

"Just so," George said. "We could extend this principle to factories as well."

"And to stock exchanges," Rudy suggested.

"And the legal profession," George responded.

We tried to determine why Rudy Thatcher could bill clients at two hundred dollars an hour for the most mechanical research while Martha Norris earned less than a twentieth of that rate.

"It's a question of economic utility," George said. "The mutual fund paying Rudy two hundred an hour expects to take the

142

documents he drafts and raise fifty million dollars to manage, which will pay a million or so in fees and expenses every year. That's excellent leverage on a twenty-thousand-dollar legal investment. Lawyers have economic utility. Artists merely lift the spirit. How does a fund manager leverage a noble feeling?"

We acknowledged the unfairness of economic equations with another bottle of Pomerol. After dinner Rudy took a tray upstairs to his sister.

When we loaded the car the next morning, Barbara was back in action. At breakfast she pressed Rudy to make a detour to the summer house she and Jack kept near Ridgefield. "The weather must have done dreadful things to the place," she said.

Rudy smothered a sneeze. "I'm sick. Ben and Martha want to get home."

"It's a half-hour out of your way."

"An hour and a quarter," Rudy said. "If we don't hit snow."

Barbara turned plaintively to Marty. "Martha, dear, I know you have to hurry home and paint, but I wonder if you couldn't spare a thought for me."

"I would love to, but Rudy's driving," Marty said.

We packed the car. George Finn bore down on us with pheasants wrapped in newspaper. His walk was stiff, as if the cold had gotten to his bones. "Ben, I'll bring a gun down on Monday. We'll bag something in the city." He laid a paternal hand on Barbara's shoulder. "I'm glad you could come up. When we get things cleared up for Jack, it will be like old times."

She managed a wan smile.

As we rolled down the driveway, she chided Rudy, "You disappoint me, being so selfish."

He hunched over the wheel. "That's me, selfish and bound straight for New York. You folks comfortable?"

She wore him down before we passed South Kent.

143

28

THE two-acre lot had hemlocks growing amid humps of worn glacial rock and scattered mountain laurel. On an evening last summer, with torches burning to keep mosquitoes away and Jack working a kettle grille, it had been a cheerful, seemingly isolated spot. A gas station and dairy store huddled at the base of the mountain, a five-minute drive when we needed ice cream.

The house looked abandoned as morning crept down the hillside. Nearby a few cedar branches had broken under the weight of snow. They lay yards from the cottage. A section of telephone line drooped suspiciously low. Marty and I followed Barbara onto the porch. As she fished for a key I peered in the windows. She said, "One winter rodents got in through the foundation and absolutely *wrecked* the place."

She needn't have worried. Inside was chilly but order prevailed. The power was off, the oil burner turned low, the pipes drained. Barbara scurried room to room in the dusk. She came out of the bedroom murmuring, "Jack must have stripped the bed."

I snooped at a small maple desk in the living room that contained bird books and fuel receipts. There was nothing vaguely connected with Wall Street. In the kitchen Barbara turned on the circuit breakers, and the rooms brightened. The desktop gleamed where the dust that lay elsewhere had been disturbed. I hadn't brushed the surface. I wondered if Jack had stopped here on his way out of town.

"Why don't I heat us some broth?" Barbara called. "Martha, the cups are over the sink. If my brother wants to sulk in the car . . ."

I went outside and waved to Rudy. He climbed out, shouted, "Tell me she doesn't want to spend the night."

"Just long enough for something hot," I said and came off the porch.

Jack had hired local boys to clear trees and split wood. Several cords of oak, cedar, hemlock and maple were stacked chest-high between the cottage and a ramshackle garage. The pile was covered with a tarp, its depressions caked with leaves and bars of ice. Overhead there was a skittering sound as a squirrel came down the garage roof to monitor the visitors.

When Rudy walked over, the animal transferred its attention to the short man in the fur hat that might be a relative.

The garage was little more than a weather-eaten windbreak for Jack's car and garden tools. I glanced through a side window and saw a tiller in the middle of a stone floor. I walked around to the driveway. The double doors sagged open a crack.

Inside were decrepit cabinets and densely packed shelves.

I stood frozen.

A wall was hung with rakes and shovels—and a man.

He dangled from a hook on the rear wall. Strands of wire had cut deeply into the wrists and turned the hands black. He wore a gray suit. His black topcoat lay at his feet, which were naked and white.

The days had seldom been above freezing. Nights had dropped into the teens. Frail but healthy, he might have made it through the first night. The garage was out of the wind. But the seepage of warmth had been driven by mathematics more rigid than any financial market's. Heat flowed to equilibrium. Flesh reached the temperature of air.

His face was stretched in a painful plea.

Rudy was stomping on the driveway, chittering back at the wildlife. The air chilled the sweat on my throat. I stopped a few feet from Rudy. "Jack is in there," I said.

29

I followed him into the garage. He sank deeper into his jacket, mouth working as he fought down his gorge. He choked, "I should have come up here, just to see."

Looking closely, I tried to understand details. Bare feet to accelerate the loss of the body's heat. Wire to hold the wrists to the tool hook. He hung a few inches above the floor, helpless—nothing to brace against for an effort to work free. Nothing to do that could make any possible difference.

Near the door were a half-dozen cigarette butts. Someone had stood and waited, at least for a while, unwilling to trust the outcome.

"Barbara can't see this," Rudy said. He backed away. "I wish we could get him down."

"Is the phone in the house working?"

He shook his head. "We'll go down to that store. We'll have to get a doctor. . . ."

We left the garage. I shut the door firmly.

She guessed something almost as soon as she saw his face. "You look—"

"Cold." He clapped his gloved hands. "Cold."

She scowled, looked at me, saw God knew what. "What's wrong? What is it? Tell me, damn you!"

Rudy stumbled, "Somebody—I guess somebody found him up here—Jack—out in the garage. There's nothing we can do."

"I don't believe you."

"We've got to go call the police."

"I'm going to Jack."

"No you're NOT." He put his arms around her.

She stood still. She said quietly, "Let go of me, please." She stared at him as if he were a nuisance. "All right, we'll do what you want."

I stayed behind. Rudy said the continuity of the site of a crime was important. Marty hesitated, climbed into the station wagon beside Barbara. I watched her until the car slid behind the trees.

I walked halfway down to the garage, then turned and went back to the porch. There was nothing left in the garage. No friendship left to recover. If I had come up to the cottage that first day, there might have been time. If I hadn't been so willing to suspect the worst about Jack Canning . . .

His letter, written under duress, had it just right.

Never trust a friend.

Never count on one to rescue you from the cold.

I stood breathing the thin air.

Longed for another chance at Handsome.

It was dark when we got home. Rudy dropped us in front of the house. His wife, a solid loyal soul I had never met, had accepted Barbara for the night. His wagon pulled away from the curb and we went upstairs.

There had been so many questions from a pair of state police detectives that I felt talked out. We'd had a stumbling, inconclusive conference call with a Sergeant Mintz in New York, who had Jimmy Doyle's folder somewhere on his desk and Handsome somewhere in the Tombs. "So why would Furbinger be involved? I'm not trying to be difficult, Mr. McCarthy. We'll certainly talk to him; he was Doyle's employer. But you haven't explained why Furbinger would have a grudge against your partner."

One of the Connecticut detectives came back and sat down. "When did you say Mr. Canning disappeared?"

I told him again.

"And you haven't heard from him since?"

I traded looks with Rudy. "I got a lettercard from him, postmarked St. Kitts. Somebody was trying to sow confusion. Jack couldn't have sent it."

"How do you know that?"

"He didn't travel to St. Kitts," Rudy said.

"You're probably right. But don't assume too much. The medical office gives a preliminary estimate that he died about forty-eight hours ago. There were abrasions on the ankles, probably rope burns. Some evidence of dehydration. From the looks of it, I would say he may have been kept somewhere for a time. Possibly in the cottage."

"Trying to get information?" Rudy said.

"There is no sign of additional physical abuse." He was a precise man who was satisfied that he had said that exactly right. No additional abuse. "Often with a kidnapping, we find there is a period of trying to decide what to do with the victim. Whether to kill him."

He looked at me as if suspecting the truth. That I had helped them make up their minds.

Rudy called at eight-thirty. "I notified George. He was devastated."

"I hope he won't call Andy Meadows off the hunt." I didn't want to talk.

"I've no reason to think he will." His tone was critical. "You sound as if you're busy."

"I was on my way out."

He could assume a party or dinner if he wanted. He said, "Don't let me keep you."

30

I told Gil what I knew, what I suspected and what I wanted to do. The sleepy look left his face. "And you need a witness?"

"A credible one."

"I will bring a tape recorder." He phoned a limousine service that delivered a driver and car at the Knickerbocker Club's front door in thirty minutes. We drove up the West Side, joined the parkway.

"I gave some thought to your other project," Gil said. "Friday afternoon I initiated a relationship that may help. We will find out tomorrow."

"Thank you."

Shrugging, he settled back until he was comfortable. "I am very, very sorry about Canning. I know he meant a lot to you."

If I said not enough, he wouldn't understand.

Vince DiMineo's house was a stockbroker's dream, a dozen rungs up the income scale from Jimmy Doyle's bungalow. Boxwood shielded the lot from Colvin Road. Gnarled wisteria met over the front door and above the windows. Stone balconies jutted from the second floor under tall French doors. The overall effect was European gentility. Bulky chimneys poured wood smoke into the clear night sky.

We parked beside the garage and walked around the house on a brick path.

When Vince opened the door, I said, "It's time you and I talked."

His hair was rumpled, his face foxlike and handsome. He wore wrinkled khakis, a green flannel shirt, new running shoes. He gave a patient sigh. "Lisa said you called the office again."

His glance reached Gil Norris. I said, "Mr. Gilman is here in his unofficial capacity."

"What does that mean?"

A woman called from back in the house, and Vince responded. "It's all right. People about work. Go to bed."

"If I were you," Gil said ominously, thrusting his belly forward, "I would be a very nervous young man. Now invite us in to a place where we can talk."

He took us back to his study. The room had big windows giving a view of a lighted backyard with a canopied swimming pool. The room was cold. An expensive cherry desk was littered with newspapers, a dirty dinner plate and coffee mugs.

Vince spread his hands. "I had to give the SEC what they wanted."

"No argument," I said gently. "But did you have to give Mr. Jesse what he wanted?"

His jaw loosened as if one of us had hit him. Until then, I had believed it was a shot in the dark.

Gil said, "We know all about it."

He drew a ragged breath, sat slowly in a leather goosenecked chair. "It's not true, none of it."

"Aren't they suspicious at your firm?" I said. "Only you took Dorchester orders from Jack. Lisa suddenly wasn't getting near our account—wasn't supposed to talk to us about Dorchester Millinery. She must wonder why."

He thrust out his chin, tried a haughty tone. "Canning demanded my personal attention. Regardless of what he says now, that was his position."

"Jack didn't know what you were doing. You loaded our account with Dorchester Millinery and sold off our other stocks. You sat on our copies of the confirmation slips. Jack didn't hide them as they came in; you never sent them. When I tell Faulkner Wells the truth, you're finished."

His tight face slackened. A list of losses might have been rolling before his frightened eyes. Commission income of three hundred thousand. The French mansion. Social cachet. "Our buddy Vince isn't just a broker—he's with Faulkner Wells." His country club wouldn't want him. His neighbors wouldn't.

"You aren't even supposed to be talking to me," he said. "You're trying to intimidate a witness."

Gil cleared his throat and said, "Mr. McCarthy has brought certain information to our attention. He has our approval for this interview."

"Nobody will believe him or Canning," Vince said.

"Mr. McCarthy is quite believable," Gil said. "If you want to save any vestige of the life you have built, now is the time to make a show of good faith."

Fingers crept up to hide his mouth. "I'll talk to my lawyer," he murmured.

"We don't care about you," Gil said, "and we're not willing to waste time. If you don't care to cooperate, there is another witness—"

Vince looked at me. "Jack is a friend. You know that."

"He was."

"I didn't have any choice. You and Jack have to understand that much. He didn't leave me any choice." He folded his hands, stared at them. "I got a call at the office. His name was Mr. Jesse. Just that, Mr. Jesse. He wanted to do some business with me. At first I. thought that meant opening an account."

"You didn't know him?" I asked.

"No."

"Describe the voice."

"High, tinny—it sounded like long-distance."

He poured out the story. That first call, in early December, left no doubt that Mr. Jesse knew embarrassing facts about Vince DiMineo. "He knew about money I had borrowed once from a client's account. God, it was three years ago. I got into trouble in treasury futures, needed eighty thousand to meet a margin call. There was this account I had. It wasn't active. The client was overseas and we had a lot of money market paper. So I tapped the

151

account for just enough to get through the mess. It was only temporary. If need be, I could have liquidated some of my own things, but that would have taken time. I got lucky. A day later rates cracked and T-bills came back. I got out about even, put the money back in the client's account. The next six months I held my breath, praying the firm's regular audit wouldn't trip me. If they found it, they would notify the exchange's disciplinary committee, and I would be out. That six months was my time in purgatory. When the ax didn't fall, I thought I had been forgiven. Then that bastard called."

Vince didn't go along with him right away. But the caller knew so much. The name of the client, the amount that had been borrowed. He told Vince that the stock exchange needn't wash old laundry if the broker cooperated. "He said it wa a harmless prank he wanted to play. When he described it, I knew it wasn't harmless. What choice did I have? He said the prank was a comeuppance for a troublemaker. If I caused him grief, I would get a comeuppance too. He said to think it over.

"I did. I thought of things like taping his call. Notifying the firm's regulatory compliance department so we could trap him. But all those ideas meant exposing myself. And you know, the chances were they would just fire me and let Mr. Jesse take his scheme elsewhere. That would be the most efficient policy.

"He called back the next day. I didn't know who was on the line at first, because he was chatting with Lisa. He told her his name was Mr. Jesse, and he was looking forward to doing business with our firm. Had she worked there long? How did she like it? When I sensed she was having an odd conversation, I was terrified. I thought he was telling her about the Levitas account—that was the name of it. A nice trusting man named Levitas, and how I had stolen money from him to get myself out of a hole. But he was chatting about nothing. He knew I would pump her later. He was sending me a message. He told her he had gone to school with the firm's chairman. He thought he might phone him later to reflect on old times. I knew which old times. When I came on the line, he said we would talk that evening and hung up.

"How could I stand up to an invisible person who could destroy

152

me with a phone call? He told me to raise cash in Jack's account—your firm's account—starting that week. Without telling you two, of course. If Jack wanted to place an order, I was to make up a phony ticket showing I had done it. I would send him a copy and destroy the others so we didn't have a record. And of course I wouldn't buy the stock he told me to. Instead I had to sell stocks gradually, the way Jack would, and start putting the money into Dorchester Millinery. That part got tricky. I had to intercept all the confirmation slips that would tell you what I was really doing. And I had to make sure Lisa didn't talk to you, because she might ask why you were selling good stocks to buy Dorchester and the whole thing would blow up. I told Lisa that Jack and you had been carping about more direct access to a senior broker and I would deal with you for a while."

He knew it was a dangerous and unstable pretense that couldn't last long. For a while he told himself he was gathering evidence against Mr. Jesse. But he knew he was trying to stave off his inevitable exposure and ruin. When monthly account statements were about to be sent to clients, he visited the mail room on a pretext and intercepted ours. At home he used Faulkner Wells forms and a microcomputer to print out substitute statements.

Listening, I understood why the burglary of our office had been necessary. The faked statements couldn't be left in our files to vindicate us.

I made sure of something. "Did Mr. Jesse understand all the trouble you had to go through?"

"He asked how I would do parts of the job. Some I didn't know. Others I told him and he said, 'Good boy, smart boy,' something like that."

"Did he tell you why you were buying Dorchester Millinery?"

"No. I guessed he had heard the company was about to go bankrupt and wanted Canning to get hurt. I looked at their financial reports and figured bankruptcy was only a matter of time. Then Grendal's offer came along and I understood. Mr. Jesse was burying Jack Canning—and you, I guess. Jack could deny buying, but who would believe him?"

"You would have had to do a convincing job of lying," I said.

"I told the bastard I couldn't do it. How the hell could I ever face Jack at an SEC hearing and swear that he had given me those orders? My voice would give me away. His lawyers would tear me apart. Mr. Jesse said my attitude wasn't helpful. Men had to steel themselves for tough jobs. Either Jack Canning's career was dead or mine was. I was a thief. By the time Jack's case reached an SEC hearing, I would have added fraud and forgery to my sins. Then he was nicer. It wouldn't be as hard as I imagined. I would be insulated by lawyers through most of the process. And since I had no ax to grind, people would believe me. Everyone is willing to think the worst about somebody the SEC is accusing. They like to see somebody cut down to size. Jack's word wouldn't be worth anything—the self-serving lies of an inside trader, trying to blame his broker for his own crimes. He was right. Once the lawyers get involved, there's no direct confrontation. I could refuse to take Jack's calls, stick to my story, and that would be that.

"In almost three years, I never stepped out of line. Not once. Not the smallest thing. I've never front-run a client's order to get a free ride. Never shifted a good trade into my own account. I've never done any of that. People who dealt with me got square treatment."

I sat on the desk facing him. Jack had never complained. Vince handled orders well. He didn't play games. He was a friend.

Never trust a friend.

Vince stared out the French doors to the patio and pool. In the summer Jack and Barbara would have spent an evening or two out there sipping drinks and carving steaks. There had been a party in August that Marty and I had missed.

"I'm finished," Vince whispered. "No, I mean *finished*! Mr. Jesse was awfully specific. Just in case my career didn't matter, I should think about household accidents. While I was down confessing to the SEC, the swimming pool might get uncovered. You know how children are around swimming pools, he said. I sent the kids away."

"Because you were going to tell the SEC the truth?" I said.

"No. Because I was afraid I wouldn't lie well enough. When Jack ran off, I knew it was my fault. Then Mr. Jesse called last week. He hadn't for a while. But he called and said Jack had chosen not to face the music. Something about his voice chilled me."

My stomach turned over. I said, "Did you ever have to get in touch with Mr. Jesse? Do you know where he called from?"

He shook his head.

"Did he ever mail you instructions, anything with a postmark or a postage-meter stamp?"

"Never anything like that. He always called, and the voice was always odd—like from inside a barrel."

"Do you do any business with a man named Bunny Furbinger?" Gil asked.

"No. I don't know the name."

"He's a stockbroker."

Vince shook his head. "I'm sorry. Is he involved in this?"

Gil didn't answer. "How many times did Mr. Jesse talk to you in all?"

"Five," Vince said quietly.

"You didn't require much breaking down," Gil said. He asked questions about the length of the conversations, Mr. Jesse's background and manner of expression. Nothing conflicted with what I'd got out of Handsome.

Vince sucked the back of his knuckle. "Have you heard from Jack?" he said.

Gil switched off his tape recorder, and I told Vince why we hadn't heard from Jack.

We roused Mrs. DiMineo, a large-boned, moon-faced woman who hadn't been sleeping. "He's extremely distraught," I warned her. "He might turn suicidal. You should call someone to help. You might also want to hire a security guard for the house. Somebody your husband did business with probably considers him a loose end."

She accepted it all as if bad news were overdue.

In the car Gil said, "Do you think you could have a talent for this sort of thing?"

"What sort?"

"Stirring people up."

"Yes." A gloomy thought. "And other people pay for it."

"Regardless of what you did or failed to do, I suspect Mr. Jesse

155

had to kill Jack. It was truly a clumsy frame-up, doomed from the start. Done in haste, I should say. Was Jack indeed a troublemaker?"

"Not normally."

"Somebody thought he was."

"Yes."

"The stakes must have been higher than a simple grudge."

Gil ran the tape for Rudy. The smaller man listened. He told me without enthusiasm, "This isn't evidence that a court would accept. You used deception and threatening—"

"Will the SEC accept it?"

"Yes. You're off the hook."

"Then so is the firm. Can you get copies made, let the SEC have one?"

"Tomorrow morning." He gave an embarrassed grimace. "Just so that you know—Barbara will want a quick sale of the firm. Quick like immediate."

Gil began putting his coat on. I said, "That might not be in her own interest. The partnership's value is depressed by the scandal."

Rudy shrugged. "I'm just telling you."

"Okay." I hesitated. "Did Jack strike you as eager to make trouble for someone else?"

"Of course not. He never had time for meddling."

"If he came across something illegal, would he look the other way?"

Rudy gave me a look reserved for innocents. "For Christ's sake. When *I* come across something, I look the other way, and *I'm* an officer of the court. Jack might stick his nose into something that mattered to him, but he wasn't out to set the world right."

"No," I agreed. Unless he had to.

31

ON Monday I avoided dropping by George Finn's office, though we had a couple of telephone conversations. The cannonade was gone from his voice. A police detective phoned and said Danny Natoli denied any part in Jack's death. He was about to be indicted for stabbing Jimmy Doyle. "The knife was similar, probably the same. Once we had a picture to shop around your office building, we found someone who saw Danny and the redhead."

Handsome's telephone number for Mr. Jesse traced to a one-room office above a shoe store on Broadway. In four months, the landlord had never met his tenant. The rent had been paid for a year in advance by a money order that arrived by messenger.

Peter called on behalf of *Investor's Week*, sounding businesslike, and asked about a rumor it was suicide. After setting him straight, I told Gail not to let any calls through except clients'.

I watched the market diligently and worked late, creating paper-shuffling chores. It didn't keep my mind off Jack. I had owed him more than I could repay. When the time had come for just a down payment on the debt, I had stood back and wondered if he was a crook.

The market danced higher in the late afternoon, like one of George Finn's spaniels sniffing game. The Fed had decided to let the good times roll, and long bond rates were down a point. My Seattle

Aviation was up six dollars. According to the tape, takeover rumors were rife. Dorchester Millinery lost two points, grudgingly, as if there were a short seller feeding stock into the market. Trionix traded heavily at an all-time high of seven dollars.

Meg Silverman showed up after the market closed, flinging her briefcase into a corner, crossing her legs with a show-off smile. She had commiserated with me about Jack by telephone. She instinctively shied away from extended mourning.

"I was just in the neighborhood and thought you could buy me a drink," she said.

"It sounds good."

We drifted down to Harry's and drank martinis. Bunny Furbinger's angel was more incognito than she had expected. Meg leaned into me confidentially. She was dressed to sell in a severe black man-tailored suit, a white blouse buttoned to the throat, a string of pearls. She complained, "Usually there is a whisper of who has bankrolled a firm. Not this time."

"No whisper that it was Lance Grendal?"

She shook her head. "I'll keep asking."

"Don't ask too often." I didn't want anyone else hurt.

"I can still keep an ear open. Are you certain it matters?"

"Yes." Find Furbinger's banker and we would find the éminence grise who called himself Mr. Jesse.

When I went home at seven and found the apartment empty, I half regretted that Meg wasn't along to dance into the bedroom eagerly, sniffing game. Then Gil called, exasperated that he hadn't reached me before. "Can you get down to the bottom of Broadway in forty minutes? I have made the acquaintance of Mr. Justin Webb, a thirty-eight-year-old senior vice president of Furbinger Associates. He is more enthusiastic than intelligent. He is *very much* taken with my intimate knowledge of the aerospace industry, particularly with my evidence that Northern Jet needs to make an acquisition and that I know which company it has in mind."

"How have you managed all that?"

"All what? It's nothing, just a teaser. I telephoned Mr. Webb last Friday and established my credentials. I had made a tidy sum on the

Steinberg play in Tiger International a few years ago. But I couldn't continue to follow the same hedge fund in and out of situations. Somebody might discern a pattern in our trading and ask about our sources. I invited Mr. Webb to lunch to discuss my opening an account with his firm. This is because I have heard from the best people that Mr. Webb is discreet. The best people do not know of Mr. Webb's existence. But once he had swallowed that line without coughing, he was hooked. He believes in me because I seem to believe in him. Also, I gave him an impeccable reference whom he won't have had the courage to consult. Today we had lunch and Mr. Webb demonstrated how savvy he is about sensitive information. Tonight I am to give him the name of the target company and its financial information. We are meeting in his office in ten minutes. Justin and I have a personal relationship now, so no one else will be present."

"Will he buy the rest of the story?"

"It has the ring of truth. Two years ago a competitor of Northern Jet adopted a similar strategy. It needed more military business to balance the civil work, so it bought a defense contractor. That is what Mr. Webb expects Northern Jet to do. I selected your Seattle Aviation as the target."

I suppressed a smile. "It's plausible."

"Not that plausibility matters," Gil said. "By the time we are finished, Mr. Justin Webb will be ready to accept Quaker Oats as the target. He will have calculated how many hundreds of thousands of dollars he can reap by using his knowledge in the options market. If there are any holes in my story, he will patch them for me."

The double glass doors of Furbinger Associates' office revealed a deserted reception area and a dark trading room. I waited nervously in the hall. A building guard had gotten onto the elevator on the fourth floor as I got off. White men in tweed overcoats did not fit his profile of suspicious characters. But he hadn't caught me lurking outside a locked office.

Gil appeared inside the suite and opened the door. "I am visiting the gentlemen's room. Mr. Webb, who runs the firm's arbitrage

159

desk, is enraptured at the thought of buying Seattle Aviation in size tomorrow morning."

He closed the door quietly and pointed out Webb's office at the end of a row of mahogany doors. He whispered, "We were almost undone by a dedicated young woman who stayed late to scream at a customer in Scarsdale. She left fifteen minutes ago."

"And Furbinger has gone?"

"Hours past. Good luck, Ben. I shall distract Mr. Webb for another forty minutes."

Gil headed back to his conference. I crossed the deserted trading room to Bunny's office. The first obstacle, the door, wasn't locked. I closed it behind me and my finger found the light switch.

Bunny's private office was tidy, with the walnut desk top swept clean of everything but finger smudges. The cleaning crew hadn't come through yet. The wastebasket was full, with discarded newspapers stacked beside it.

I sat in Bunny's red leather chair and opened desk drawers. The stock promoter took Maalox pills and had Lincoln Center tickets. He kept a toy oil derrick in one deep drawer, jumbled cassette tapes in another.

His bookshelf behind the desk was no more revealing. More than a yard of space was taken up by multiple copies of prospectuses for stock offerings that his firm had organized. No matter how many of those confessionals got printed, or what ugly truths they revealed about the president's past, the deals went through. The customers Bunny attracted never read fine print. I had done a bit of research and learned that F.Y. "Herb" Butler, of ConCom International, was also a founding stockholder of Trionix. Two of his earlier corporate brainstorms had landed in bankruptcy. His winning smile kept the customers coming back.

Bunny's computer system was state of the art, offering prices from a dozen U.S. and foreign stock exchanges, several levels of over-the-counter markets, reports from the commodity pits, news and analysis from various wire services, plus a filing system for maintaining customer accounts. Computers that big never sleep. I switched on Bunny's terminal and wondered how tough they had made the security obstacles.

One code would permit all Furbinger Associates brokers and the support staff to gain access to general record-keeping files. It would be something fairly simple, if Bunny's setup was typical, because the idea was to get the offerings sold, not to have brokers lumbering from desk to desk asking each other if they remembered the password.

I typed FURBINGER and hit Enter, and the computer said I had used an invalid code. It invited me to try again.

So I tried BUNNY and the system opened up.

After a minute of scanning directories, I tried looking over customer lists. There were too many, and none of the names meant anything. I asked for specifics: GRENDAL, LANCE; GRENDAL OFFSHORE LTD.; GRENDAL HOTEL ENTERPRISES; PARADISE ASSETS.

None of them drew a response.

I searched for Jimmy Doyle's client roster, but it was empty; the names already had been reassigned.

For ten minutes I pulled up files looking for the firm's own house accounts. But Furbinger kept them well hidden and I gave up.

I switched off the terminal.

The desk top was bare except for a telephone and Rolodex file. The telephone was a complicated one with an answering machine built in. The file was mostly blank cards; apparently a secretary took care of most of his phoning.

Then another explanation for the blank cards occurred to me. The telephone set was impressive, with two key pads, numbers on the right, letters on the left, a cassette tape peeking from a window at the top of the machine, a half-dozen line and conference buttons, a liquid crystal display that showed the time. I punched a letter at random and the time was replaced by a lighted B. The display would flash the name and number being dialed from the machine's memory.

I rewound the tape and listened to snatches of conversations in which Bunny Furbinger veered from profane to solicitous. The people he talked to were entrepreneurs looking for financial support, a couple of clients who sounded like heavy hitters, a woman who wondered why she hadn't gotten a check. I skipped around on the tape wishing I had a lot of time. Nobody on the fragments I heard dropped a mention of Dorchester Millinery. Trionix seemed to be on a couple of people's minds, and Bunny told one elderly-sounding man that he thought the shares could trade at 15.

I opened the desk drawer and stared again at the pile of tape cassettes. Not all were faceless blanks. Scattered in the heap were some commercial recordings of modern composers: a couple of Adams, a Crumb. Unlikely choices unless you were having a bad day in the market and needed comfort that someone else felt worse. I picked up a Crumb and put it on the machine. Screeches announced humankind's doom. I jumped ahead. Bunny Furbinger's voice leapt out of the speaker. ". . . and Harvey can go elsewhere if he doesn't like the terms." I pressed fast forward. A woman's voice. "Got a report for you on—" broken off in midbreath. Other fragments followed, pieces of conversations that he had not wanted to preserve in full. At least a hundred plastic cassette cases filled the drawer. If each was from the telephone, Bunny was going out of his way to keep a record of something. There was no way I could sample more than one or two of the tapes. Little hope of catching anything significant.

I could try getting out the door with a box full of tapes. But if Bunny incriminated himself on any of them, I would have destroyed the usefulness of the evidence.

My first choice was having the SEC find the cassettes on the premises.

Which they wouldn't if Bunny got nervous.

I found his supply of "blanks" in a credenza, a stack of forty or fifty commercial tapes, many of the same recordings. The collection had the look of close-out merchandise that could be bought cheaply and recorded over. I checked a couple and found the orchestral music intact. He hadn't used them yet.

I exchanged the tapes in the desk for those in the credenza, left a handful of blanks on top. He would use those first. With luck it would be a while before he began recording over his own conversations. If he began throwing away evidence, modern music would go into the trash.

A handful of telephone tapes were left. A compromise. I dropped them in my overcoat pockets.

It was eight-forty.

I went back to the telephone. Unlike the computer, its memory would be limited to a couple of hundred names and numbers, all accessible. I pushed a READ button and a STORE button—not much different from our own system—and scrolled through the list alphabetically. The list was long. A lot of BARBER, BRICKLAYER, COMPUTER, SAG HARBOR (a summer house?), TICKETS, personal trivia. Strings of names that could have been straightforward or unintentionally cryptic. IGGY, MERCER, SALLYKIN. All had local numbers. I wasn't sure what I was looking for, but it probably wouldn't be as clear as an entry for GRENDAL or PARADISE or PHIL.

Several names appeared to be gibberish. A couple of others were either shorthand or Bunny's idea of code. There were local exchanges and out-of-town area codes that I didn't recognize. I scribbled down each puzzler as I came to it and got seven in all.

I turned out the light and crept out of the office.

Wind sweeping from the Hudson lifted rubbish along the building facades like spiraling kites. As newspaper pages circled on dirty wings, Gil Norris crossed the street and we ducked into the subway station. I had been waiting at the unprotected entrance for twenty minutes.

"He wouldn't let me go," Gil apologized. "I told him it would be six weeks before a deal is announced. Young Mr. Webb says we can scatter our buying of Seattle Aviation shares through several brokerage firms and nobody will be the wiser. I am supposed to meet him Wednesday with my check."

"What do you tell him when he wonders where the check is?"

"That I have heard there has been a hitch—nothing fatal to the deal, but reason to move cautiously. Naturally I will keep him on top of everything I hear. Disappointment will accumulate slowly." He blew into his hands and asked, "How did you make out?"

We took a cab uptown, and in the safe rooms of his club I showed him. Listening to one tape from start to finish, we heard ninety minutes of mostly five-second bursts from traders reporting back to Furbinger. A couple of conversations stretched on but were so elliptical that the subject was lost on eavesdroppers. Other calls

163

made very good sense. After hearing one, Gil commented, "I would venture that he makes a habit of manipulating the stocks he brings to market. If I were public-spirited, I would want to put him out of business for the good of the market."

"I don't think what he does is much of a secret," I said. "A stock like Trionix wouldn't be trading at seven dollars if somebody hadn't done an energetic selling job. Part of selling is creating an appearance that other people want to own your product."

We took a break and I called home. Marty said she had a new commission from Danton's theater. "A real leading man," she said.

"Congratulations."

"Mrs. DiMineo called a little while ago," she said. "Vince's lawyer checked him into a psychiatric ward. She holds you responsible."

If Vince was in the hospital, he might not be talking to Mr. Jesse.

"How late are you and Gil going to be?" she asked.

"It may take a while. Don't wait up."

Gil had sandwiches sent up around eleven. We took a couple of breaks to discuss what we had heard, or hadn't heard. The job of not hearing much took us until dawn. When we were done, we knew that Furbinger played loose with his stocks, his clients and stock exchange rules. Nothing suggested that he played with Grendal.

"There were eighty or ninety more tapes," I said.

Gil massaged his face. "Not worth the risk, Ben. I would guess that Furbinger is reasonably careful about what he records. What about telephone numbers?"

I unfolded the list of odd numbers. Gil ran a finger down the entries. "We should check them all," he said. "Except this one: PHX is short for the Philadelphia Stock Exchange, and 215 is Philly's area code. Nothing mysterious there. Look at these two. MEDONE and MEDTWO. They sound like doctors' offices, but the area code 809—the Bahamas or Bermuda. Where is Grendal based?"

"Paradise Island."

"Huntington Hartford's old fiasco," Gil said. "They used to call it Hog Island."

I used his telephone. The first number didn't answer. The second was answered by a recorded male voice reciting the number's final four digits and inviting a message. I hung up.

164

I was ninety percent certain that I had recognized the rich baritone. When I looked at the code and reversed the first three letters—getting DEM instead of MED—all doubt vanished. "We've got our link to Grendal," I said. "This number belongs to his troubleshooter, Chet Demming."

I took a cab home, drank two cups of tea and phoned Peter Bagley at his apartment. It was only eight-thirty. Nobody at *Investor's Week* got to the office before ten.

"I'll trade you an exclusive interview," I said, "for whatever new poop you can find on Lance Grendal by this evening."

"Why should I want the interview?"

"In the next day or two, the SEC will drop its investigation of us. The new target is a broker at Faulkner Wells. I'll give you a prime quote on the quality of SEC investigative work."

"Then I get on their hit list, right? Okay. Are the services for Canning public?"

"Tomorrow at eleven."

"I'll be there."

I caught Gail with her coat on. I fed her the line to use and told her to try lining up an appointment with Lance Grendal. "Preferably in the next forty-eight hours," I said. "If he's not in New York, I'll go down to the Bahamas."

32

GRENDAL Offshore Ltd. put a lot of money out front where visitors could admire it. Blooming hibiscus and rhododendron plants crowded the borders of a fiftieth-floor garden, enclosed by glass walls that overlooked the frozen meadows of Central Park. Grendal's operation rented two floors of the Gulf National Tower. So far I had seen a hallway full of sculpture and a garden full of vegetation, but nothing that looked like a desk or a file cabinet. For all I knew, Lance Grendal ran his empire off a pocket calculator and a notebook. I followed a flagstone path through the garden to an escalator that swept up along the windows to the executive deck.

A Eurasian girl swinging a leather portfolio waited at the mezzanine. She had a quick smile and a businesslike handshake. "Bet 'chure Mr. Murphy. I'm Miss Bell. Would you like coffee? Lance is on the transatlantic phone."

Miss Bell's post was a neat square of desks and couches. She threw the portfolio onto one of the couches. "Lance was intrigued when he got your secretary's message. That's why he agreed to see you. Are you serious that Dorchester Millinery should acquire Trionix?"

"We think the benefits might outweigh the odd business mix."

She shook her head in disbelief. "I'll let you sell the idea to Lance. I don't know how people found out that he left Paradise Island, except that the executive assistant down there is a blabbermouth."

166

I said, "You don't work in the Bahamas?"

"No. I'm Lance's New York Miss Bell. There's another one down there, my sister. She's the blabbermouth."

"She must take after a different side of the family."

"We're twins. But that's very perceptive of you."

There were a few potted trees nearby to shade us from the recessed fluorescents. A pastel wall was broken by a single Chinese print of a wave hitting the shore. A couple of carpeted corridors led off to the executive offices.

Lance Grendal loped into sight, dressed for a day hopping around the outer islands: crepe-soled topsiders, tan corduroys with pockets on the thighs, a blue turtleneck shirt. An ancient suede jacket hung like a cape from his prominent shoulders.

Every step aged him. At thirty feet he was tanned and wiry-haired, a black moustache flaring above square teeth, a Vandyke showing two handsome streaks of white. At fifteen feet, the Caribbean sun had cut furrows around the nose, crosshatched the cheeks, bleached the color from the eyes except for reddish rims. The left eyelid sagged, its withered muscle giving him a permanently lecherous wink. He sized me up as I reached for a category for him. *Frayed* was my word. Just as a guess, he had been going to seed in the sunny ports, eating too many rum breakfasts.

He waved a summons. "B.J., honey, we'll have some almond tea. Come on, Murphy."

His office was empty except for a pair of bamboo trees, a shelf full of malachite temple jars, and a painted screen on which an old bearded warlord perpetuated his dynasty with a contortionist. The screen blocked a couple of low wicker and steel chairs and a table that were the only hint that Grendal worked here. They were next to a window that offered another dreary view of the park. Grendal sat down and propped his feet on the window ledge and waggled them. His ankles were hairless and heavy-veined.

The remnants of an earlier tea littered the table, nestled among annual reports and green-barred computer paper. There was no quotation terminal, no news wire, only a telephone.

"Mr. Murphy, is it? Yesterday I had little B.J. cross-check the

167

telephone number you left. It's listed to a firm called Canning & McCarthy. Ain't that queer?"

"I'm Benjamin McCarthy."

"I've read about you. Your privates are on the chopping block. A week ago, three federal lawyers wanted me to explain how your firm got wise to one of my deals." He spread his palms and made a lifting motion. "I didn't know, so I couldn't tell them. But I'm curious myself. So I let you come up here."

He rocked back in his chair and stared at me. "You made yourself a first-rate pain in the ass in Dorchester. Old Roscoe Tullman got so upset he was calling me twice a day. 'What's this guy McCarthy want? He acts like he's out to blow the deal!' I couldn't tell him. Then when the SEC jumped you, Tullman just about had a stroke. He figured we tipped you about the deal."

"Have you tried to set the record straight?"

"Really and truly, I don't give a damn. I'm stuck here where I don't want to be, which is away from my boats and my beach. I got nothing to do but pacify B.J. a coupla times a day—that and talk to munchkins like you."

"I don't want to waste your time," I said. "But I've got a theory on how word leaked on Dorchester."

"What is it?"

"You had your boy Chet Demming tip Bunny Furbinger."

"Who the hell is Furbinger?"

"His firm brought out a company you're involved in called Trionix."

"Trionix I know. We own a little. As for the rest . . ." He gave a long-toothed grin. "I don't know any Furbingers. If I did I wouldn't let them in on my deals. Why should I? And—"

"The thing about Furbinger," I said, "is that he has been selling short Dorchester Millinery stock. As though he expects your offer to flop."

"That shows both of you don't know what you're doing. My offer is the best one Tullman will ever see."

"Maybe Furbinger knows it's so good you're planning to withdraw it."

"Jesus. Now I'm sorry I took the time to entertain you."

Miss Bell brought in a teapot and cups, both decorated with pastel flowers and birds that had faded to pale blushes. She poured two cups and left.

"Why are you so fixated on Furbinger?" Grendal asked. "Or is he just someone to take you off the hook?"

"I'm off the hook. Somebody went to a lot of trouble to set us up, and it didn't work. As for Furbinger, he just keeps turning up. In Dorchester Millinery. In technology stocks you own. In Chet Demming's circle. Do you recognize this telephone number? I got it in Furbinger's office." I recited the 809 number that rang Chet Demming's line on Paradise Island.

"So you got Chet's phone number."

"Furbinger had it."

Grendal leaned toward me, puffy eyes slit. "Well, partner, listen. If Chet tipped anyone, first he'd have to be crazy, because he knows I'd have his cock and his balls for earrings. That's the first thing. The second is, anyone he tipped wouldn't be selling Dorchester Millinery short. They'd be buying. Now you say, Maybe old Lance plans to welsh on the deal. Let me walk you through it. Just so you'll know how stupid you sound. Dorchester has lost money for most of the last ten years. Those losses are on the books, so if the company ever managed to make a buck they wouldn't have to pay taxes on it. Not for a long time. Now, once I get this thing into Grendal Offshore, here's what I can do. I can fold a couple of my little profitable companies into Dorchester. Right there I've cut my tax bill maybe five million a year. Then I can do a few other things. I can sell off the Connecticut real estate, recoup about ten million of my cost there. Again, no taxes. The textile production we can run cheaper out of a plant I own in South Carolina. So if the corduroy market doesn't tank altogether, we might generate some free cash from the business. Lastly, I've paid cash for the shares I bought on the market. But the rest I'll buy for junk bonds. So I figure I can recapture my cash investment in about twelve months. Would you back out of a deal like that?"

"Could Tullman back out? The stock has been weak."

"The union's been making some noise that they don't like me.

They're gonna have good reason when they all get walking papers. The deal is going through."

"Does the town know you plan to scrap the mill?"

"I haven't advertised the fact. But hey—if we can get the wage problem settled, I'm flexible. Nothing's carved in stone. I may keep the plant open. I may put in new machines and have those townfolk knit nothing but crotchless panties. Or I may bulldoze every brick. Once I own it, it's all up to me."

He glanced at a black-and-chrome diver's watch on his bony wrist. "Sorry, partner, but I'll walk you out."

"There's still your connection to Trionix."

"Buy yourself some of that one, McCarthy. Ride my coattails legally. Nobody can touch their technology."

We turned a corner and walked into Miss Bell's austere domain. She sat on a corner of her desk, telephone to her ear.

I asked him, "What is Trionix's technology?"

He scowled at me, shrugged. "I don't bother keeping that stuff straight. That's what detail men are for."

"Trionix is just a promotion," I said. "Once the price gets pushed a little higher, Furbinger will cash out. Who got you into the stock?"

"Beats me. One of my usual bird dogs."

"One named Demming?"

"Chet doesn't prospect companies for me. He's got other uses." He clapped his hand on Miss Bell's shoulder. "B.J., darling, phone the traders. We'll take another twenty thousand Dorchester Millinery at thirty-one or better. This deal's going ahead, McCarthy. Believe me."

"Is that what Jesse says?"

His eyebrows rose. "Jesse?"

"Doesn't the name mean something to you?"

"Sure it does. Jesse James. Jesse Jackson. Jesse Livermore. You know Livermore? He ran bear raids in the twenties. Lost his fortune in the thirties. Had a drink at the Sherry-Netherland one day, went into the gents' and shot his brains out. We should all be man enough to do that when the game's over."

170

33

GIL Norris was waiting at the edge of the fiftieth-floor jungle. "There's a very pretty girl up on the balcony," he said. "Do you suppose she administers Mr. Grendal's high colonics?"

He waved and Miss Bell waved back.

"Well, what is Grendal like?"

"Crude even by Wall Street standards. Can out-tough every other boy from the Bronx. Slipping, aging, insecure. Says he's going ahead with Dorchester. Denies knowing Furbinger, much less owning him."

"You wouldn't expect him to tell you otherwise."

"No. But if he plans to scotch the merger, it should worry him that we've spotted his tracks. It didn't seem to."

"What does that tell you?"

"That he doesn't plan to."

"Yet Furbinger has sold short, and Furbinger knows Demming."

"A puzzle," I agreed.

He ceased gawking at Miss Bell and ambled to the elevators. He unwrapped a cigar, and when a car came, intimidated a prim, white-haired passenger by waving an unlighted match. As we walked out onto Madison Avenue, Gil said, "Several possibilities come to mind. Check me on them. First, Grendal deliberately had Demming feed Bunny a bad tip. We cannot dismiss the idea. But

171

if he doesn't know Furbinger, why should he bother? Perhaps an old grudge we haven't stumbled across, yes?"

"If there's a grudge, Bunny would be wary of tips from Grendal's people."

"True. Unless we suppose that Furbinger doesn't know that Grendal is out to get him. Perhaps there was a slight he thought he had gotten away with."

"It's stretching," I said.

"I agree. So is the second possibility. That is that Demming fed Bunny bad information at his own initiative. Again, why? The third possibility is more intriguing. Suppose the information was good. What does that imply? Either that Grendal does not plan to go through with the deal—an idea you reject—or that Chet Demming has reason to doubt the deal will be completed. In the latter case, he may have shared his information with Furbinger but not with Grendal. That would be very disloyal."

We took a taxi down to the Plaza and had drinks. "What will become of your firm?" Gil asked.

"Barbara wants to sell it. Finding somebody to take over what's left of the client list will be easy. The price won't be what she hopes."

"Have you thought about buying the firm yourself?"

"It crossed my mind."

Peter Bagley arrived and shook hands with Gil. They had met that morning at Jack's funeral. I brought Peter up to date on Handsome and Vince DiMineo, kept all speculation to myself.

"Do you know who wanted you shut down?" Peter asked.

"Not so far."

"You're luckier than some other people have been. I went through the last eighteen months of stories. I thought you would like to see this." He handed a page from a memo pad across the table. I unfolded it and found a list. Nine names, stacked like obituaries, which they were. Markey Wahl. Wister Securities. Rensselaer Company. Six others, a few recognizable, going back to October a year ago. That was when the government had closed down Rensselaer, a small discount brokerage firm, for violating minimum capital rules.

"All deceased?" I said.

"Yeah. A couple deserved to be. There's a little clearing house on the list that was playing games with inventories. Another firm had a vice president who started shorting treasuries in ten-million-dollar lots. Interest rates had just started down. I covered that mess in my column. I looked for common denominators among the others. There aren't any. Rensselaer was taken over by Furbinger Associates. None of the others were. A firm called American East Securities in New Jersey absorbed two other of the healthier failures, if that's not a contradiction in terms."

We got another round of beers, and Peter said, "Finding out about Grendal was easier. I talked to a hedge-fund manager who used to go in with Grendal sometimes. Following Lance's forays hasn't been profitable for a while. My guy thinks Grendal has lost his touch. He says there are two big banks Grendal used to deal with that won't take his calls."

"Men like Grendal have fallings-out with bankers all the time," Gil observed.

"I know. They play them off against each other. Who will lend the most money on the thinnest collateral? My guy's version is that these banks had been extremely cooperative and rue the day. Grendal has a billion-dollar operation, if you put all the pieces together—"

"If you can find all the pieces," I said.

"And if you can find the pieces, how many of them have been hocked to the limit? You know, an offshore player like Grendal could break the rules. How could a banker in North Carolina or New York know if the asset he's lending against has already been pledged to banks in Panama or Brazil? Anyway, there's a rumor going around that he's borrowed everywhere he can, twice in some cases."

I thought back to what I had read in Peter's office. Grendal had always been a borrower. He had built his empire on debt.

"The magic of leverage works both ways," Gil said. "When your deals work, the profit is multiplied. Your equity rises like a hot air balloon. If a deal flops, the balloon collapses. That would be a good

173

time to be an offshore operator, with your assets spread around, hard to find and seize."

"There was a small buyout a couple of years ago, the Moliere Department Stores, that went sour," Peter said. "It didn't make the papers. The company was private. The Molieres padded the inventory before selling to Grendal. Two months later he had a bankrupt on his hands. That may have been the first time he got careless."

"I think he has gotten careless again, if he owns stocks like Trionix," Gil said.

34

ON Thursday the Securities and Exchange Commission issued a press release stating that a prosperous stockbroker was being investigated in the Dorchester Millinery case. The commission said it expected to bring charges against other persons as well. It appeared, said Gordon Trapp, the enforcement chief, that there had been a conspiracy to obstruct justice.

Trapp didn't mention that the commission had agreed to support Rudy Thatcher's motion for lifting the order freezing the assets of Canning & McCarthy.

On Saturday, patrolling the perimeter, I caught a flash of orange hair under a watch cap. Bongo Harris slipped out of sight on Hudson Street. The police drove through the area without finding him.

On Monday, Dorchester Millinery broke off its merger agreement with Grendal Offshore Ltd. Roscoe Tullman said only: "The board of directors has determined that the sale of our company is not in the best interest of our stockholders, employees, or the community. The proposal encountered resistance among our largest investors. We have terminated discussions."

The large investors I had talked to were eager to sell. I wondered what Tullman had left out.

I tapped the symbol for Dorchester on my terminal. The last

transaction had been at 30¼. Trading was halted as the floor specialist sent out indications it might reopen between 22 and 26.

It was bank day for Furbinger. If he had sold short in the low thirties, he could clear ten dollars on each share. Times, say, three or four million shares equalled a decent few weeks' work.

Where did that leave Lance Grendal?

I called Sol Lehrman on the exchange floor. "Is there any sign that Grendal has sold his Dorchester Millinery?"

He phoned back in five minutes. "Not a share. The specialist says he's sure. But your friends at Furbinger are short twenty percent of the stock."

I tried Grendal's office. Miss Bell said the master was in conference and would be occupied all day.

Waiting for Dorchester to resume trading, I watched the quotes of other stocks march across the screen. An amber chain of ticker symbol, price, symbol, price. When a large block traded, the size showed in a condensed code. After a while you could watch the hypnotic rhythm of symbols and numbers and gain a visceral instinct for the direction of the market. Were big chunks of stock crossing as prices went up a few pennies or on declines? Was the passion to own suddenly greater than the passion to sell? The mood could swing wildly twenty times a day.

Gil came around and I told him the news. The stock of Dorchester Millinery had opened at 24⅜ and acted weak.

"If Grendal is borrowed up, his bankers must be worried about their collateral," Gil observed.

"They should be. The stock was in the midteens a few weeks ago. Once people decide there's no buyout coming from anyone, the price will head back to the teens."

"Which means what for Mr. Grendal?"

"If he has five million shares, he must have bought a lot as the price was rising. Say his average cost is twenty-five. If the shares collapse to fifteen, he'll be fifty million in the hole. He won't be able to unload many shares on the way down."

"A fatal blow?" Gil wondered.

It would depend, I thought, on how other Grendal ventures were faring. If he had debts piled around and weak collateral, fatal indeed.

Gail came in simpering and delivered a mug of tea to Gil. He rewarded her with a look of extreme pleasure, as if life seldom brought such kindness. When she had left he said, "Is it coincidence that what works out so well for Mr. Furbinger is so unhealthy for Grendal?"

He relaxed in Jack's chair, listening on the extension as I phoned the company. All I could get from Roscoe Tullman was the fact that old E. H. Parsons was the major shareholder who had turned against the merger. He had managed to sway another director, who, Tullman implied, waffled hourly.

"Do you know what changed Parsons' mind?" I asked.

Tullman let his breath out. "If I do, it's not something I will discuss. If you want to talk to Edgar, he's staying in town at the Roosevelt."

We took the evening commuter flight up to Dorchester. Gil had insisted on coming along. He had a drink and went to sleep, lips sputtering, cheeks pale and damp. I glanced through the afternoon paper and worried about him.

He dozed in the cab that carried us to the drab business district. Once we entered the Roosevelt Hotel, he shook himself, yawned and issued orders. "You check us in. I'll find the house phone."

I signed for our rooms, turned the luggage and keys over to a bellman, and went around the corner. The phone desk was empty. Gil beckoned from the doorway of the New Deal Saloon. "Parsons is coming down. Look at this!" He waved the afternoon edition of the Dorchester *Tribune* under my nose. The front page bore photographs of Tullman and Grendal. The headline announced:

GRENDAL DIRTY TRICK SINKS MERGER

We found a table near the door. I skimmed the article. The dirty trick wasn't specified. The article said vaguely that "family considerations" had helped turn board member Edgar Parsons against

177

Grendal. On the article's continuation inside was a picture of E. H. Parsons III and his red-haired wife at a black-tie charity affair.

Other useful news: Dorchester's stock had closed the day at 22¾. A local banker applauded the deal's collapse, saying, "Grendal possesses a terrible reputation for destroying jobs."

Reading over my shoulder, Gil said, "That's a gentle way of putting it. Chet Demming should have been quieting such concerns."

"I think he was busy doing other things," I said.

Edgar Parsons came into the bar pushing his double-knot of chin like a swinging fist. Gil stood up and nodded, and Parsons came over. His gait was rolling. There was spunk in the watery blue eyes. He focused on Gil. His voice was gravelly with a waver of hoarseness. "Always happy to meet shareholders. You said your name is Norris? You probably think I've knifed you in the back by rejecting Grendal's offer."

"Not if it was a bad deal," Gil said quickly. "What are you drinking?"

Parsons ordered a Jameson's, then sat down and pinched his chin between thick fingers. "The more I looked at what Grendal was offering," he said, staring straight through Gil and reciting as if from memory, "the worse the contract looked. The payment was to be in low-quality bonds, along with enough cash for beer money. I felt the shareholders deserved better."

Gil nodded.

I said, "Grendal's offer had a face value of thirty-six dollars a share. You can't be surprised that it sounded pretty good to us."

He squinted, half-recognizing the voice. "Face value isn't real value. I've had my ear to the ground, and I know things you presumably don't. I am skeptical of the safety of any bonds issued by Grendal Offshore Ltd. Some of Grendal's financial backers appear to be, ahm, unsavory."

Gil spun a beer cracker with his thumbnail. "Is the board open to selling assets on its own?"

"We have discussed it. I have insisted on that. Roscoe Tullman is unalterably opposed because we would be writing off eight hundred jobs in this city. That would blemish Roscoe's standing with the Rotary."

"In some towns he would be lynched," Gil observed.

I asked, "Could the company be sold as a going concern to its workers or the town?"

Parsons's mood shifted. He gave a deep, choking laugh into his whiskey. "Neither the city nor the workers are big enough fools to buy Dorchester Millinery. They plan to milk the cow until she gives her last kick."

I said gently, "Are there other considerations in your decision?"

He raised his eyes and didn't answer.

"The newspaper said Grendal had engaged in dirty tricks," I said. "What sort?"

He shrugged. "Crude attempts to gain influence with the directors. I'm certain it goes on all the time, but—"

"Were they trying to gain influence through the directors' families?"

A look of sickness spread up his face. He had guts enough to ask, "What exactly does that mean?"

"The newspaper said something along those lines."

"Well, it backfired."

"It might never have been meant to succeed," I said. "You know there have been heavy short sales of Dorchester Millinery shares. Somebody has been betting that Grendal's deal wouldn't go through."

When another Jameson's arrived, his hand found it unerringly. "Don't some of you smart boys down in New York make a living second-guessing takeovers? This time the short-seller got lucky."

"Luck wasn't involved. The selling has been out of a small firm called Furbinger Associates. Furbinger had somebody working inside Grendal's organization to wreck the merger. I think I know who. You can tell me if I'm right. Grendal has a troubleshooter on the payroll named Chet Demming. Young, good looking, rough around the edges, but apparently attractive to women. Roscoe Tullman's secretary, Miss Wegner, gets dreamy-eyed when Chet Demming walks into the office."

Gil shot me a warning glance, and I stopped. From Parsons's look

179

of pain and humiliation I knew I was right. The old man stared at the table, got up mechanically with a rasped "Excuse me."

After he left, Gil said, "That was pretty brutal."

I knew.

The bellman had unlocked the door between our rooms. They were dowdy, with faded armchairs, ancient wallpaper and a dusty view of Allen Street. Gil lay down without removing his jacket and leafed through a dog-eared booklet on the entertainments of Dorchester. Leaving the door ajar, I watched television for almost an hour before hearing a rap on Gil's door.

Edgar Parsons stood in the hall. "They said you were registered, Mr. Norris." He looked me over. "I'm missing bets this evening. You're the fellow who telephoned me. McCarthy, is it?"

"That's right."

"What's your connection to each other?"

"I'm Ben's uncle-in-law," Gil said. "I look after him. Why don't you come in?"

"Demming's skills must have been apparent to everyone but me," Parsons murmured. The pain that suffused his face didn't reach his voice, which was hard and factual. "For weeks my wife has been carrying on about what a great opportunity Grendal represented. About how we could sell out, move to a place with more of a cultural life. I had no idea where she was getting it. Or why she was laying it on so thick."

He stared at the ceiling. "When I walked in on them, it never occurred to me that Demming was being too clumsy. They were in my parlor, my parlor, and she had . . . I came back from the bank and found them. I guess I was meant to. It was just too careless, being there like that. If I had been thinking clearly, I would have wondered about that. Instead I went into a rage and tried to throw him out. He was younger and stronger. It may be close to the ultimate humiliation, being pinned to your own carpet by a man with no pants on. So I sat there while he got dressed. He took his time. He kept grinning at me."

"Heavy-handed," Gil said.

"But effective. I moved in here yesterday afternoon and phoned

180

Roscoe at home. I told him I would never vote my stock to Grendal. I got Phil Nicodemus behind me. Between us, our families own almost twenty-five percent of the company."

"If Demming was working as a well-poisoner, he has been a great success," Gil said.

"Now that I reflect, he let a few things slip in conversation that I thought at the time were damn careless. A couple of times he hinted that Grendal Offshore's finances were precarious. Other times that his offshore bankers handled tainted money."

"Not what one expects from a man who is supposed to make the deal go smoothly," Gil said. "It appears Grendal entrusted Demming with too much knowledge of his affairs. Accompanied perhaps by not enough money."

"Who is this other firm you mentioned, Furbinger?"

I answered, "A junk-stock issuer."

"And you are certain of the connection? May I know how?"

"I'm certain they're in touch. I can't say how I know. A stock called Trionix may have brought them together. Somehow or other, Demming heard about Trionix and took the idea to Grendal, who bought shares."

He shook his head, not really caring. He was a tough old bird, able to put his pain aside. But he was exhausted, his inner eye distracted by an ugly domestic drama that must have been playing nonstop since yesterday. In his mind he would kill her a hundred times, kill himself a hundred. Kill Demming when other images lost their gut-twisting intensity. A bleak way to spend winter evenings.

"The way it looks," I said, "Furbinger and Demming will split about thirty-five million dollars from the stock's collapse."

"Godspeed to them," Parsons sighed.

Gil hoisted his overnight bag onto the bed, rummaged until he brought out a bottle of whiskey. As he unscrewed the cap, he said, "Ben, weren't you going to dinner? I'll be along in a while."

When he showed up it was almost eleven and the kitchen had closed. I took the lid off the steak I had ordered for him. He nodded and sat down. "Mr. Parsons's initial feeling was that we could let the market sort this out. He had, you see, been hoodwinked twice. He had been a fool about his wife. And he had reacted the way Demming wanted him to. We drank a little and he decided that he needn't reward people who've made a fool out of him."

"What else?"

"He mistrusts you. I vouched for your reliability. And I told him that vengeance is good for the soul. To prove that every old man could be maudlin, I told him about Dorrie and what I thought about doing after losing her. I told him that if he could take Furbinger's prize away, he would be in line for an honorary O.O.B."

"An O.O.B.?"

"Yes, a membership in the Order of Old Bastards. Freddy Laker, who you may recall founded a discount airline, was a charter member. Jimmy Goldsmith would be a good candidate. I have passed probation. Old bastards keep coming back. They come back swinging."

"I think you invented the order on the spot," I said.

"Not true, but thank you."

Old Uncle Gil. Marty had invited him in on our problems for more than emotional support.

35

I went upstairs and called home. On the fourth ring Marty answered, sounding breathless. "So how did it go?" she asked.

"All right. You're still up."

"Burning midnight oil. I had to run down to the phone."

"What are you working on?"

"You'll see, maybe. It's preliminary. I spent the afternoon with Barbara. She's settling into her tragic rôle pretty well."

"Why did you see her?"

"She wanted to talk about Jack. So I went. For that good deed I got my reward. She told me she was certain Jack had been in love with me. From afar, of course."

"It's possible."

"Come on, Ben! Loving anyone but his wife would have violated Jack's standards. He believed in obligations."

People had done worse, I thought. Worse than believe, worse than violate the belief.

"Well, he should have loved you," I said. "He had good taste otherwise."

"I'll sleep on that nice thought," she said. "By the way, Sol Lehrman phoned. He said not to call him after ten because he would be in bed."

183

* * *

We met Edgar Parsons at nine A.M. in his room. It was a sunny corner suite, probably the best the Roosevelt had to offer, with a sitting room cluttered with a sofa, chairs and a desk positioned between tall arched windows that looked straight across at the Connecticut National Bank. A sleepless night had left him haggard. His jaw worked monotonously as if savoring an unpleasant taste.

"Perhaps I should agree to do business with Grendal," Parsons said. "If the stock gets back to thirty, we'll have settled Furbinger and the other fellow's hash."

"It would take away their profit, but it wouldn't ruin them," I said. "Besides, Grendal's offer is poor. He could loot the company, default on his bonds, and you wouldn't end up with much."

"You've got something else in mind," Parsons said.

"I thought you might want to buy more shares of Dorchester."

He started to laugh, looked at me and cried, "In heaven's name why?"

"Every share that can be taken off the market is a share that Furbinger can't buy."

"He hasn't been buying, at least according to you. He's been selling short."

"That's right. But at some point he will have to buy to make good on those sales. If he can get stock easily and cheaply, he goes home fat and flush. If he has to pay up, he might suffer a little." I let him think about that, then added: "He might suffer a lot."

"You say he has sold short twenty percent of the company's shares," Parsons said.

I nodded and helped him along. "You and other directors own twenty-some percent. Lance Grendal holds twenty-five percent. The Dorchester Farmers Trust has about six percent, mostly for former Millinery employees. There isn't much loose stock around."

"Roscoe says we have a plethora of mom-and-pop holders with a couple of hundred shares each."

"If Bunny Furbinger had to cover a million shares in a hurry," I said, "how high do you think he would have to push the price taking in two hundred shares at a time?"

Parson couldn't manage a smile. But he asked, "How high?"

* * *

We flew back to LaGuardia and shared a taxi into town.

On the flight Gil had dozed, but in the cab he came alert. "We need to find an office," he said, "away from yours."

"What's wrong with my office?"

"It lacks mystique. Furbinger knows who you are and where you are. It would help us psychologically if he has an enemy he cannot identify."

I stopped back at our building, unsuitable as it was. For an hour I returned calls that couldn't be put off. Then I reassured myself by checking with Faulkner Wells that our trading account was indeed free of restrictions. Lisa Merchant said that Vince had been fired. Jack's old stocks were back in place. She did a bad job expressing sorrow over Jack, tiptoed around asking whether Vince had been involved in that. I told her he hadn't. "That's a relief," she said. "Do you mind if I tell some of his friends?"

"Go ahead. Lisa, did you ever get a call from someone named Mr. Jesse?"

She didn't recall one.

I told her not to be surprised if I sold some of Jack's old stocks and bought Dorchester Millinery. "Down here it looks pretty cheap," I said.

"Oh, God—you're not kidding, are you? No, you haven't got a sense of humor." She gave me the account balance, just over five hundred thousand dollars, including idle cash. Only fifteen percent of that was mine, but Jack had let me trade the account in his absence. I never had without asking what he thought of an idea. Now I would—until Rudy got wind of what I was up to. Money meant a lot to Furbinger and Mr. Jesse. To me it was a useful tool, a hammer of vengeance.

I had trouble getting past Miss Bell at Grendal's office. "He doesn't want to talk to you, Mr. McCarthy."

"Tell him I learned things in Connecticut last night that might interest him."

"He won't care," she said. She left and came back in a minute. "Would you like to drop by?"

185

Before leaving I checked the quote on Dorchester Millinery. It was 22¼.

Grendal was sallow. He sagged in a cane chair in a stream of balmy Caribbean air that washed silently from wall vents. He wore sandals, cutoffs and a white cotton beach shirt with pink embroidery that rippled in the trade wind. "Your bit about Trionix got me curious, McCarthy. So I asked one of my accountants where he'd heard the idea. He said Chet had mentioned it and told him it would rack up a few brownie points with me."

"Did you know that Chet was sleeping with Edgar Parsons's wife?"

He shrugged. "Chet was supposed to work the big shareholders, line them up for me. If it helped the cause to fuck a couple of wives, he was allowed to do that too."

"He arranged to have Mr. Parsons catch him at it."

"Lordy. I always figured Chet was too dumb to be disloyal. My guys up there say he left the hotel Sunday and hasn't been seen since."

Miss Bell came in unannounced and sat on the window ledge. A pearly slim leg swung from her kimono.

"I guess Parsons freaked," Grendal said.

"He should have freaked at your Chink paper," I said. I smiled apologetically at Miss Bell.

"Ain't life funny. Chet's daddy must've been a donkey."

Miss Bell investigated her nails. In response to Grendal's questioning glance, she said, "He's infantile."

"For flushing your deal, Demming probably gets a cut of Furbinger's profit," I said.

Grendal reached for a phone, asked for the latest. He winced and hung up. "Dorchester Millinery is twenty-one and a half."

"You must have bought a lot of stock above thirty," I said.

Grendal rolled his eyes. "B.J., honey, take your ears out of here. Rustle up some tea, chop-chop."

A month ago I wouldn't have been able to push him. Pushing people for what I wanted came reluctantly, with distaste. I was learning. I said, "Does she work for you or for your bankers?"

"You're an asshole. Bankers love me."

186

"Maybe they used to. But Demming and Furbinger must know that you're borrowed to the hilt. If you could raise more money, you could push the stock up and ruin their day."

"Ruin their fucking week," he muttered into his hand. He added mechanically, "I've got all the borrowing power I need."

"If they get away with this, there are going to be other people trying to take a bite of you. A lot of them. They'll circle you the way you circle weaklings like Roscoe Tullman. If losing the Dorchester deal doesn't bring you down, all the little nibblers will, a piece at a time. That prospect won't reassure your foreign bankers—whoever they are."

He got up, stretched, stared down at the wintry city. He kicked one brown leg, then the other. He was a tough guy, a professional ball-squeezer, being talked to as if he were a loser. It had to bother him. If a nobody from downtown thought he was a loser, the big boys might start getting suspicions. A spray of ice crackled against the window. The afternoon was alternating from rain to sleet.

"You're so interested in my bankers, someday I should introduce you," he said.

"No, thank you. One way you could keep them happy is not to end up looking like a chump. You could do that if Furbinger comes out a loser."

He tucked his hands into his back pockets. "If somebody else offered to buy out Dorchester Millinery . . . but we both know that won't happen. The deal worked for me only because I wouldn't pay cash for most of the company."

"You could buy more shares," I said.

"With my bank lines tapped out? Not that they are. . . ."

I said mildly, "You could hock the shares a second time with your brokers."

He stopped watching the weather and looked at me. He couldn't resist grinning. "Apart from the fact it would be illegal, why would I want to?"

I gave him the same rundown I had Parsons on Furbinger's exposure to being squeezed. "If the buying was strong at the outset tomorrow, the price might jump several points before Furbinger knows he's being attacked. A quick reversal of fortunes hurts morale."

"What's in it for you—besides helping out Lance Grendal?"

"I want Furbinger squeezed."

"Have you got buyers besides me lined up?"

"Yes. But there's a caveat. At the first sign you've dumped even a hundred shares on us, the buying will stop."

He sucked his yellowed teeth. "Not real gracious of you."

"You can join the fun or not. You can't sell into us."

"What you're planning sounds a lot like stock manipulation. But I guess us girls don't care about that?"

"I think the shares are a good value," I said. We both knew he was right.

I didn't see Miss Bell on the way out.

A timid young man who worked for an old friend of Gil's showed us the office at five o'clock. It was in a midtown building with most of the space taken up by small merchants and accountants. The Twenty-eighth Street subway station was a block away. The room held two folding chairs, one steel desk and an empty waist-high box marked with a moving company's logo. A battered Quotron terminal and a telex machine sat on the desk.

"Tell Moe it's perfect, Noah," Gil said. "Did he buy those Todd Shipyards bonds when I told him to?"

"I don't know, Mr. Norris."

Noah left, and Gil spread his hands. "We couldn't get a telephone for several days. We'll get by with the telex."

I told him I was impressed anyway. "How did you manage the telex?"

"I leaned hard on my broker at Yancey Queen and Fender. I told them that it had to be done this afternoon. I will buy the first five thousand Dorchester."

"Are you sure you want in on this?"

"Definitely." He saw my expression of worry and said, "This could be a profitable venture. That is my only reason for taking part."

"It might not work," I reminded him.

"What odds would you put on Grendal going for your scheme?"

I couldn't think up odds. If he had spent enough time stewing, bile would overcome fear of his bankers. He couldn't sell what he had. He couldn't stand by while the price was hammered down. His only solution was to buy more. If it weren't for his years in the sun, I would have been confident.

36

DORCHESTER Millinery opened at 21⅞ on two hundred shares. Ninety minutes later it traded at 29. More than thirty thousand shares had changed hands. Gil and I had bought only six thousand. Parsons and Grendal were intangible presences behind the numbers.

There was no sign that Bunny Furbinger was running for cover. Some of the stock we had bought around 24 might have been additional short sales from his firm.

Once past that level, the price rose briskly. When Wall Street smells a short squeeze, traders would join in the ruin of their mother.

"Kenneth Furbinger must feel his world is going awry," Gil said.

"He hasn't lost any money yet."

"No. But if I were he, I would be nervous about other things. He has seen Jimmy Doyle and Jack murdered, Vince DiMineo ruined. His silent partner must have more the aspect of a devil than an angel."

"Mr. Jesse has kept his other henchmen in the dark about his identity. Bunny may not know who he's working for."

Gil rubbed his nose. The old eyes watching the quote terminal were watery, the flesh pale. "I suppose that's possible—more cash in the mail with a note attached—but for more than two years?"

"Why not? His benefactor could phone Bunny when it suited

him. It would be just a detached voice. 'Do you have any favors for me?' Furbinger would understand he could provide useful information, or when Mr. Jesse wanted it, help wreck a firm like Markey Wahl or Canning & McCarthy."

"If you're right," Gil said, "Bunny's information that Grendal wanted to buy Dorchester Millinery would have been useful twice over. Mr. Jesse could construct a scandal to ruin Jack and you. And Furbinger could make money on the side if Demming wrecked the merger."

In the next hour the price of Dorchester Millinery fell all the way back to 27½. Some of the selling looked like shorts. But we were guessing. The office had neither windows nor wall decorations. Nothing distracting. We sat and watched changing amber numbers and tried to discern what the changes meant. At 27¼, a buyer appeared and took almost three thousand shares in pushing the stock up to 29. Grendal? Parsons? Some bored hedge-fund manager in Pittsburgh or Baltimore who had decided the stock could be goosed?

I tapped out a message on our telex, which printed out almost simultaneously two miles south on the trading desk of Faulkner Wells's Water Street office.

FAULKWEL.

BUY 500 DOR 29¼. BUY 500 DOR 29½.

CANMAC.

Ten minutes later the telex gave a muted burp and printed out a report that we had bought five hundred shares at 29½. I had gotten only half the order. The stock had moved away from me. The Quotron showed a buyer willing to pay 29¾ for eight hundred shares. The only offer to sell was at 30⅛ for three hundred shares. I put in an order to sell five hundred at 30 and got the report a few minutes later; somebody had taken the stock. The quote on the screen remained 29¾ to 30⅛.

When I bought the three hundred at 30⅛, Gil said, "You will never make your fortune selling at thirty and buying at thirty and one eighth."

The next trade was at 30¼. Gil tapped out a telex message to Yancey Queen and Fender, his broker.

YANQUEN.

BUY 500 DOR 30½.

NORRIS.

He gave the sellers something to think about. The only stock offered for sale, suddenly, was at 31½. Just one hundred shares. Traders watching the action were tightening their grip on any Dorchester Millinery they held, sensing high prices ahead.

In midafternoon the stock crossed 35, survived a blizzard of short-selling, and jumped ahead to 35⅝. The higher prices improved our buying power and Grendal's. We took in fifty-six hundred shares at 35⅞. Then, without our intervention, the price rolled ahead to 37½.

At two-thirty I left Gil in charge of the cubbyhole and took the train downtown. Gail was stern. "You've got a dozen messages, and Mr. Thatcher wants to talk to you. So does Mr. Finn, and so does Mr. Lehrman. It would be nice if somebody told me what's becoming of the firm."

I called back the clients, missed George and Sol, avoided Rudy.

When the market closed at four P.M., Dorchester Millinery had just traded at 38¾. An hour later the news wire carried out a paragraph citing the stock's remarkable surge of 17¼ points without takeover news. Market sources said a trader may have been caught with a large short position.

Peter Bagley caught me. "Have you been watching Dorchester Millinery?"

I admitted I had.

"What about the short rumor?"

"Our old friend Bunny Furbinger has the largest short position," I said. "I hear he's in trouble."

"Are you kidding me?"

"Check it out. It's all yours."

The more the word on Furbinger got around, the easier my job.

Gil arrived at the townhouse a minute ahead of me. At the bottom of the street, a taxi was pulling away, lights flashing, onto Hudson. "Good timing," I greeted him at the steps. I had walked from the West Fourth Street IND station. The night air was so cold and clear that bodegas and distant skyscrapers seemed equally dazzling.

"Describe Bongo Harris," Gil said, puncturing my mood.

"Reddish hair, lumpy face, sallow, large nose, big hands, six foot—"

"He may have been waiting in front of the next building when I drove up. The man I saw wore a knit cap and a running suit."

"Where did he go?"

"Over to Bleecker."

We walked east to the corner, split up and circled the block to the north and south, met in front of the house. I hurried upstairs.

She met us with hugs, a kiss on the cheek for Gil, one full on the lips for me. "I was watching and you walked off."

Gil's hand lingered on her shoulder. "One of Mr. Jesse's Dobermans is prowling. You'll keep your eyes open?"

"Of course. Don't worry."

He smiled and nodded. "Of course."

She took his coat, threw it over the sofa back. "You two look ineffably smug. Is it working?"

"So far. If we don't stumble in the next few days, we've even made a few dollars. Ben said you were interviewing for a commission."

"I got it."

"So prosperity is contagious."

She didn't answer for a moment. Then a secret smile widened. "I've landed two jobs, actually."

"What's the other one?"

"I can't tell you." She danced into the kitchen, at least as self-satisfied as we were.

Looking after her fondly, Gil called, "About Mr. Jesse's creatures—you know I wouldn't hector you. . . ."

She appeared with a salad bowl, pointed him sternly to the dining room table. "I told you not to worry," she said.

37

TWICE in Thursday's first ninety minutes, trading in Dorchester Millinery stalled as buyers soaked up the paltry amount of stock for sale.

When the exchange asked Dorchester's management whether some corporate development was about to be announced, Roscoe Tullman's reply was crisp and affronted: "We have not been formally contacted by any new party about the acquisition of this company."

Gil shook his head, pretending bewilderment. "I don't remember bribing Tullman to say it just right. That 'formally' and 'new' will keep speculation buzzing that something is going on."

He was right. When the specialist resumed trading, DOR was 40¼.

Another halt came ten minutes later, and after it the stock jumped to 44. Gil and I watched the numbers roll across the screen like a body count in an imaginary war.

. . . DOR 44¼ . . . 5,000 DOR 44⅝ . . . 25,000 DOR 44⅞ . . .

Dorchester Millinery touched 46 an hour later, and Gil sold five thousand shares he had bought the day before at 30. I told Faulkner Wells to sell half of Canning & McCarthy's thirty thousand shares of Dorchester. The account had made almost eight hundred thousand dollars. When Rudy found out, I hoped the profit would soften his indignation.

Sol Lehrman met me at the members door of the exchange. We walked in a light rain toward South Street. He said, "You're in on this somehow, Ben. Furbinger was still shorting, naked, this morning. So were others. But after that last halt, some people on the floor started putting numbers together. They figured that something like six million shares have been sold short. That's almost a third of the company's issued stock. This afternoon Furbinger Associates used another broker to try to buy back stock, but you can't keep that kind of thing secret."

"How much did he buy?"

"Less than twenty thousand. Every couple thousand pushed the price up another half-point. He's like a man with his feet tied to his neck sitting in front of a train. If he gets up to run he chokes himself. If he stays put he gets run over."

"It may not matter," I said. "His losses must exceed his firm's net worth."

Sol's expression wasn't altogether friendly. "If you ever decide you're angry at me, give me a chance to set it right before killing me."

"Has there been any sign of Grendal selling?" That was my main worry, that Grendal would double-cross us.

"Dribs and drabs from one broker he uses. Not much."

We stopped in Crazy Joe's for coffee. Sol chatted amiably about his horses. He had made enough in Troubadour Industries to buy his wife a hot car and add a nag to his stable. He thought the pressure of trading on the floor was killing him. He ran down. "I was trying to get you the other day. I thought you might want to know that Furbinger had company in selling Dorchester short. One of the big houses came in Tuesday and Wednesday, almost as heavily as Furbinger."

"They probably heard that the takeover was dead."

"Yeah. It's not the kind of firm you normally see playing with Furbinger Associates."

"Which firm?"

He told me.

I didn't answer.

He remembered he had a beef going with one of the horse trainers who otherwise would be a good buying agent. I made perfunctory noises. Sol gave a pitch for the investment qualities of American saddlebreds.

It wasn't proof, I thought numbly. The name wasn't proof.

They could have sold short for a dozen reasons. For a client. On a trader's hunch.

A lot of reasons.

I thought of Jack's last message. *Never trust a friend*.

If you know the truth, I thought, *it sets you free*. And makes you sick at heart. Perhaps it had made Jack sick enough to go confront the friend who had betrayed him.

"Which firm?" I had asked Sol.

And he had told me.

"Brooker Finn," Sol said.

He had been such a good friend to Jack. Such a good friend, George Finn.

Somebody else at the firm, I thought.

A vice chairman, a head trader, a rogue broker.

Eyes closed, I listened to a piping voice, shrunken by distance and thinned by dense cold air. *"Get Ben up to the house."*

A voice of a friend, stunned by freezing water, filled with fear, exhausted—I had thought.

Instead, the voice of an enemy, terrified after the lethal trick had failed. He must have dreaded the accusation that his clumsy thrashing had a deadly purpose.

"Get Ben up to the house."

Shrill, bleating, unrecognizable. Like another voice that had been mechanically distorted.

"How dare you defy me!"

Opening my eyes, I stared at Sol's long face. "Are you all right?" he asked.

"It's been a long day," I said.

"How dare you defy me! How dare you!"

George Finn dominated the stock exchange disciplinary commit-

196

tee. An ideal place for learning about the lapses of Vince DiMineo. Or for steering an inquiry into Markey Wahl or Canning & McCarthy. The fact that Brooker Finn had joined Furbinger in shorting Dorchester was proof of nothing—at least not the kind of proof that the exchange would accept. Nor would that coincidence be strong enough for federal regulators to act. If I made an accusation, George Finn could voice pity and dismay over a friend's nervous collapse. "I'm certain that young Benjamin will soon come to his senses. His friends wish him a speedy recovery."

There might be tracks he had left, fragments that could be tied together. But would anyone look for the fragments that pointed to an eminence of the stock exchange?

It was barely six-thirty when I got home, to an apartment empty and desolate-feeling. She had made a decision, I thought, afraid of what it might be. She wasn't one to run from conflict, but she might run from causing misery. What could be worse for an Irish prude, she would ask herself, than a restless wife?

Losing the wife.

I went into the kitchen planning to phone Gil.

A large rectangle of sketch paper was suspended by grinning-cat magnets on the refrigerator door. A message printed neatly across the top announced:

COULDN'T KEEP GOOD NEWS SECRET
FIRST SITTING TONIGHT

Below was a sketch. It was a caricature of a massive face with tiny features, round glasses, a tweed hat, a benign and slightly puzzled smile. She had done him up in a shooting jacket with a bird hanging from one pocket.

A sketch of tonight's subject, George Finn.

38

WHERE would they be? Not Finn's office. He had a house or an apartment somewhere in the city, but I had no idea where. Jack probably had visited.

I had been insane to think he would feel safe. The brutality of the attacks betrayed rage and fear, feeding each other.

I turned my back on the drawing, opened the utility cabinet and pulled out the phone book. The pages held a half-dozen George Finns scattered around Manhattan, several times as many G Finns. A largely hopeless task, even if my man was among them. Wasted time if his number was unlisted.

Sol Lehrman's friendship wouldn't extend to finding the home addresses of exchange governors.

Barbara Canning might have it. When I rang the apartment she answered immediately. "Of course we've gotten together. George admired Jack tremendously, you know."

"I need his address and telephone number."

"Benny, I couldn't give you that without George's permission. I know he invited you to his farm, but you shouldn't presume on Mr. Finn's kindness."

I stared at nothing, trying to decide what to say.

She offered, "I suppose I could ask George whether—"

"No."

"I beg your pardon?"

I couldn't trust her with the truth, couldn't risk her calling Finn. I took a deep breath, chuckled in a way that I hoped was convincing. "It would spoil the surprise. Rudy thought that a case of good brandy from the firm would be a suitable thank-you for his hospitality."

"Oh, well, I had been thinking of sending a gift of my own. But it's so difficult deciding what might be right for a bachelor. . . ." She went away, embarrassment concealed in businesslike heel clicks, and came back with an address in the East Seventies.

I put down the handset, prayed that she could resist phoning him to give away our secret.

Would Finn assume that Marty had kept their secret? If he asked her casually, she would laugh and confess. He would be sure to ask.

That she had kept the appointment would tell him that I didn't know he had been selling Dorchester short. Within a day or two, the name Brooker Finn & Company would reach me. Buyers and sellers were notoriously curious about who is playing the opposite side of the street. Gossip would find me even if I didn't seek it, like water leaking from a dozen buckets.

He would know that, would prepare a way to remove that threat.

I left the lights on, went downstairs, waited in the vestibule for several minutes watching the frozen sidewalks, the doorways of other buildings. Bongo would be somewhere, or another dockworker's helper. Almost certainly tonight.

Across the street and a few doors up, a red sports car sat against the curb with its lights off and the engine running. The windows were steamed. Two shadows moved in the front seats. If I left the house at the right time, when another vehicle was coming up the narrow street so the sports car couldn't back up, they would have to scramble after me on foot.

The exhaust from the sports car sputtered and quit. Doors opened and two men got out. Both wore leather jackets and tweed caps. One joined the other on the sidewalk, draped an arm over his shoulder, and they walked toward Bleecker.

I looked toward Hudson Street. No plumes of exhaust betrayed another occupied car. But I waited. Eventually a momentary flicker of red light glowed on the bumper and chrome grille of a car midway down the block. Somebody in the van just ahead, half hidden by a tree, had touched a brake pedal.

The van's occupant was bored and cold, I supposed, possibly nervous as well. From the van he, or they, could see the lighted apartment windows and feel confident the quarry was still in the nest.

If I went out the door fast, I could be over to Bleecker before anyone in the van got moving. With luck and a taxicab, I would be uptown in fifteen minutes.

Provided the van was where my trouble waited.

I could call the police, hope to reach Teeger. Then hope he would send someone because I didn't like the looks of the van. Time-consuming in any case. Dangerous if he sensed there was more going on and got me to confide about Finn. . . .

I went back into the hallway. Under the stairway was a door to the basement. The apartment owners had different sections cordoned off for storage. I found the right key, unlocked the door, then sprinted back upstairs to the apartment.

Timing was everything. How long did it take the police to respond to the average emergency call in the neighborhood? How long would it take them tonight?

Next problem. How long would it take my watchdogs to respond to an invitation to come upstairs?

When you had two variables, neither predictable, there was no point trying to be scientific. I switched off the apartment lights, from the back rooms to the front, and stood beside the phone counting.

. . . thousand forty-eight, thousand forty-nine . . .

They might not have an eye on the windows every moment. Fifteen seconds could pass before Bongo or a friend noticed that lights were going out. Thirty seconds as they waited patiently for me to appear at the front door. Thirty seconds more of deepening frowns. Thoughts that maybe there was a back exit they didn't know about.

Thirty seconds leaving the van and walking a half block.

I dialed 911 and said breathlessly, "There's a burglary in progress in my building." I described Bongo, a dark blue van, gave the house number and said it was the top apartment—

. . . thousand eighty-one, thousand eighty-two . . .

I closed the door behind me, but didn't turn the lock. When I got to the bottom of the second flight of stairs, nobody had reached the front steps or vestibule. I spun around the stairway, stepped through the basement doorway.

The front door opened an instant later. I stood in the blackness as two pairs of feet tromped to the stairs, climbed past my head. It would take them a couple of minutes to determine that the apartment was empty. If the police arrived soon, I hoped I wasn't drawing them into a shootout.

I pushed open the door and saw Bongo standing at the foot of the stairs, looking up. He wore a blue pea coat and a knit cap. His bare pink hands held a gun with two barrels cut off just beyond the stock. Instead of two sets of feet going upstairs, there had been only one.

The door's movement caught his eye.

He looked at me with gleeful smugness, swung down the muzzle of the shotgun. He called out, "Luis!"

I pulled back, and he followed.

He came through the doorway a little too eagerly. Flattened against the wall, I grabbed the snubbed barrel and yanked. Though it wasn't a very deep basement, the stairs were notoriously steep. His toe snagged one step midway down and he began a somersault. He tried to break his fall without letting go of the weapon. He hit the concrete floor and the shotgun under him discharged.

I groped for the light switch. Bongo lay with an arm doubled under him, his forehead smeared with blood. I went down, pried the shotgun loose. The pellets had hammered off into God knew what basement treasures.

Luis had gotten halfway down the basement steps in silence when I looked around. He was dressed all in black, with shoulder-length hair, a sparse growth of beard like pencil scratches on his chin, an olive complexion, a tight and determined expression. His left hand held a long knife inconspicuously beside his leg.

I aimed the shotgun at his belly.

He stopped with a tennis-shoed foot in the air. He took in Bongo. "Did you kill him?"

"Come on down and see."

He backed up instead, graceful as a panther. He made no noise in the hall. The front door clicked.

I followed. Rhoda Heinbach came out of her apartment in dungarees and a frazzled sweater and looked at me as if hoping I hadn't chosen tonight for a murderous rampage.

"We have a burglar downstairs," I said. "Is Oscar home?"

He came to the door and I handed him the shotgun. "One barrel is loaded. The police are on their way."

"I thought the boiler had exploded. Did you shoot someone?"

"He fell down the stairs."

"A burglar," Rhoda said.

"Maybe we should lock the basement door until the police come," Oscar suggested. "Unless you shot him?"

I locked the door. When I started out the front, Rhoda said, "Aren't you waiting for the police?"

"There were two of them. I'm going to look for the second. Could I borrow your car?" It was as brazen a lie as I had told in an hour. Luis was the last person I wanted to run into, and a policeman was next to the last.

It was a nice neighborhood. Small apartment buildings bumping shoulders with large old townhouses, a line of sandstone broken by darkened brick. I'd parked the Heinbachs' car on Second Avenue beside a restaurant. I walked along a stretch of three-foot fence that had probably been tall enough a century ago to keep the world at bay. Most of the lower-story windows now were decorated with iron bars.

I was just in the neighborhood, George, dropped by because my wife can't keep a secret. So how is the sitting going?

A small Oriental woman opened the door and regarded me through a metal gate. "Mr. Finn not home," she said.

"I was supposed to meet Mr. Finn and my wife here. I'm Ben McCarthy."

202

Silently she climbed a little hill of reluctance. "They went to country."

I held my breath. "That's a long trip. Mrs. McCarthy usually doesn't like to travel."

"Oh, she laughing!"

He was still getting by on charm, holding out the prospect of a breakthrough commission. *The country house is where I feel most at home, Martha. Could it be the best setting for a portrait?*

Had she told George about giving away their secret?

I smiled. The housekeeper didn't.

"Will you talk to Mr. Finn tonight?" I asked. "Does he call for messages?"

"He have answering service. He call them."

39

IT began snowing before I passed Wilton. The wipers kept the windshield of Rhoda's old Honda clear, but off the main highway the road was hard to follow. At the base of a mountain I crept through a hamlet that had snuggled in for the night. The only lights shone at a volunteer fire station as I left the village. A couple of furrows cut the snow ahead.

When I came over a hill ten minutes later and crossed a stone bridge, Finn's country house had to be just ahead. I slowed to five miles an hour. The roads were empty. Lights from farmhouses had been infrequent and distant. I switched off the headlights and inched down the next quarter mile.

The approach to the house was long blurred by snow. I pulled the car off the road, beside the gate that led to Finn's horse barn. Wondering if the old retainer had given the mares an extra blanket for the night, I climbed out of the car.

The snow was several inches deep, drifting over hollows, still falling heavy and wet. After plodding ten yards, I was puffing.

A hundred feet from the house, I left the driveway and circled through an overgrown pasture. At a wire fence, climbing with a grip on a shaky post, I wished for gloves, boots, and Bongo's weapon.

Sounds were muffled: my stumbling toward the side of the house,

204

the crackle of brush beneath the snow. When I fell, my grunts were smothered in frozen breath. I got up and went another twenty feet before hearing the car, its engine whining and tires buzzing on a small grade.

Finn's Bronco nestled under snow a few yards from the front door. The car worming up the driveway flashed its high beams. I ducked instinctively. The driver was lucky if he could see ten feet.

The visitor stopped behind the Bronco as I reached the trellis-clad west wall.

The car's headlights stayed on, and a horn bleated.

The front door of the house sighed open. George Finn stepped out wearing a bulky sweater. The driver stumbled out of his car and waded up to Finn, arms gesturing back toward the road. The newcomer's broad-brimmed tan hat looked ridiculous, as did the tightly belted trenchcoat. Neither was built for the squat proportions of the little man whose face peeked from under the brim.

Bunny Furbinger knew Mr. Jesse better than the other servants had.

Furbinger was describing something alarming encountered behind him. I knew what. He had passed a strange car, windshield just dusted with snow, hood steaming.

Finn's head turned in a slow arc. He took off his heavy glasses and squinted uselessly into the hushed night. Bunny's whole body turned as he followed the line of inspection. Finn put on his glasses and retreated indoors.

He was back in less than a minute—a long time for Bunny, an impatient time for me. When Finn reappeared, it was obvious that he and his henchmen had the same dreary turn of mind. He held a pump-action shotgun under each arm. He passed the left weapon to Bunny, sent him slogging down the driveway in his city shoes.

George stood on the front step, seeming to enjoy the snowfall.

I backed along the wall, peered through the first window. Marty sat with a glass of port or something else a well-mannered host would provide, slumped in an old Hitchcock chair with her feet stretched toward a fireplace.

I thought of Jack's bare feet in the slatted garage and felt my teeth clench.

She seemed comfortable and unconcerned. I wondered what Finn had told her. *Rumors of a fox in the neighborhood, my dear.*

Through the fogged glass, with light inside and night outside, she wouldn't see who tapped on the window. She might call George.

I tramped the rest of the way around to the back. George might come looking for footprints. In that case he would be certain that the car's presence wasn't innocent. He was probably certain already.

The boom came from a long way off, followed by a second and third. Either Bunny was shooting at ghosts or Rhoda Heinbach's car was getting his attention.

I tried the back door, which was locked.

I returned to my window.

Finn had stepped inside, was shrugging on a field jacket. He pulled a mitten onto his left hand, left the other bare. Smiled at Marty. God knew what jolly line he offered. *This won't take a minute. Would you like to phone your husband?*

If Bunny came back and he and George circled the house in opposite directions, especially if they circled wide, the pincers could catch their quarry.

I moved away from the window, then ran straight for the pasture. The wire fence stretched parallel to the house. From a dozen yards south, I could see the front door and the top of the driveway. Finn had switched off the outdoor light and was standing still near a barren wisteria trunk. Whether he was trying to spot movement through the wavering snow or was trying to be invisible I couldn't tell. He had donned a floppy hat and knee-high boots in addition to the heavy jacket and mitten.

My topcoat felt flimsy.

A short, forlorn figure struggled up to the house. The tracks that his car had left had almost vanished, and the shape of the driveway itself was disappearing. If Bunny and Finn dallied, my own tracks might be lost. In just a few minutes they would be hard to follow in the dark.

If the pursuit reached this spot, the scar would be obvious. I lay almost flat, propped on elbows, collecting a good snow cover on the back.

They conferred, George bending forward. Anybody watching would have thought of two gentlemen planning a sport hunt.

They set out and found the tracks near the window. A muddled path led to the rear of the house and came back. They followed the tracks and found that the visitor had stopped outside the back door.

I got off my belly and retreated. The pasture rose in an easy slope to the left. After fifty or so yards, a gray scrim of trees appeared. It turned out to be little more than a windbreak between properties, three or four yards deep. Around the trunks crusts of pine needles had gotten only touches of snow. Without the deep footprints to guide them, Bunny and George would have a harder time pressing the hunt through here.

If I stayed among the trees, leaving no evidence, they could only be certain that the tracks didn't appear where the field resumed. The quarry could have veered left, toward deeper woods, or right, to meet the road.

Where the land hadn't been cleared, boulders and clumps of broken rock still poked from the ground. Between the rocks were depressions filled with pine needles and leaves. The air possessed greater clarity than in the field.

Once they inspected the snow on the other side of the windbreak, they would know I had headed for the road. They would rush ahead to intercept me.

I would be fifty feet behind them, toward the thickening band of forest.

A minute later they reached the edge of the trees a hundred feet north of me. On the forest side, where a sweep to the road would drive me ahead. My unfeeling fingers touched the bark of a large, tilted hemlock. The two hunters went on to scan the next field. I crouched and tried to be invisible.

207

40

I was huddled in a cluster of glacial stones when they stumbled across me. Hiding had seemed a better gamble than running. If they overlooked me as they headed for the road, I could backtrack to the house. In the dark they should have passed by.

Worst of luck that Bunny crossed a few feet from me and noticed that the boulder looked like a doubled-up man with a coat over his head.

He screamed in surprise.

When my head came up, he stumbled back, voice screeching up the register. "He's here! Here!"

Finn was only a few steps away. He clucked when he saw me. "Yes, so he is. What are you going to do about it?"

Bunny looked at the shotgun in his hands, tried to bring the weapon level. "We should kill him."

"We should. Go ahead."

"Here? Now?"

"Why have we been pursuing him, Kenneth?"

Bunny made another effort to steel himself. He tried pointing the gun while looking away, and the muzzle veered. He peeked and saw that he was aiming at a boulder two feet to my right. It was too dark to read his expression. He jerked his head at Finn. "You go ahead."

Finn nodded. "It would be easier if the target were moving. Or resisting. More like a game." He looked at me. "Well, we'll have to manage something. You've been a dreadful nuisance, Benjamin. A lot of money is at stake, more than you can imagine."

"You managed with Jack," I said.

"It was necessary to improvise," he said, perhaps aware of his matter-of-fact sadism. "I believe we'll find the road down this way."

We crossed a stone wall and assumed that the clear stretch between overhanging trees was the road. The ruts left by our cars had vanished. The air was clear and empty. The temperature was dropping.

When we passed Rhoda Heinbach's battered little car—windshield blown out, front tires in shreds—I guessed what Finn had in mind. We waded through knee-deep snow to the barn. The building was electrified. George snapped on an overhead light. A small structure, good for two mares and high-stacked bales of hay and straw. Kept from freezing on the coldest nights by a couple of fan-driven electric heaters with glowing orange wires, which hummed on a cinder block ledge away from the straw-bedded floor.

The barn felt warm after an hour in the open. But in fact the corner farthest from the horse stalls, where George nudged me, was little warmer than outside and our breath escaped in white gouts.

George came back from a workbench holding a coil of bare wire. He pointed the gun at my middle and said, "Kenneth, help Ben remove his overcoat."

Bunny laid his weapon on the floor. He tugged at the coat buttons.

I did nothing to help. He yanked first one hand from a pocket, then the other, pulled the sleeves down. He began enjoying himself and became rougher. He threw the topcoat onto a straw bale.

The suit coat followed.

"Very good," George said. "Throw it over there. Now the shoes. It's all right if you knock him down if he doesn't cooperate."

Bunny tried a two-handed push but I stayed on my feet. I backed a few steps, hoping vaguely to get the little fat man between myself and George's shotgun.

"Never mind," George said quickly. He tossed the roll of wire to Bunny. "Would you permit Kenneth to tie your hands, Benjamin?

So that I needn't shoot you right now? Tie in front of him, Kenneth."

Bunny's silly hat had come off, and yellow hair matted his forehead. His lips and cheeks near my chest were rosy. He said, "Hold out your hands."

I did. He looped several quick turns of bright wire around one wrist, then pulled my hands together.

George's voice was patient. "Make sure it's tight, Kenneth."

When he was done, it was tight.

"Behind you," George said, "on the hook—get the rope. Put an end of that between his wrists. Make several knots."

Bunny took the coiled rope off the wall, forced a loop between my palms. There were beams overhead at roughly three-foot intervals, big hand-hewn six-by-tens. Bunny cast the line over a beam. George had to lay down his weapon and help to hoist my weight off the floor.

It was a matter of having my arms and shoulders torn loose. When my swinging feet cleared the straw by six inches, George tied the rope to a tool hook on the wall. He breathed heavily. "Now, Kenneth, remove his shoes and socks."

I tried to kick, but he dodged and grabbed my legs. He fumbled. The laces were caked with ice. He finally tore at them with a pair of wire snips. He pulled the shoes free, peeled the socks off. He flung the shoes across the barn. The socks fluttered down in midflight. He stared up at me. His eyes seemed to have found sensual pleasure in bare feet. "You're not so smug now. Not like when you thought you could fuck me."

He waited for an answer.

I said, "I did fuck you."

My belly was the easiest target for him to hit. He swung twice, which set me turning like a slow top.

As I came around, George stood with the guns propped on his shoulder. Behind the glasses, his shrunken eyes blinked quickly. He said, "Why did it matter so much to you, Benjamin?"

The jovial boom was out of his voice. That had been a fraud too.

I noticed with creeping dismay, that I no longer could feel my hands. I said, "What did Jack know about you?"

210

His lips pursed. He shrugged. "He found out—I don't know how—that I had pressed the stock exchange to investigate a man named Noble Wahl. He thought it strange as I was a friend of Noble's. A few months ago he learned that indirectly Brooker Finn had taken over much of Noble's business. Your partner could not believe his own suspicions."

"Weren't the governors of the exchange suspicious?"

"They believed that I was doing my duty in seeking Noble Wahl's expulsion. Taking over his client list was an act of charity, which maintained continuity for Noble's customers. Honor and convenience often appear to march hand in hand. Don't you agree?"

I didn't answer.

He came close. "Aren't you going to tell me that I needn't harm your wife?"

My mouth barely moved. "You needn't."

"She came to the door and saw Kenneth. She didn't recognize him. But someday she might, and our relationship must be confidential."

He turned to Furbinger. "Open his shirt."

Bunny obeyed with relish.

They left.

On the way out, George flicked off the light.

I hung in the darkness and froze.

There was nothing else to do. Not for a while. I didn't know how long.

It was Bunny who came back. A half-hour later. An hour.

He stayed only a moment. The hanging man's head was down, his fingers were purple, his feet were white. He was shivering uncontrollably. Struck across the knees with a gun barrel, he responded sluggishly.

A ghastly sight, a dying man. Bunny's feet scraped away. His voice was a denying whimper. "You had it coming, you bastard." The barn door closed.

He had left the light on, which helped marginally.

Hurt marginally too. When I looked up, the sight of the dead hands set off a wave of despair. The damage had to be permanent.

211

The beam was about two feet above the hands.

I could see a way, had seen it as soon as they flung the rope overhead. Seeing didn't make it possible. Being stripped of my topcoat and jacket helped, because they would have restricted movement.

I tried lifting my legs. Gravity was a harsh opponent.

I tried talking myself into it. The barn was a high school in Utica and my hands held gymnasium rings. No matter that the hands wouldn't work. Arm muscles would do the lifting. Shoulders and head would swing back to shift the center of gravity, legs cantilever up. When it worked right, you hung upside down from the rings.

It was no great trick in theory. Every reasonably nimble seventeen-year-old could manage it. But the seventeen-year-old had hours to practice, and had useful hands gripping two rings to balance his weight, and didn't work in a torn shirt in a thirty-degree barn.

If I could lock my ankles over the top of the beam, get the weight off the rope, there was a chance. I brought my feet up. When my knees got to waist level, the center of gravity was still in the hips. No leverage, no cantilever, just weight that I couldn't hold aloft. I let go with a gasp.

Hung blinded by tears. The hands might be dead, but the wrists were agony. I couldn't do that again.

Couldn't think of an alternative.

The second try was a bust too, but my left heel brushed the rope.

On the third attempt I had a better notion of balance and a desperate indifference to discomfort. I brought my legs up hard. Both heels locked around the rope. Sliding upward, the frozen toes bumped what had to be the joist.

Hanging upside down in a fetal ball was one accomplishment. More doubtful was defying gravity long enough to slide my feet upward on either side of the rough beam.

Locked around the rope, my ankles stored a lot of energy from gravity. When the feet left the rope to shinny up the joist, it would be like undoing a spring clip. I tried crab-walking the heels up the joist. With feet that could feel, it might have worked. If I hadn't been shaking from chill, it might have worked. When the inevitable happened, it cost my feet a bit of skin that I barely felt scraping away. The jolt as my legs swung down knocked the breath from cold lungs.

I closed my eyes, gasping and sobbing.

Came to with a moment's disbelief. Reality hadn't changed, and consciousness hadn't rejected ownership of the abused flesh. The mind said, *Yes, this is me.* I hadn't dreamt I was hanging from the rafter or seen some square-jawed hero do it in a movie. That was too bad. Dying was a dreary reality.

There was nothing in particular I should have taken care of.

I had chased down the most striking girl I had ever met, caught her and loved her. . . .

Turned her over to George.

The barn was colder. Looking up, I saw that the door was open. A compact figure stood in the doorway, just out of the light. Staring at me. God knew for how long.

My movement stirred him. He looked behind.

"Don't go," I croaked.

He didn't answer. He stepped inside. Well bundled against the frigid midnight air, a quilted jacket, felt cap with ear flaps, plaid muffler, wool pants and knee-high gum boots. A small countryman. I barely recognized him. George's old retainer.

"What's your name?" I said.

"Gibson." He stared up at me. "Got up for a piss and saw the light. Thought the horses might be sick."

He had slogged through the snow to check. He squinted. "You—you're the boy that saved Mr. Finn."

"Get me down. Please."

He couldn't untie the knot at the tool hook. He opened a pocket knife, held the rope with one hand, sawed through. The gnarled fist's grip was powerful. He lowered me gently, put a shoulder under my arm, let the rope go.

"Over by the heaters?" I said.

"How—uh—long?"

"What time is it?"

"'Bout two." He sat me down on the floor near one of the mares, brought the electric heaters down to ground level.

"A couple of hours. Can you get the rope and wire off?"

He surveyed my hands with distaste. "The rope, sure enough. The wire—I'm no doctor. You have to take a tourniquet off slow."

"Get it off now. It can't be any worse."

He carved through the knot, brought the snips from the floor where Bunny had thrown them and went to work on the wire. "Least you wasn't hanging by the wire," he said conversationally. "Ain't deep. Your feet look frostbit."

Good news indeed. He followed my directions and found both the suitcoat and topcoat, my shoes and socks. I huddled under the garments as my feet thawed. The hands felt like blocks of ice.

Gibson squatted beside the heater. The mares stirred. "Who done this?"

"A man named Furbinger. He's holding Mr. Finn hostage."

"Goddamn."

"Do you have a phone?"

He shook his head, then suggested, "There's a car right up on the road—no windshield."

"That was mine. Where is the nearest place with a phone?"

"Besides the house . . . couple miles toward the village. I could walk."

"If you saddled the horses, we could ride." It would take hours to get there and back . . . too long.

He set about it with energy. The mares seemed puzzled as blankets and saddles appeared. But they were placid old girls, ready for whatever their friend wanted. Gibson paused in fitting a bridle. "Are you sure about this? How are you going to hold the rein?"

I tried to flex my hands. Got a quiver, accompanied by an electric jolt that took my breath away. "No problem."

He snorted. He turned off the heaters, hunted in vain for a stray pair of utility gloves before stripping off the old leather pair he wore. He ignored my protest, which was feeble, and slid the gloves gently over the awakening flesh. "You get on Gigi. She's tamest."

Gibson helped me onto the saddle. The mare looked around with sleepy eyes, shook her head.

214

"Give me the wire snips," I said. Gibson handed them up without question, led both horses to the barn door.

He didn't mount until he had walked almost to the road. Then he climbed up, with a minimum of fuss, stubby legs barely reaching the stirrups. He handed me a rein. "You don't need to tug. She'll follow me."

We followed for all of fifty yards. Then I pulled the reins up clumsily, and she stopped. When the snorting fell behind, Gibson looked back. Breath billowing, he called, "Ye all right?"

"One of us needs to keep an eye on Mr. Finn. You know where to go for help and I don't, so it's got to be me."

He considered that. "Guess we wouldn't want any bastard to haul Mr. Finn away." He nodded brusquely, rode off on his mission.

I climbed down and led the chestnut down the culvert and up to the edge of the pasture. The barrier here was a dry stone wall, tangled with brush, tumbled down in spots, all those details hidden and made treacherous by the snow. We walked until we came to a spot where the hump seemed lower. I wrapped the rein around my left wrist and led her across a faltering step at a time.

The next fence, at the far side of the pasture, was made of wire strung between posts. I tied the mare to a section and pulled out the snips. I knelt in the snow. Through the fence I could see the rear and south side of Finn's house. We were only a dozen yards from the back door. The first floor was all lighted. So, in unnerving clarity, was the field. I fumbled the snips with both hands. The snap of the wire giving way sounded like a cracking tree branch.

My teeth rattled, almost as loud.

I cut the wire and went through, trying not to run.

In the living room Bunny sat with a shotgun across his knees. I couldn't see George but could hear him, loud and boastful. Marty was on the battered sofa, elbows on her knees, bare feet on the floor. Her head was forward, face hidden. I wondered about their plan. A barefoot walk in the snow would be consistent.

Two men, two shotguns.

I turned away and trudged back to the fence. Left the old mare tied. Forced speed from legs that didn't want to move at all. Gasped at every step like an old man at the end of a marathon.

215

The trek to the barn seemed to take forever.

I plugged in the heaters and turned them high. Off the tool rack I lifted down a pitchfork. Kicking loosened a bale of straw until I could work it with the pitchfork. The straw smelled moldy and damp on the outside, dry and summery inside. I rolled two bales against the north wall, scattered the loose dry straw over them. No lumber lay at hand, but the lid of a feed bin was held by rusted screws that came loose under my hammering. I split the planks with a heel, stacked them in a teepee over the straw. Hunted furiously for kerosene, but Gibson kept a safe barn. A gallon can of wood preservative held a few cups of liquid that I emptied over the straw.

A dampened twist, thrust through the grille of the nearer heater, ignited with a flash.

I dropped it onto the mound I had built.

A shattering, accusatory snort greeted my return to the fence. I set the pitchfork against the post, stroked the animal's neck. Her saddle caught small dark flickers of red from across the road.

My vantage wasn't nearly as good as George's living room. As the flames rose, I heard his front door open.

George Finn bolted into the driveway, struggling with a parka. He waded past the parked cars, gestured at the plump figure that stumbled after him. The message was clear: go back to the house.

I slipped through the cut fence.

When I rounded the front of the house, Bunny stood in the doorway. He held the shotgun at present arms. With the barn burning and George gone, the last thing he expected was the hanging man coming to get him. When the pitchfork tines touched his neck, Bunny shrieked. He jumped back and struck the doorjamb.

He started to point the gun. I pushed the tines gently against his chest and his motion froze.

"Put it down."

He let the gun drop.

"Stay here." I picked up the shotgun, walked past him down the short hall to the living room. Marty looked up.

"You're keeping bad company," I said.

She flew off the couch, face alight, and hit me with the force of a young lion. "Oh, Ben!"

Holding a shotgun in one weak grip, a pitchfork in the other, I still managed to hug her. "Get your coat. And boots if you can find a pair."

Bunny was on the front step, looking tempted by the cars. He backed away as I flung the pitchfork into the snow.

I looked inside George's Bronco, then into Bunny's runabout. Neither had keys in the ignition lock. He saw what I was doing and hands dived like panicked rodents. He pulled a key ring from one pocket, flung it toward the field and smiled vengefully.

I lifted the shotgun and fired. The windshield of the Bronco disappeared. I killed a front tire, then gave Bunny's car similarly disabling treatment.

Marty came out the door, wearing her shearling coat and zippered boots.

Bunny pedaled backward, but she caught him. He raised his hands feebly. She shook him like a child, drew back a fist, her teeth clenched, her eyes wide, dark hair billowing—a formidable sight. He collapsed hugging his knees.

George would have heard the gun's discharge.

She looked at the crippled vehicles. "Do we have another car?"

"Yes, but it's in worse shape."

We crossed the field to the fence where the mare waited patiently. It was cruel to ask her to carry both of us, but she plodded gallantly down to the broken wall and allowed herself to be led across to a road that was empty and silent.

41

WE coaxed the mare two miles down the road to the fire station. The lights were on, and a wagon with state police insignia sat in the driveway spouting exhaust. Gibson was inside, patting Kate and telling a skeptical trooper about Mr. Finn's kidnapping.

Our arrival deepened the confusion. I said that several cars had been shot up and that my wife and I had ridden for help. We didn't know what had befallen George.

The trooper walked outside, saw the flickering red glow in the sky and dashed back. "Got a fire due west—could that be Finn's place?"

"Could be," Gibson said.

The station's duty man sounded the village alarm but acted despondent. "On a night like this, we're going to find a pile of ashes."

It suited me fine. Volunteers came trickling in. A crew left on the pumper truck, followed by the trooper. Mr. Gibson rode along.

Pleading frostbite, Marty and I stayed behind.

"Why didn't you tell him the truth about George?" she demanded.

"Why didn't you?"

"He's insane—he was talking that way. I don't want to get within a mile of either of those two ever again."

"My reason was more prosaic. No proof. It would be their word against mine, and my reputation is in disrepair."

"The SEC dropped its charges."

I shrugged. "If it was someone other than me, wouldn't we assume he had just had a good lawyer? The taint sticks."

"So what do we do? George could have you arrested for setting fire to his barn."

I led her into a tiny office, which had a telephone. "Not to mention vandalism and horse stealing. See if you can wake up Rudy."

Leaning against the wall, I snuggled my hands under my arms. I didn't want to remove Gibson's gloves in her presence. The hands ached and the wrists would be gruesome.

She got the number, dialed, and Rudy answered quickly. She held the receiver away, and I could hear his sharp command: "Put your husband on!"

"Hello, Rudy."

"The police want to talk to you. Your neighbors turned over a man with a broken arm and a sawed-off shotgun."

"One of Mr. Jesse's deputies. One of George Finn's."

"What the hell does that mean?"

"They're one and the same."

He didn't scoff. "Are you sure?"

"Yes."

"Do you have proof?"

"Not a shred. He and Furbinger must have left tracks that someone with a subpoena can find. Could you come and get us? I would rather talk to Teeger in New York than get tied up with Connecticut troopers."

"What have you been doing up there?"

I thought of possible responses. "Just hanging around," I said.

Marty fell asleep on the drive back. When I told Rudy about the time in the barn, he insisted on collecting a camera at his apartment and snapped Polaroids of my wrists and hands while Marty showered. He took my statement on a microcassette recorder, then questioned Marty as she sat in an old terry robe. George had ranted about young money, nouveaux riches, who had destroyed a gentleman's industry. When George spotted an especially promising firm making inroads among the traditionalists, he put it on his list of targets. She didn't remember the names he had rattled off. Several had gotten a "comeuppance," according to George. His position on the disciplinary committee brought access to the names of potential agents he could recruit—people like Vince DiMineo, who hoped their indiscretions were forgotten. People with much to lose.

His friends at the Securities and Exchange Commission descended ferociously on upstart rule-breakers whom George reported.

"Did they hurt you?" Rudy asked.

She shook her head. "They were working up their nerve to do something." She didn't look at me. "What did they do to Ben?"

He told her.

She pulled her knees up.

Rudy said, "Like Jack." I nodded. He promised to bring around a videocam in the afternoon and go through it all again. When he left it was almost dawn.

We slept until early afternoon. I found a towing service and sent them around to collect the Heinbachs' car. I went downstairs and more or less explained the damage to Oscar and Rhoda, promised to make good on it. They responded better than I would have.

A little before three, Rudy came back and so did the police. Teeger sat and listened, his pitted face as empty as if we were reporting a flying saucer at Washington Square.

He put down his coffee cup. "I talked to people in Connecticut. Mr. Finn said that persons unknown shot up the cars and set fire to the barn. He was grateful that his man found you in the barn. He suggested that you had been under pressure because of legal and financial difficulties and might not be rational. That assessment was shared by a trooper who met you." He smiled. "I guess it's probably good you didn't tell him about Mr. Jesse."

Rudy said, "What are you getting out of his two punks?"

"Stoic silence. Certainly nothing to link them to Finn. We may not be able to prove anything against him."

Rudy said he had hired a firm of detectives to dig up dirt on Finn and Bunny Furbinger.

When they left, I phoned Gil and made plans for the following week.

42

MONDAY morning the shares of Dorchester Millinery opened
weak. In the first half hour of trading, the quote tumbled to 45,
then 44¼. Watching the action, Gil and I had the same reaction.
I pulled Sol Lehrman off the exchange floor to the phone, and he
confirmed our suspicion. "Brooker Finn has been a heavy seller," he
said.

"They don't have stock to sell," I said. "They're going short."

"The sales are not marked as shorts and they're getting executed
on downticks." Both were violations of the exchange rules. I didn't
imagine that George cared.

I said, "Sol, why don't you ask around and see if the stock can be
borrowed. I think Brooker Finn is shorting naked. They won't be
able to deliver shares to the buyers."

He went off with that dangerous thought. I asked Gail to line up
calls to Edgar Parsons and Lance Grendal. I told them both what
was happening.

Grendal laughed. "Let the bastards dig themselves in deeper."

The stock bottomed at 41¾ at ten-thirty, then began to recover.
Sol called back and said the exchange had told Dorchester's specialist
to make sure that any short sales could be delivered. The specialist
turned back a block of five thousand shares from a small New Jersey
firm. A dozen people on the floor had noticed.

I hung up as the price jumped past 43.

I bought a few thousand shares.

Sniffing a squeeze, other traders came in. One bid for ten thousand at 44. Somebody topped him at 44½. No stock was for sale.

When Dorchester Millinery hit 48, the spread on our terminal suddenly widened to 48 bid, 51 asked. The bid was for ten thousand shares; five hundred were offered for sale. An instant later the stock traded at 51.

The screen blinked. The bid for Dorchester Millinery was five thousand shares at 49. Two hundred were for sale at 52½.

Gil leaned forward. "What do you imagine is going on down at Furbinger Associates' office? If word is out that he's getting squeezed, nobody will lend him money. Except George, and that would bring him further into the open."

Brooker Finn would have deep pockets. The firm could bail out Bunny Furbinger and sell Dorchester Millinery short until the cows came home. Except that very soon, Brooker Finn would get a call from the surveillance department at the stock exchange. More apologetic than stern. *Must be an oversight, gentlemen, but you've been selling Dorchester Millinery short on downticks—of course you wouldn't violate the rules—but by the way, can you deliver the shares you're selling?* The question would go to Brooker Finn's compliance department. George's directors would hear. It would be out of George Finn's hands.

New York's financial district is compact. We left Gail in charge of the office at eleven-fifteen and walked down to Brooker Finn's building, arriving just before half-past. The mannequin behind his Louis Quinze desk in the marble lobby deigned to notice only the familiar faces.

The public boardroom was crowded. The market was having a strong morning, and everybody wanted to watch the foot-high numbers dancing to the jingle of prosperity. I thought it was our version of the British tradesman's motto: *I'm all right, Jack, I've got mine.* Union card, stock account, what was the difference?

Getting a chair was out of the question. Gil and I edged to the back rail, near a telephone. He grabbed my shoulder, nodded to the

223

quotation board. Dorchester Millinery's latest trade marched past, DOR 54½.

Finn would be watching the buy orders for signs of weakness. If only a few buyers were aligned against him, he could survive.

Bunny would be watching, sickened.

Every point the stock rose would be agony.

I picked up the receiver, asked for the young broker who had taken over the client accounts we transferred. I told him to buy Dorchester Millinery shares as high as 60 in ten of the accounts. When I asked him to ring back on extension 802, he gobbled in surprise. "You're downstairs, Mr. McCarthy?"

"Downstairs and buying Dorchester Millinery," I said.

As I hung up, Gil leaned close. "The SEC will want to talk to you—to us—about this."

"Let them. We've got a legal right to buy a stock we think is going higher. We also have a right to tell Lance Grendal and Ed Parsons we think it's going higher. If Finn and Bunny start closing their shorts, it will go a lot higher." I spoke with more confidence than I felt. Real short squeezes were rare—Home Shopping, Martin Processing, Resorts International. When sellers finally panicked and tried to cover at any price, just to salvage something, the action could be explosive. But you never knew what price would mark the top.

Several thousand shares of Dorchester Millinery crossed at 57.

My purchase or somebody joining the party?

I saw Lance Grendal walk through the doorway, elegant and forbidding in a black topcoat, burgundy tie, navy double-breasted suit. Heads turned. He inspected the tape-watchers with the benign contempt of a professional for amateurs. He walked over to us.

"My boys on the floor say the shorts haven't even begun covering," he said. "Unless the exchange halts trading, the stock will go to a hundred." He sounded authoritative, confident, at peace with his bankers. The disaster that had almost broken him was on the way to being forgotten.

He lighted a cigarette, spit out a mouthful of smoke. He watched the patrons, mostly well into their sixties. There were more spectators than traders. "A room like this is a waste of money," Grendal said. "They should serve prune juice and bran."

DOR 58⅜.

Every point would fuel the anger.

I lifted the receiver, got the young broker. "Let's spread another ten thousand shares in those accounts. Pay up to sixty-five."

As I put down the phone, Grendal chuckled. "Who do you plan to sell to?"

Looking over heads, I spotted Sergeant Teeger drifting along the far wall. He kept his distance.

The phone rang. "Mr. McCarthy? In those accounts, you've bought twenty thousand DOR from fifty-six to sixty-two."

The print came across almost as he spoke.

DOR 62⅛.

Every point enraging him.

"Ten thousand more, limit seventy." I hung up.

Grendal sighed. "I think I should be selling, easing out just a little."

"Stay away from the outside phones," I said.

"I could already have placed the orders," he said. "I could be feeding you my stock right now."

"You're too greedy to do that," I said.

The man upstairs would have been checking, would know by now.

DOR 64 . . . 64½ . . . 66 . . .

There was a stir among the tape-watchers.

George Finn burst into the narrow, high-ceilinged room, momentum carrying him like a primal force. He was impervious to shoulders and elbows. He brushed bodies aside. On the broad, smooth face, the sharp little features remained composed. The lenses that shrank the eyes caught reflections from the quote board, red dots that marched like an army of rampaging ants, devouring, destroying. He threw a glance over his shoulder at the board.

DOR 77.

He saw me then—and Lance Grendal—and hurtled forward, the rage erupting. He shouldered past an elderly man who spun like a child and collapsed. He bore down on us, mewling as if he had been robbed of speech.

Then the voice erupted. *"You impertinent bastard!"*

He slammed Grendal aside. His massive hands grabbed my neck. My heels left the floor. Telephones jangled and fell.

I could read his face, contorted and crimson. Not insane, I thought abstractedly, just thwarted.

The world grew hazy.

Teeger threw an arm around his chest and pulled. "Here—none of that!"

When my vision cleared, George Finn treated Teeger to an indignant glower. He cried, "These men are criminals—stock manipulators! Right in my own boardroom!"

Teeger kept his distance. He extended his badge. "Mr. Finn, I want to talk to you about men named Danny Natoli and Bongo Harris. And about James Doyle."

"Well, of course we can talk about those things!" George boomed. "I am a governor of the stock exchange. I will be happy to talk to you."

I said softly, "Start by talking about your friend Jack Canning."

George's face rippled as boiling hatred sought release. His words choked, stumbled. "What—about—Can—ning—?" Shaking his head, he stepped forward. Teeger spun under a blow and collided with me, took us both down.

The policeman got up first, rubbing his cheek. George was gone. "Goddamned fool, where's he think he's going?"

George had left a wake of astonished customers, who gaped as we headed into the lobby. The brass door to the street was closed. A uniformed guard stood beside it, looking puzzled.

"Where did Finn go?" Teeger demanded. The white-faced mannequin rose from his desk, fingers to his lips.

The ornate dial above one elevator door showed a car had just left the ground floor and was speeding past the second.

"He's on his way back to his office," I said.

"Does he keep a gun there?"

"I don't know."

Another elevator car emptied. We stepped in and I pressed 21. Neither Gil nor Grendal had made the elevator.

I imagined Jack, suspecting George, confronting him after the burglary. Bad luck. In a couple of days the scandal Vince had contrived would have erupted. Nobody would have believed a word Jack said about anything.

George Finn's secretary was a short-haired, handsome woman in middle age who was highly agitated, perhaps for the first time in her career. She seemed unsurprised by our arrival. Loyalty took command. "Mr. Finn asked not to be disturbed. If you would like a seat?"

Teeger brushed past. She seemed to expect it. He banged on the mahogany door. "Mr. Finn!"

There was no answer.

"Just before you arrived," the woman said diffidently, "I thought I heard glass breaking."

Teeger slammed his foot into the door. It crashed open into a room of Persian carpets and sunlight.

Beyond a shattered corner window, fingers clung to a ledge. He had changed his mind. Decided to try to brash it out.

Icy wind swept past us.

In a moment the ledge was empty.

43

GIL bought me lunch at the club. He fussed with his sandwich, set it down and said, "Bunny Furbinger says he never connected the stock fraud to the murders."

"Nobody can prove he did," I said.

"You're awfully unperturbed for a man he tried to kill."

I shrugged. The exchange had halted trading in Dorchester Millinery at 102. We had sold most of our positions and all the clients' positions on Tuesday in the mid-eighties. Grendal had said he wanted to stay with his shares for more of the ride. When the short sellers were bought in, it would be from people like Grendal who owned the stock—and at the price they set. Furbinger Associates' assets were frozen by court order. A preliminary audit showed Bunny was still short about a third of Dorchester's outstanding shares.

I couldn't see that I had much to be unhappy about. The welts on my wrists drew curious looks in some restaurants, no notice at the better places.

"They had a long-standing business," I said. "Furbinger would promote junk stocks, make money as they rose. Brooker Finn would sell them short near the top and cash in as they collapsed. Very lucrative. The more small investment firms that George gained control of, the more places they could hide the manipulation.

Rudy's investigators say that Brooker Finn had been losing money under George. He got even with the upstarts he loathed at the same time he kept his firm afloat."

I didn't tell him how much a part hatred had played in selecting targets like Markey Wahl for destruction. Old Noble Wahl had been a self-made man of integrity who had run his firm with quiet rectitude. A stiffer-necked Jack Canning.

Gil smiled sourly. "The stock exchange appointed an investigatory commission. They are supposed to determine how many times Finn might have abused the information and authority he held as a governor. The early line is that the Dorchester Millinery affair was an aberration—that George Finn's judgment slipped from overwork."

"That sounds reasonable," I said.

"You're too young to be such a cynic."

"Is cynicism a sign of maturity?"

"No." He laughed. "A sign of old age."

"So Old Bastards are cynical as well as persistent."

He folded his spotted hands, tapped a finger pointlessly on the base of his water glass. "Old Bastards keep coming back, with extraordinary persistence, which is not a characteristic of great cynicism. Nor keen intelligence, perhaps. On both counts, you qualify."

He pushed his plate away and settled into the flowered wing chair. Old, unhappy in his way, tremendously loyal, peeved because I hadn't totally confided in him. "In fact, you've become a little bit of a ruthless S.O.B.," he muttered.

I nodded, complacently grateful that we both disapproved.

"It would be interesting to know how a gentleman of Finn's stature became acquainted with a rent-a-thug agent in Brooklyn," he said casually. "Every Wall Street house should have such friends. Imagine sending out margin calls by Bongo Harris!"

"If Brooker Finn handles longshoremen's union money, we might have a clue," I said.

"Not that it matters."

"Not that it matters," I agreed. An answer might never come. Answers to other questions would come and seem unimportant.

Until last night I had puzzled over Jack's handwritten note to me, so clearly his own, mailed from St. Kitts, where he hadn't gotten. Last night I remembered George's sister, who lived in the Caribbean. Her winter home, I found, was St. Kitts. It must have seemed an odd request when George's letter arrived, full of chatter about the farm and the mares and an aside to cover the lettercard that was enclosed. *Just drop this in the mail with a local stamp, would you, dearest? A friend's son collects stamps.*

Gil ordered a brandy. It was a late lunch, he explained, and he planned a nap. "Ed Parsons thought you might like to manage some of his profits."

"That could be arranged."

"He's filing for divorce."

"I'm sorry to hear it."

He cleared his throat. "And what about you?"

I didn't pretend to misunderstand. "We're standing pat."

He smiled with relief. "And how is my niece?"

"No different."

I went home. The Lady Vermeer was painting. The subject was square-jawed, a future matinee idol, done from a series of sketches. I hoped I wouldn't meet him. If he made it into the movies, I vowed I wouldn't see them.

But I stayed and watched her work. "Gil's angry," I said. "He thinks I've caught the Norris disease."

"Which is?"

"Recklessness." A kinder word than ruthlessness.

She held my gaze, not smiling. "Poor Bunny and George."

She went back to work and I watched the cleft jaw take on reality. After a while she asked, "Do you want to talk about something?"

"No. I'm seeing how you work under pressure."

"Not well. Go away."

She would never be completely mine. Never come apart on my shoulder. Just as well.

"Go *away*," she repeated, not meaning it.

I went downstairs.